PAGE LEFT INTENTIONALLY BLANK

C000179193

© **A Hidden Past**

A Hidden Past.

By Marilyn L Palmer

© *Mysterious Butterfly Series*— 01

Worldwide Copyright by: © Marilyn L Palmer April 2020

Independently Published— All rights reserved.

ISBN: 9798631350083

First printed by Amazon UK— April 2020

Also, available in kindle book format—

This is a book of fiction, Therefore the locations, people and events mentioned within are imaginary and fictional, even if they appear to reflect names, facts, circumstance and places in the real world.

Dedication.

I couldn't manage to have achieved completion in such a short time without the comments and encouragement from my betrothed.

Thank you sweetheart, for the hours spent pointing out glaring mistakes, to ensure I ended up with the result I was looking for— The reader wouldn't be tripping up every couple of pages with my 'quite not perfect,' proof reading.

(I rest my case...)

Please leave comments good or bad— on the dedicated Amazon Web page. Much appreciated—

Marilyn L Palmer 2020

© **A Hidden Past**

© *Mysterious Butterfly Series*— 01

© **A Hidden Past**

Chapter / Timeline   Page

#1   Saturday Ten AM

May 3rd 2021

The unexpected loud ring of the doorbell, made her jump slightly, recoiling in shock.

"Who the heck is that?" thought Kim Chapman, already making her way quickly across the lounge, towards the front door.

Dodging Roger her elderly Tortoiseshell cat, sitting as usual in the middle of the hallway. She reached out to the door lock and sharply twisted it open.

"Miss Karen Chapman?" Inquired a refined baritone voice, the owner out of sight to the right of the porch.

She decided to step outside, with the intention of advising the caller her name was Kim, not Karen.

Kim stumbled slightly, as she caught the heel of her shoe, while stepping over the threshold. A capable arm reached forward to clutch her elbow, and steadied her balance.

Looking up to thank her white knight for his help, she unintentionally took a sharp intake of breath. After finding herself confronted by a charming smile, attached to a hunky man dressed in leather and denim. Slightly stunned with his good looks. It took a couple of moments to be able to ask him the question that had recently come to her mind, "Karen Chapman?"

He held up a package gripped in one hand and politely offered it to her. "Sorry, I saw the initial K and just sort of assumed it would probably be Karen." The courier shrugged and smiled once more, "My mistake."

Kim nodded and hesitantly returned the smile. "Not a problem, it's actually Kim." She could feel this nagging feeling inside. "I have seen you somewhere before haven't I?"

"Probably," he replied mysteriously and turned to walk back up the drive. Climbing a powerful antique motorbike and donning a helmet, he kicked down on the starter and roared away.

Standing slightly perplexed at his cryptic reply, she suddenly remembered the parcel in her hand.

Walking back indoors to the comfort of her leather settee, Kim placed the shipment onto the adjacent coffee table.

From its size, it appeared it was possibly a large hardback book. She hefted it up to examine it closer.

Kim noted it appeared to be relatively heavy, adding further credence to her assumption it possibly contained reading material. Upon checking the label, she noted the name and address had been written by hand. And no return address appeared to be present. The handwriting itself was full of swirls and curls. Suggesting the sender was conceivably a female.

The outer packaging was waxed brown paper, simply sealed with transparent tape. "Oh well," she thought. "Definitely not sent by one of the global online shopping sites."

Kim hastily looked at her watch, and took a sharp intake of breath. "Damn, I had almost forgotten— Maureen Hutchison has an appointment at ten-forty, and she always moans like hell if I am late."

Kim snatched up her appointment diary and phone and finally left the cottage. Seizing her keys from the hook by the door, on her way out.

✳✳✳

Having missed lunch, due to a succession of appointments following after Mrs Hutchison. Meant, Kim was now absolutely ravenous.

Slamming the car door shut, she opened the front porch. Pushing an indignant Roger, meowing loudly up against the wall.

Leaning down to fuss him, "You stupid cat, it's your own fault— you will always lie somewhere awkward in the hallway." She lightly scolded him, and then remembered the delivery she had abandoned earlier. Snatching a packet of biscuits from the tin in the kitchen. Kim sat down on the settee, already nibbling at a digestive in her hand.

Unable to resist the suspense any longer. She tore at the wrapping paper, revealing what she suspected was a book.

To be more accurate, 'a book' would most likely represent an overstatement— It consisted of an 'A5' ring binder, with protected sheets of paper nestled within.

"What the hell is this?" She thought to herself, totally surprised with the package and its content.

Turning the binder on the table, so the rings lay at the top. She lifted the cover upwards, revealing a loose heavyweight paper sheet, lightly folded in the middle.

Its contents were still not visible, only available after she had unfolded it. Revealing what appeared to be, an old-fashioned birth certificate.

Reaching into the top pocket of her light blue smock. Kim slipped out a rounded pair of reading glasses and carefully positioned them on her nose and ears.

"Why would anybody send me a birth certificate?" Kim thought, gathering it slightly closer towards herself for a better look. Now she was intrigued and sought the identity of whom the documentation belonged to. Eyes roved over the certificate, until she found the owners name. Kim raised an eyebrow in confusion, "Karen Taylor, I don't know any Karen."

Then it sort of made sense. As she suddenly recalled the parcel, it had arrived addressed to herself. The courier— Had distinctly asked for Karen and explained he naively assumed it was her name.

"Was it just a coincidence, or did he know more than he was letting on?"

She read a little further— and gasped. The date written on the certificate was her own birthday.

Eager eyes began to dart all over the certificate. Following each line of text expectantly, hoping to discover anything at all.

That would maybe explain the unknown reason; she of all people had been sent this conundrum.

Kim surmised, that if anyone else had received it. They would at least have an explanation why it had even been sent— possibly contained within a simple covering note.

The father's name was Adam— the mother's Helen.

Kim had nearly dismissed that fact as of no particular interest, but she couldn't put her finger on why something was still pestering her inside. She looked intently once more, at both their full names.

'Adam Bridges and Helen Taylor.' She took a sharp intake of breath. Apart from revealing the fact, they didn't seem to be married— Kim had just spotted something glaring at her in the certificate.

She couldn't believe what she had seen was just sheer coincidence. Kim bit on her lip, Gran's surname was Taylor as well.

Her eyes began to well up, as she thought of her late grandmother Angela.

Kim had spent most of her happy childhood holidays at Gran's house.

When she was young, her mother and father were constantly busy. Travelling and working, all corners of the United Kingdom.

They had never explained their employment, or the reason they were always unavailable. Kim would have done anything they had asked. Just so they could share her holidays as a family.

It was always the same routine at term end.

She would normally be shuffled off to her Gran's on the first Saturday of the holiday. Then picked up again on the following Sunday, just before the school term resumed.

Feeling a tickle on her cheek, Kim began wiping the corners of her eyes dry. With an ever-present paper hanky, strategically concealed up her sleeve. Kim let loose a long sigh, before resuming her investigation once more.

Other papers— consisted of an intriguing mix of receipts, combined with numerous handwritten letters and lists.

Each article of paper was carefully protected. By a sealed clear plastic document sleeve, safely attached to the rings of the binder.

After carefully laying the documents, neatly down into a pile— to nestle onto the table once more. Kim sat back, deeply sinking into the folds of her comfortable settee.

Roger sensing an opportunity for a fuss. Deftly leapt onto her lap, nudging her elbow to garner her attention.

Deep in thought, she unconsciously began to stroke Roger behind his sensitive ears. Sensing the incessant sound of his loud purring, finally bought her back from her mental deliberations.

"Well Roger," she asked out loud. "What do you suppose I should do?" The cat continued to purr noisily, with no obvious intention to ruminate on her questions.

Unabashed, Kim continued testing his opinion— By pointing to the folder on the coffee table.

"Do I altogether forget the whole lot exists and hope it was completely a mistake?— What was the reason Kim Chapman ended up receiving it? Not a Karen Taylor instead?

Maybe 'motorbike man' will knock on the door and announce he has to recollect it for the proper recipient?"

Kim looked at her cat, imagining his feedback.

Roger coughed slightly with a hairball irritating his throat. Interpreting his response as a probable negative answer. She offered instead, "Perhaps I should ask somebody else's opinion as well?"

Kim thoughtfully considered her own suggestion. "Hmm, That way— I suspect I wouldn't feel so uncomfortable, after keeping it all to myself.

I reckon I could easily make, far too many incorrect decisions.

By examining them without any external advice, I could easily come to wrong conclusions."

Mind made up, feline heaven was about to end— As she picked up Roger by the scruff of his neck, depositing him unceremoniously back onto the uncomfortable wood floor.

Forging her way over to the traditional pantry, at the corner of the kitchen. Kim extracted a large taffeta bag. Garishly decorated with the mural announcing, 'I love cats' faded on both sides.

Returning to the coffee table, she made certain the plastic sleeves were carefully folded back into the binder. Gently placing the whole thing, inside the taffeta bag.

Kim picked up her mobile phone and began pecking at the touch sensitive screen to compose a short message.

To: Maria Lockyer: Kirstie Hanson: Nancy Myers
Subject: Need your advice?

Hi Hunny-Bunnies,

I have received a couriered parcel this morning, and it contains papers and stuff. Am looking for the wise man, but can't seem to find him. So you will have to do... LOL.
You all okay to meet at the library cafe in an hour?
Let me know ASAP.
Xxx Kim.

She pressed the send button and leant up against the door jamb waiting for a response from her dearest friends.

Three sets of 'ping-ping' on her phone arrived seconds later. Each reply displaying just a large letter X signifying their approval, prompting her to make her way to the upstairs bathroom for a quick shower.

Peeling off her chemical stained smock, and launching it into the clothes bin. She turned on the shower head already anticipating the powerful jet of water. Stepping inside, she began to relax as the steaming spray struck her shoulders.

✳✳✳

After completing her ablutions, she made her way to her wardrobe, pulling out a couple of smart blouses and a pair of casual slacks. Deciding the silky cream blouse went best with her shock of red hair, she dressed and began putting on her makeup.

Kim had been extremely glad when she had reached her late teens and finally abandoned school. The ever-present calls of Carrot head and other derogatory titles, that were shouted wherever she went. The cruel taunts had eventually accumulated inside, causing the combined resultant stress and the lack of confidence, to claim an unforgiving damper on her psyche.

Combined with the fact puberty had scarcely taken hold at the age of sixteen. Meant her boyish figure and angular facial features, had only increased the volume of cruel harassment she had to endure.

It was only after she had connected with her 'crew' while at college on her hairdressing course. Was when she began feeling more confident with her body and hair.

Raven-haired Maria Lockyer had been redoing her 'A-levels.' Trying to get higher grades in Maths and English.

With the intention of qualifying and satisfying her employer, the local supermarket chain known as 'Dingles.' They were adamant she acquired certain qualifications, before they would even validate an application to become a Staff Supervisor. They also had to be present before any internal training and placements could take place.

Kirstie Hanson shared the same 'A level' classes as Maria. Naturally White haired, now dyed a shade of red like two of her friends. Kirstie was preparing to become a Bank assistant at the local branch of 'The Bank of Devon and Cornwall.'

And last but not least— Kim's 'best of all best friends' Nancy Myers— Infant School Teacher at St. Mary and Whitelaw.

At the time they met, she was helping out at the college as a lab assistant. While waiting to receive her police check documentation, so she can officially work with minors.

For some reason, it had undergone an inordinate amount of time to process. So, she had practically spent a whole year at the college, before finally achieving full employment at St. Mary and Whitelaw.

Nancy was practically Kim's double, with naturally vibrant red hair— cut in a bob, and possessed a willowy figure to match.

Last year— The four of them had celebrated, after successfully achieving their qualifications. By sharing a two-week holiday together, on the sunny beaches of North Majorca. Growing to know each other's likes and foibles, while living together in a small villa, was an essential part of their bonding.

They had managed to occupy all of their time together, until landing back home, without a single bad word being uttered in anger.

All four had therefore decided it was a sign— that shouldn't be ignored. The whole experience had culminated into a strong bonding, and they had since spent most days meeting together as firm friends since.

Pulling the stiff bristle comb, down through her unruly hair one last time. Kim dabbed it and allowed herself a final look in the mirror.

Satisfied— she packed her phone and purse into an unusual green denim bum bag, and suspended it over her left shoulder.

Taking the stairs down two at a time, she intercepted a disappointed looking cat on his way the opposite direction. Kim scooped him up under his shoulders, and after reaching the bottom of the stairs. Deposited him onto the sofa instead.

Roger had been planning to console himself by sleeping on her bed. He had felt annoyed at having his 'fussing' aborted, disappointed for yet another puerile reason for it to stop.

Grabbing the taffeta bag from the table and lifting her keys from the hook by the front door. Kim got into her sporty Milano Red Honda Jazz, and headed purposely towards the library café.

✳✳✳

#2   Saturday Three-Thirty PM

May 3rd 2021

Clipping shut her mobile phone case, Kirstie Hanson was quite excited. The message from Kim had initially puzzled her, "Who would deliver a load of papers via a courier? I'm sure it would have cost more than it was worth."

Thinking about it, Kim was normally quite blasé about most things, hefty bills and costly repairs to the car went straight over her head. Her mantra was ordinarily 'just getting on with it and don't worry.' This is probably the first time she had contacted her friends to help her make a decision, instead of the other way around.

If anybody else had a problem, the first person they would turn to would be Kim. She repeatedly provided the appropriate answer at the right time, so Kim seeking help was unheard-of.

Kirstie's twin brother Dave shared the ex-council maisonette they both rented from Pandora Estates. He had moved in, when he had abandoned the army.

Eventually reaching the minimum service period of six years, after enthusiastically joining the forces at sixteen— Dave had just as eagerly finished his contracted term.

He had left after becoming disillusioned with political interference. Into funding, and theatres of engagement.

12

Unlike most other of his ex-army colleagues. He had walked straight into a permanent job, as a well-paid electrician.

Dave looked up from behind the newspaper he had been reading. "What's up Sis'?" He queried, stretching out his muscular legs on the leather sofa.

Kirstie looked at him wordlessly with eyebrows raised.

"What? I only asked if the message was interesting." Dave noticed the defiant stance had not changed. "Err— have I done something wrong Kirstie?"

"Dave," she said, stretching out the single syllable of his forename. "Not only are you sitting on our new sofa, in only your boxer shorts. But, you have the temerity to do it, while wearing your work boots as well. If one ounce of mud or oil is found..."

Dave raised a solitary pointing finger in response. "And who actually paid for it?— me." He laughed, playfully throwing a soft pillow at her head.

"Right that's it," she smirked. Leaping onto her brother, pinning him down on the sofa. Kirstie began tormenting him mercilessly, by tickling his underarms and waist. He squealed in an unmanly voice, "I give in, I give in— please make it stop."

She rolled off him with a thump, onto the floor. "Big brave military man, surrendering to the wimpy Bank Clerk— Whatever next?" They both giggled childishly.

Climbing up off the floor, she glanced at the clock on the wall. Remembering Kim's 'call for assistance', she flew into the bathroom for a quick wash.

The Library café was only a five-minute walk away, but she sailed out the front door as soon as she was ready. Intent on being the first to query her friend.

✳✳✳

Maria had painfully watched the till operator slowly drag each item over the laser scanner. "C'mon, both of our shifts finished five minutes ago," she thought. While observing the displeased expressions. Plastered on the faces of the customers, in the lengthy queue for the till.

She felt sympathetic. "I'm not surprised at their reaction. Everybody— including me. Will be more than pleased when I finally get her off that damn till."

The operator sat staring uncomprehendingly, focussed on the last item to register. It wouldn't scan. Finally, looking up implorably at her Supervisor. Signifying blatantly, she hoped Maria Lockyer would assist her.

Maria sighed, "This really is not the reason I worked damn hard day and night, to obtain this job." Leaning over the operator's shoulder. She inserted her master override key, activating a supervisor mode on the till.

Maria lifted the recalcitrant item, and simply typed in the code printed at the bottom of the barcode. With the product accepted, and final till total printed. She released the device back to the operator, allowing her to complete the transaction.

Young Jordan had only just arrived at the till to start his own shift. Maria nodded slightly, to signify that he should jump straight on. He was normally quick, Maria smiled. Knowing he should start clearing the grumpy queue, impatiently waiting to hand over their money.

After spending a few seconds, looking around to make sure the fresh shift Supervisor was available to take over. She determinedly marched directly to the staff room. Cleverly concealed behind a code secured door, at the rear of the store.

Grabbing her coat and large handbag from the assigned secure locker. Maria left the building, via the rear staff entrance. Exiting toward the multi-story car park, located conveniently behind the store.

Arriving at her car, Maria was about to click her remote locking key fob. When she suddenly remembered, receiving— a texted request earlier on. It had invited her to meet up with her friends at their favourite café.

"Oh shit, I had nearly forgotten," she exclaimed out loud. Maria turned around, to head for the car-park 'exit' stairway instead.

A heavy hand was firmly placed on her shoulder, making her jump slightly with shock. Twisting around, now completely hyped up. She prepared to use her self-defence skills, obtained on-line.

Maria stopped short of stamping on her potential aggressor's ankle. As she had unfortunately, just recognised the culprit.

"Miles Quinn— and what can I do for you?" She asked icily. "I thought I had already promised you just one thing. There is no way, I want to sell you my house..."

The man standing in front of her simply smirked, "I'm confident you will change your mind and see sense sooner or later," he chided with barely concealed venom.

"You are wasting your time," she said clearly and began walking away.

"Don't you dare dismiss me— Bitch." He replied with a stare. Miles began executing a menacing step forward towards her. "I think you need to listen to me for a bit longer— don't you?"

Standing at just over six feet three. With a muscular physique, he presented an imposing figure. Miles managed to improve muscle mass every day at work. Self-employed as a builder, specialising in refurbishment. He was selfishly hoping to obtain Maria's property, as a potential investment.

Miles presented to the world a facade of respectability.

He had originally chatted up Maria at the local night club 'Heroes.' Appearing to represent the courteous handsome young man, that any father would be amiable to releasing his daughter's chastity in marriage.

His genuine intentions were eventually made clear. When Kim had found out from a client that he was wed with two young children— a third on the way.

Further conversations with more of his previous conquests revealed the man enjoyed intimidating females. They all had one thing in common. They had belatedly discovered the real Miles Quinn.

After the instant, these facts came to light. She had instantly discarded him from her life— like a hot potato. But unfortunately, he did not seem to receive the hint. Still turning up occasionally, at the most inopportune moments.

"How are you?" he asked disarmingly, "Have you replaced my charming personality with another, since sadly losing mine?"

Maria exhaled sharply, "No, and after your despicable charade. I have no chance of being confident now— do I? There is no way I will be able to rely on any men— Full stop. Especially for the foreseeable future— you chauvinistic pig." She angrily spat unladylike at his feet.

Miles smiled disarmingly, "You might regret uttering that sentence one day, you know."

He rudely inspected her up and down. Making it obvious he was admiring her curvy figure and silky raven hair flowing down past her shoulders.

"Don't forget we enjoyed this conversation, and maybe I will pop round sometime, to see if I can convince you to change your mind." He concluded in a menacing tone, turning to head in the opposite direction, where he had parked his ostentatious Aston Martin Rapide.

She walked slowly and nervously backwards— Witnessing him disappear into the plush seating of his car. Only then could Maria breathe again. She twisted around walking at a swift pace towards the exit stairwell and the certain company of her friends.

✳✳✳

Kim had already found her 'best friend' Nancy Myers, sitting comfortably in one of their favourite leather chairs, at the library café.

Nancy held a steaming Americano coffee in her hands. Unconsciously blowing softly across the top of the cup, so it wouldn't burn her lips.

While they were waiting for the other two to arrive, they had fallen into conversation easily. She took a sip of the hot drink and looked Kim in the eye. "So, how's Andy? I haven't glimpsed you two together for a while now— is something up?"

"*Straight to the point,*" thought Kim, there was no way she could lie— So she came right out with it. "Andy and I have decided to cool the relationship for a bit. He wants to get married and put bluntly— I don't."

Nancy raised one sculptured eyebrow. "Are you serious?" She challenged Kim, surprised at her answer.

"That's precisely the problem— I am the one who is not interested, while Andy is fully committed. I appreciate him and all that, and couldn't think of anyone else I would want to settle down with. But..."

She looked down dejectedly, towards the centre of the table. With a hint of moisture, glistening at the corner of her eyes.

Nancy stood up and bent over to cuddle Kim in response. "I am really sorry about that Hun, I thought you two appeared to be made for each other."

"Yeah, so did I— and then one day it dawned on me. I am only twenty-three. I feel like I still want to spread my wings and not be tied down with a baby and the like."

Kim examined Nancy's greenish eyes. "I sound horrid, don't I? Andy's dad had already hinted that we could initially move into the empty flat over his grocers shop as well.— I think I have made the sensible decision, though— Do you agree?"

Noting her friend's bottom lip starting to quiver, Nancy bobbed her head briskly in agreement. "Kim sweetheart, you know the three of us will back you up. Whatever decision you have made. Speaking of which— where have the other two got to? We are supposed to be helping you out with another decision?"

As Nancy looked over Kim's shoulder, she spotted Kirstie and Maria walking towards them. They also sat down in their habitual chairs.

The lady behind the counter had just recognised them.

She grabbed another two large cups from a shelf and promptly began priming the coffee machine, for their customary orders.

Kim tactfully wiped her eyes with a flourish. Pretending to adjust her slightly heavy eyebrows, whilst wiping away any remaining tears. She greeted her friends with a forced smile.

After noting Maria didn't seem her usual chirpy self either.

The miserable look on her face was enhanced by the stoop in her stance.

Prompted by her close friends gathered around her. Maria recounted her earlier run in with Miles in the car park.

"I can't understand why I let him get to me. There is no-way on earth, he is going to convince me to sell my house to him— the man is a ..." Before she could utter an expletive, Maria was interrupted. Their fresh coffee order was being carefully placed onto the table, by a handsome middle-aged man.

The intruder smiled apologetically. "I hope you don't mind; the lady was about to bring it across, so I offered to help her out," he explained.

"Motorbike man," thought Kim in recognition, while simultaneously turning a deep shade of red. She felt herself shrinking downwards, as Kim saw he had recognised her as well.

"Miss Chapman— initial K, we meet again," he offered his open hand which she declined to respond to. The man gave no comment and simply put his hand in his pocket instead.

Kim felt the focused stare of her friends, and they were obviously fit to burst. Readying themselves, to ask her questions about the unknown hunk standing before them.

Noticing their rapturous puppy dog faces. He silently looked each girl in the eyes and offered an introduction.

"My name is George Walsh, and I really must apologise! Forgive me, I am obviously disturbing an important conversation."

The sound of silence echoed back. "Maybe we can all chat another time then?" Without waiting for an answer, George walked hastily into the adjacent Library itself.

Three pairs of raised eyebrows faced towards Kim in anticipation.

Kim laughed nervously. "I didn't know his name— until now," she smirked. "He is part of the reason I am sitting here asking for your help today." Kim took the cups off the tray and placed it now barren onto an unoccupied table beside them.

Having made some room. Kim continued by lifting her taffeta bag, and carefully removing the content. Placing the binder gently onto the table.

She hastily explained how she had come to possess the collection of documents, and in particular— The improbabilities shown on the birth certificate.

They all stared at the captured accumulation of paper. — Frozen, as if a magic spell was about to be performed.

Maria broke the pathetic silence, gesturing at the folder on the table.

"I suppose we should actually have a look at them then? I'll make a start." She took the birth certificate carefully from its plastic sleeve, and began to pore over the content.

Inspired by Maria's investigative attempt. The others began plucking random sleeve contents with gay abandon, from the ring binder.

Kirstie thrust a hand into the air, "Hang on," she called out excitedly. "This looks very interesting." Kirstie received stern looks from other people in the café, who were sitting closer to the library doors.

Staring back with her hands on her hips, she mouthed deliberately in their direction. "WHAT IS YOUR PROBLEM?"

The recipients of her frigid stare, quickly started paying closer attention to their beverages instead. Whispering to each other behind raised hands, and opened paper menus.

Holding a small notebook, with fragments of mould encrusted paper in her hand. Kirstie directly placed it and two sheets of paper, onto the top of the pile of loose documents already extracted from their plastic protection. She explained, "I found it stuck between some bills."

She pointed towards the ominous paper remnants, and the matching missing areas on the edge. The white covers of the notebook appeared to have been previously adhered by a green patch of damp. Probably the source of damage to the invoices, during its life in the plastic bag.

Kim lifted it up between two fingers, and carefully prised it apart between the cover and the first page.

It disappointedly revealed a simple shopping list, and something gold and triangular fell out landing by her feet.

"The package that just keeps giving," she mused, picking up the item, and laying it onto the edge of the table for everyone else to view.

"It looks like a guitar plectrum with three holes drilled in it, one hole at each corner," offered Kirstie. "I know it's a plectrum because Dave keeps losing them every time he plays his guitar at a gig. The flat is full of the darn things— in teacups, the fruit bowl." She took a deep breath. "I once even found one in the Frosties, although that one might have been a free-gift..."

Kirstie noticed her friends were looking at her strangely. "Okay— maybe I got a bit carried away— Anyway plectrum it is." They all laughed at her, as Kirstie's face was now a deep shade of pink.

"Okay, has anybody found anything else?" Kim glanced at the handwritten shopping list, "Of interest..." she added grimacing.

"Some receipts in Spanish or something," offered Nancy, brandishing them in the air.

"Loads of photos in this sleeve— They look like they belong in a family album or something," observed Maria. Now removing them from captivation and handing them to Kim.

Ignoring the boring receipts, Kim spread the clutch of photos out onto the constantly growing pile of paper. One photograph in particular, instantly caught the focus of her interest.

She gave a sharp intake of breath. "Oh my god— That looks like Gran and my mum when she was young." Kim said out loud— Ignoring the accusatory stares from other customers.

Her friends glimpsed a white face, discoloured by shock. As she lifted the offending photograph, to gain a more thorough look.

The black and white picture had faded to sepia at the edges, but otherwise it appeared to have been taken care of.

The image portrayed a typical family scene. Two adults with a pair of adolescent girls, enjoying themselves on a sandy beach somewhere. The man and the woman sat on two old-fashioned, striped deck chairs. The girls were sitting on a patterned beach towel, with their knees shyly pulled up towards their chest.

Excluding the adults for a moment, her eyes flicked between the virtually identical teens. Kim had recognised her mother straight away. She was sporting on her left temple, the 'Harry Potter' scar mum had received in a horse riding accident. "But who was the other girl?"

Kim observed her own hand trembling, as she tightly held the mystery photograph.

Recognising that her friend appeared to be highly stressed. Nancy stood and wrapped her arm consolingly around Kim's shoulders.

"I think we have investigated enough for today," announced Maria. "Perhaps we can pick this up another time — When Kim has completely recovered from her shock?"

They quickly gathered the loose papers and thrust them safely into random sleeves.

Nancy led the way out, heading towards the Library car park outside. No one appeared to notice the lonely guitar plectrum. Which had again been knocked onto the floor, finally resting hidden underneath the table.

A tall man slipped aside the square pillar he had been leaning up against. He had been watching the antics of a group of young women with interest, out of sight of their view in the shadow of the pillar. He reached under their table and deftly swiped the plectrum into his large hand.

George wiped off some remaining mould, and noticed minute lettering at one corner. He took one last look at the plectrum— then deposited it safely into his denim jeans.

George smiled— absolutely over the moon with his random find.

***

#3   Saturday Six PM

May 3rd 2021

Nancy and the other girls had been fussing over Kim all afternoon.

Two hours ago. They had bundled Kim into the back of her own Red Honda Jazz, with Maria consoling her as best she could. Nancy had slipped into the driver's seat, and Kirstie had followed behind in her own clapped out Ford Fiesta.

Pulling up outside the cottage. Nancy could see Roger pacing backwards and forwards, across the internal windowsill. His tail flicked slowly from side to side like a pendulum— Roger was totally convinced. That Kim 'must' be aware, he was impatiently waiting for his tea...

Spotting the girls and Kim getting out of her car. He quickly disappeared— Racing to meet them at the front door.

The rattle of the key was followed by the door rapidly swinging open. Once again, Roger was unceremoniously flung roughly to one side. As Kim and her entourage swept inside, heading for the sofa.

"I'll get the tea on," shouted Maria, already rattling cups and filling the kettle from the tap. Kirstie followed her into the kitchen. Immediately searching cupboards, for a fresh packet of sweet digestive biscuits.

Nancy continued consoling Kim, who now seemed to be slowly responding with short one word answers. Noticing the guilty photograph, still being gripped tightly between Kim's fingers. Nancy carefully prised it free to prevent it from getting torn and placed it safely onto the coffee table.

Roger took this as a signal that his mistress now had both hands free. His life revolved around her ability to fuss him. Already purring at high volume, he confidently jumped up— landing safely into her lap.

Kim smiled, as Roger contentedly began to slowly pat her legs with his forepaws, making himself more comfortable.

A contented cat, finally curled up into a fetal position— Immediately falling asleep with his whiskers twitching, as she softly stroked the fur down his back.

Maria walked back in with Kirstie in tow. Carrying a tray with four cups of tea and an already open packet of digestives.

"Tea up." Announced Maria, already stuffing another biscuit into her mouth. Kirstie placed the tray onto the coffee table, after Nancy moved the inciting photograph out of the way.

Kim gratefully took her cup of hot tea and took a long refreshing sip. "Ahh, that's better, thanks girls for looking after me. I have to admit I wasn't expecting— that." She sighed, gratefully taking another deep gulp.

Eventually, the final empty cup was placed neatly back onto the tray.

"Well Kim, the big question is what will you do now?" Asked Nancy. "I suppose if we make a list, maybe things might look just a smidgen clearer."

"Okay," agreed Maria, while Kirstie simply nodded in agreement.

Nancy again took the birth certificate from the safety of the folder. Lifting it up in the air, and using it to make a statement. "Right— point one, the names on this certificate. Who is Karen Taylor?"

Maria took charge of recording the minutes. Writing the salient points down, onto the back of one of the larger receipts from the folder.

Nancy continued, "Karen also has the surname, of Kim's Gran on her mother's side. Could she possibly be a missing sister?" Although that fact had passed through everyone's mind already, it still seemed to be no more than a strange coincidence.

"The real dilemma as I see it— Is Karen Taylor having the same birth date as Kim Chapman," continued Maria.

"Plus the biggie for me. -- Who the heck sent her the paperwork and photos inside the parcel in the first place?"

Kim nodded her head in agreement. "I have, to be honest, I am a bit suspicious of that bloke George.

I think he knows more than he is letting on— What do you guy's think?" Kim asked her friends.

They all agreed he was not only suspicious but rather tasty too. Maria even hoped he was not only involved, but single and available for grabs as well.

They all laughed out loud, teasing Maria that she was looking desperate for another man already.

They were disturbed when Kim's mobile phone shrilly rang. She picked it up and noticed the caller id was displaying the name 'Andy.' She ignored it and let the incoming call time out.

"I will talk to him later, sorting this out, will come first at the moment. I've got lots of things to unravel," Kim explained. She was not exhibiting the slightest sign of remorse, after deliberately blanking her boyfriend.

"Well— I have to start somewhere, don't I? Mum is somehow involved in this, so I had better confront her with the binder first— and see what she has to say."

❋❋❋

After Kim had finally fed an impatient cat, filling his dish with his evening meal. It was over an hour later, before her friends had left her alone.

She once more, looked at the photographs still in their plastic sleeves. Her eyes were drawn to the photo on the table and wrinkled her nose in apprehension.

Knowing full well, she would have to ring her Mum soon. The thought of building up the courage to use the landline phone— Was making her feel distinctly nervous.

Trying to distract herself. She ambled over to the front door, extracting today's newspaper from the letterbox. Kim had forgotten it was still here— After all the excitement experienced today.

Taking it into the cosy study, she laid it down on the old oak table at the side of the snug room. Hoping to try to calm herself. By immersing herself, deep into its professional content.

Usual political antics were headlined on the first page. Announcing calls for the House of Lords to be devolved. Not surprisingly in Kim's mind. Happily— it appeared consensus had somehow decided, in agreement with Kim. The whole pack of 'Humph-Humbug' supporters were now apparently deemed surplus to requirements.

As the fallout after Brexit, was finally being brought under control. Some politicians were now looking for another fight, to validate their existence.

While others were rumoured, to now being rewarded with a peerage... Unbelievably— in recognition of the damage inflicted against the incumbent party, at every juncture of the drawn-out fight for independence.

"BORING," thought Kim. Idly flicking through the pages, looking for something actually interesting to read.

Just as she found an article that looked interesting— The house-phone began to insistently ring. Lifting the handset from the charger cradle, she glanced at the caller ID identifying it as a likely spam call.

"Hello, Constable Smith— Fraud squad, how can I help?" She uttered confidently and was rewarded by a click. Followed soon after, by the sound of a dialling tone in her ear.

"Never fails," she murmured, and was about to put the handset down— When she paused in thought.

Feeling extremely annoyed with herself, for being a coward, and unable to ring her own mother. Kim decided to begin dialling, Mum and Dad's number right now. Her fingers automatically flew over the keypad.

Kim normally found herself, randomly dialling her Mum. A couple of times a day at least, for a friendly chat and chin-wag. Now she was ringing her in confrontation instead— Kim decided this felt really weird inside.

Mum and her, were so close. They were always finding things to laugh at. Having the same sense of humour. Often inspiring Kim, to refer to her mother as Sis.'

The monotonous dial tone disappeared. Replaced, by the sound of the number tones being dialled instead.

Now changing to a ringtone in her ear, she waited for her Mum or Dad to answer. The seconds ticked by, and she was about to hang up and try again later— When the phone was answered.

"Hello— who is this?" queried a monotone male voice.

Kim sighed, Dad was useless with technology. If he had looked at the display on his handset, it would have displayed her name. "Hello Dad, is Mum about?" She asked.

Instantly recognising her voice, he replied happily. "Oh, Hi Kim, she is just coming through the back door. We have been tending to the garden— Everything okay with you?"

She winced, before answering in a falsely bright voice. "I'm Fine Dad— Just ringing for a chat as usual." Kim hated lying to her Dad, as he was such a worry-guts.

She heard a rustle on the phone, and then she was greeted by her Mum Pamela saying hello.

"Kim, you're ringing a bit earlier than usual, it was lucky we were in the garden. Your Dad had suggested earlier that we spend a day at the coast as it has been lovely weather."

Kim carried on the mundane conversation, trying to sound trouble free. Explaining she had been spending a normal Saturday routine, with her friends at the café.

Pamela had sensed, there was a slight tremor in Kim's voice. It was telling her something was deeply amiss. She found herself interrupting her daughter mid-flow.

"Kim— is there anything wrong?" She asked in a concerned tone, now confronted by an unnatural silence from her daughter's end of the phone.

"Are you still there?— Kim? Speak to me. Tell me what it is?" She was now extremely worried, this was not the daughter she thought she knew inside out.

"Yes Mum, there is something wrong," admitted Kim. Now with a definite tremor in her voice. "I have got something that I need to ask you."

Pamela waited silently. Mentally urging Kim to 'spit it out' and divulge the source of the problem.

She heard Kim utter, "Did you have a sister— Mum?" This time it was Pamela's turn to reflect total silence.

"Mum— please answer me," her daughter pleaded. There was a tearful note in her voice, followed by a gentle sob. Pamela held her silence for a little longer. Until unable to suffer her daughters torment, any longer. "Yes," she answered timidly in a tremulous voice, "Why?"

"I received something Mum, and it contained amongst other things, a photo of you and another girl with Gran, and I assume Grandad.— Who, and where is she?"

Trying calmly, to avoid the straightforward question. Pamela slyly countered with, "Where was the photo taken?"

"Mum— why don't you want to answer?" She accused her mother unbelievingly."It was the seaside, why does that even matter anyway?" Kim began to cry, upset with the tension between them.

"Her name is Helen," Pamela said in a monotone voice.

Kim exhaled loudly in shock, without revealing why— She asked her mother if she could come around their house tomorrow, as she had something that she wanted to show her. Pamela swallowed deeply, and softly agreed.

"Thanks Mum would Sunday lunchtime be okay?" Kim asked hesitantly. "I really fancy a roast for a change. Something tells me, Roger would definitely appreciate any titbits of meat."

She was already beginning to relax a little. Hopeful, that her suspicions were likely to be answered in full.

Pamela chuckled softly. "As long as you don't bring the scrounging moggie with you. Last time you did, I lost a complete side of salmon. I should have known better I suppose. I was the one who foolishly left the fish on the worktop— remember?"

Kim smiled to herself in acceptance. "That's a deal then Mum, I'll be there two-ish. I will bring along the mysterious item with me, to see if you can put any further light on it— Love you to pieces— Bye."

She placed the phone into the cradle with a satisfying clunk.

✳✳✳

Kim opened the fridge door and peered inside— Empty.

She declared, in annoyance to herself. "Damn it. I forgot I needed to visit Dingle's Supermarket, after meeting the girls at the café earlier today."

Kim was still thinking aloud, while holding her grumbling stomach. "I suppose I could do a quick shop, then call into Asian Ari's for a nice hot curry, Hopefully it will help me sleep. If not, at least I have a happy and full tum…"

She washed her hands carefully in the kitchen sink, and proceeded to mentally recall the shopping list— While trying to concentrate on that. She found herself dragging a shopping carrier, from the back of the old pantry at the same time.

Now ready to leave the house. Kim automatically locked the back door and made her way to the front porch and outside.

✳✳✳

For the third time today. Kim again found herself sitting in her Honda Jazz and reflected it was only the second time she was actually in control of the vehicle.

34

Driving carefully to avoid the potholes left in the road, still unfilled from the previous winter. She looked upwards.

Noticing dark and heavy clouds had rapidly drawn in overhead, promising showers— Or maybe, even a storm.

The change to inclement weather, wasn't promised on the latest weather report. It was only a short while ago that good weather ahead, was being being touted. Only a few short seconds ago, on her car radio.

Kim was beginning to feel annoyed. Neither had they hinted at the amount of traffic, trying patiently to get into Dingle's Supermarket car-park. Independent spots of rain began falling onto her windscreen, quickly escalating to a full-on downpour.

Remembering, Asian Ari's was adjacent to the multi-storey car-park. Kim's current preferences had instead now altered. Preferring a short run to his restaurants front door, rather than the trudge across a large car-park.

The thought of sitting soaking wet while eating her meal— after shopping. Rapidly changed her immediate priorities.

Manoeuvring back onto the main road, avoiding the traffic entering Dingle's. Kim found herself, navigating towards the town centre instead.

Flashes of almost blinding sheet lighting, reflected on the water logged road surface. Was followed by loud claps of thunder, drowning out the radio programme she was listening to.

Kim could just about make out, a glowing purple sign ahead on her left. It was quickly followed by the multi-storey car-park entrance. She turned onto the ramp and started to look for parking spaces.

Parking safely, She paid for a parking ticket, lasting for two hours. Dingles didn't close until 22:30— So there wouldn't be any need to hurry her meal.

She popped the ticket face up, onto the corner of the dashboard. Then leant over to the back-seat picking up her yellow umbrella and a waterproof cape. Slamming the car door shut, she walked the short distance to the lift entrance.

Soon after finding herself a car space on the sixth floor. Kim had already convinced herself that she didn't mind using a lift in the car-park alone at night.

Kim had reckoned her decision could be easily reinforced. Especially after a large meal and having to face five long flights of steps.

Once she was in the position— where she had to decide how to make the return journey, back up to her vehicle. Kim was convinced, she knew which method she would choose.

Just as the doors were about to finally close before descending, she thought she saw a shadow moving slowly outside.

Slightly nervous— She pulled on her cape as the lift doors opened. Kim put up the umbrella, in anticipation of the inclement weather outside.

Feeling the wind and pelting rain on her face. Kim ran the short distance to Ari's front porch, and burst through the half-open door.

Ari Barindi recognised Kim immediately. Complete with still open umbrella. The man ushered her to a table, sheltering her behind short screening.

Kim looked embarrassingly at the open umbrella. While in the process of closing it, and rolling it up.

She nodded towards him, uttering a breathless apology. "Sorry Ari, I was in a rush to get inside to get out of that rain. I genuinely forgot it was still in my hand," Kim hastily explained.

Ari raised his hands in recognition of her plea. "Don't worry Missy Kim; I am just glad it was not a sabre or something. I would have been annoyed if it had ruined my ceiling," he joked.

He reached into a large pocket, handing her a large menu. "Would you like to start with your usual Lentil soup?"

Kim again simply nodded her head once.

"Okay, I will return during your starter, to collect your choice for a main meal from the menu."

Ari bowed respectively and headed away towards the kitchens, with her initial order.

Without even opening the Menu, she already knew she was going to say as soon as Ari returned with her soup. "Pilau rice and Chicken Bhuna, with boiled eggs on top."

Kim supposed he left a menu out of habit. As she had eaten the same menu every week, for the last two years. She was proud to have been a loyal customer, since his shop had first opened.

Slightly hidden behind the screening. She took advantage and began to browse around the rest of the restaurant. She enjoyed being nosey and began half-listening to other customer's conversation.

Her ears perked up. Kim thought she had just heard a familiar voice. Now reasonably certain, it was coming from the adjacent booth.

"You wouldn't believe what she said next?" The male voice dropped in volume slightly, so she couldn't hear how it continued. A few seconds later, it was rapidly followed by a female— shrilly, laughing out loud. The man had a distinctive braying laugh.

Kim swallowed deeply— "Andy! Oh my god..." Inwardly, she began feeling frantic. "Who is he with, and who the hell was the woman he had been talking about?" Were just some thoughts— ricocheting around, inside her mind.

Leaning towards the couples voices. Kim concentrated harder, to clearly listen to the ensuing conversation.

The man again brayed loudly, with cruel laughter. "She had no idea what was going on— I thought the 'babies' bit would have convinced her to marry me.

Duh, big mistake on my behalf. Looks like I will have to take another tack, to get her to tie the knot. I want that house, and the money it will fetch after the quick divorce. Regardless of her feelings..." Andy King, chuckled at the thought of his deviousness. Calculated to eventually swindle Kim, out of half of her cottage's equity.

He sighed, "It would probably achieve £325,000 in the open market, due to its size and location. A cool £162,500 in our pocket, just for the inconvenience of sharing a few months of marriage." Kim could hear a fork dropped onto a heavy plate.

"Changing the subject, how are you getting on with your fella?" Andy asked the mystery woman.

Kim looked up to see Ari silently placing in front of her, a steaming bowl of Lentil soup. The enticing spicy aroma, almost distracted her attention.

Taking her purse out of the bumbag. She carefully extracted three crisp five pound notes, and placed them under the drinks menu holder.

Kim made sure they were poking out slightly, so that Ari would quickly notice them.

Pulling her cape back over her shoulders. She picked up her brolly, tucking it firmly into the pit underneath her arm.

Standing up. She picked up the napkin on the table, wrapping it around the edge of the still steaming soup bowl.

Realising the amount of emitted heat, could badly scald her. Especially if she mistakenly placed her hands— In the wrong place.

Mindfully, Kim carefully gripped the circumference firmly. With both hands touching the protection of the napkin.

Looking around to check that Ari was not wandering aimlessly about the floor. She walked the few steps to the adjacent booth, and stared accusingly at Andy.

Initially, Andy and his companion had not noticed Kim standing next to their table— Bowl in hand.

He caught a slight movement out of the corner of his eye and turned expecting to see Ari ready to serve the next course, with their meals on a trolley.

Instead,— He faced a furious Kim, who uttered an explicative and poured the hot soup onto his lap. Andy rose rapidly from his seat, with his arms waving around in shock.

One hand, caught a two-litre jug of cheap Indian lager. Knocking it over and landing away from him. Its contents drained into the already shocked females lap, soaking her lower half with chilled liquid.

Kim ignored their curses and shouts in her direction. She readied the umbrella and began marching directly towards the restaurant door.

Instinctually expecting trouble with all the shouting. Ari had just left the kitchens, with a large chopping knife in his right hand.

Andy had by now, managed to wipe off the majority of burning soup that lay on his crotch. He stood slowly and carefully, and was now steaming meaningfully towards Kim. He balled both his fists, into a pair of tight balls.

"Hang on just one minute, Mr Andy— Please do not make threatening stances in my restaurant, or I will be forced to call the police." Ari stood defensively. Pushing Kim the final few feet towards safety, and out of the door.

Kim didn't need telling twice. Flinging open the door, and shouting behind.

"Thanks Ari, I will see you in the week to explain." She ran effortlessly, towards the car park lift— Leaving far behind, Andy's angry shouts into the wind and the rain.

The gales had blown a large amount of moisture over the open walls, and onto the Multi-storey tarmac floor.

In her haste, Kim began to aquaplane across its surface. She slid uncontrollably for a couple of feet. The soles of her shoes, eventually purchased a grip.

Losing her balance. Kim began to fall to the floor, just outside the lift doors. As she started to fall for the second time that day. A strong arm caught her and prevented her lying in a heap on the floor.

Before she looked up, she already knew exactly who was going to be standing there— George!

Kim stood open-mouthed as he let go of her arm, and wiped away rain from his sodden hair.

Totally shocked. She could only flutter her eyelashes helplessly. Finally, regaining the power of speech, Kim managed to croak out loud. "You have got to be joking George, not you again."

George pulled back his head in mock horror, and smiled disarmingly. "Don't you mean?— thank goodness you had finished your meal, after sadly eating alone at McDonald's.

Then by incredible chance, to have spotted you running across the road like a bat out of hell. Finally, the miracle was complete. As I managed to reach you, seconds before you had a nasty accident?"

He looked at her with a pathetic smile. Just like a puppy dog— expecting some praise.

Kim couldn't help laughing, at the hapless look on his face. "Thank you— I think," she said with a final snigger, now also sharing a smile on her face.

George's facial expression changed to one reflecting deep concern. "Are you okay? He asked. "If you don't mind— I will ride upwards, with you in the lift."

Kim looked at him oddly.

He sympathetically offered an explanation. "It's okay, I have no intention of doing anything else. I just want to make sure; you get back safely to your car."

George noted, Kim still looked doubtful of his offer. "My car is on this floor, so I won't hang about to wave goodbye or anything," he chuckled.

Kim heard distant sirens. Combined with shouts still coming from Ari's, convinced her to make up her mind.

She shook her head signifying a yes. Kim found herself pushing hard on the lift door button. As the doors slid open, she stepped inside the metal cabin. Feeling a lot safer, with George following in tow.

Distracted by smelling his aromatic aftershave. Kim automatically looked up at him and shivered slightly. As the adrenaline was now wearing off.

Up until now. Kim hadn't really appreciated how handsome George actually was. Firm jaw, cleanly shaven with perfectly white teeth. Short brown wet hair, probably curly when dry. The hairdresser inside her, easily surmised.

The ping of the lift, announcing it was now reaching its destination. Had instantly accentuated her awareness of her surroundings and left her disappointed as her daydreaming suddenly ended.

Kim realised, she would love to be spending more time with the man beside her. He was gallantly now standing against the door edge, blocking it to make sure she exited safely— without the doors closing in on her, unannounced.

She stepped gingerly out of the lift and could see her car parked opposite the lift entrance.

"Thanks— George," she said coquettishly. "You are a gentleman; I'm glad you appeared when you did. That fall would have finished off a crap night with a bang otherwise."

He noticed the signs of tears, beginning to build up in her eyes. "I know you don't really know me. But, If you want to talk anytime, you can find me working hard in the library— most days."

George saw her contemplate his new offer with a quick nod of the head.

"Okay— drive safely, the roads are very slippery— Nite." Said George, slipping back into the lift.

"Nite," whispered Kim, getting into her car. "See you soon Mister Walsh. You can be sure of that..."

✳✳✳

#4   **Sunday Eight AM**

May 4th 2021

George wasn't sure what time last night, he had actually dozed off on the sofa— but, after scratching his head trying to provoke a sense of wakefulness. He realised something else may have added to his tiredness, a few short hours after falling asleep.

He vaguely remembered waking agitated, at around three O'clock in the morning. With an aching back and an almost full bladder, stabbing him deep in the groin.

After finding relief, he recalled exiting the upstairs toilet — For an unattractive brief moment, George had considered making his way back down the stairs.

Hoping to perhaps reboot his laptop and work some more on his novel— Before deciding that would probably be pointless, as Microsoft Windows had indicated it was ready for an update, as the computer finished powering down.

The last time it had updated, he had found himself staring at a single message of 'Please wait.' He had wasted four precious hours of his life waiting for it to finish, before finally allowing him to use it again.

Logic told him, he might just as well be crawling into his comfortable warm bed instead.

George had made the short journey back to his bedroom. Picking up his mobile phone off the bedside table, after noticing a flashing light indicating he had received a message.

A few quick flicks on the screen revealed. It was an anonymous message. Asking him when he was next going to be announcing a book signing, as they would love attending anywhere in the United Kingdom.

George mentally tried recalling his book promotion schedule and after only a few minutes, he shook his weary head in defeat. "I don't need this crap this early in the morning, I need my sleep..." He thought to himself while stifling a large yawn.

Decision made— he pulled back the heavy duvet, crawled inside fully clothed, instantly falling sound asleep.

❋❋❋

His head was now pounding. Unable to think clearly, George had risen early and sauntered downstairs. Making his way into the modern kitchen.

George was dog-tired, after spending the best part of the night, laying on the uncomfortable couch.

The metallic clunk of the toaster as it was loudly ejecting his toast from the heated interior, had caught his attention.

Leaning heavily against the tall fridge freezer, George was currently distracted. He had been going over in his mind,

45

yesterday's activities for the umpteenth time. Before finally giving in with the lack of clarity he was achieving, and deciding he should be consulting his notes instead.

Thankfully, he had recently gained a new Hi-Tech-habit. Where at every opportunity, he would make sure he dutifully recorded his thoughts, using his new essential tool. 'Google Docs.'

George had downloaded and installed the 'App' on his mobile phone, with the intention of using it to review stuff later— if needed.

However, there was no-way If George could help it. Would he even be thinking about looking at those?— or indeed any other notes.

His growling stomach would be overriding anything else happening. Until he had drunk at least two coffees, and devoured his unhealthy breakfast.

Reaching forward. George plucked the Tiger bread toast from the still hot cavities of the toaster, dropping it still hot and golden brown, onto an awaiting plate.

A loud ping from the microwave announced the fillings for the toast were also ready— perfect timing.

Pulling the flap on the front of the appliance and opening the tinted door. George Walsh took out the white plate inside, complete with a number of steaming Frankfurters nestled at its centre.

His next ritual step was rapidly completed. By smothering the dry toast, with lashings of brown sauce.

Now the recipe was nearing the end. As the taste enhancing sauce was followed by a shake of pepper and a handful of grated cheese.

The pinnacle had been almost reached, as George carefully arranged each juicy Wiener. To sit across the bottom piece of toast, into calculated parallel lines.

George smiled contently, as he completed his creation. By finally covering all the contents, with the other buttered crisp slice of toast.

Preparation completes, and raising what he believed to be a culinary masterpiece to his mouth. George took a large satisfying bite, out of his regular sandwiched breakfast.

He was rudely interrupted from taking a second tasty mouthful. As his mobile phone, began to loudly play a nondescript jaunty tune.

Recognising the caller ID on the display. Prompted him to take his time, dithering before he could be bothered answering.

"Amber Prevett— and what is so important that you have to ring me, so early on a Sunday morning?" He asked in a sarcastic tone, looking pointedly at his watch.

"As your literary agent, I think I have the right to contact you day and night.

Do you realise George, by encouraging you to actually do something? There is then a strong chance, we can both make some more money." A honey toned voice, sarcastically flowed like poison, spilling from the telephone speaker.

"I'm still at the preparation stage," George advised her. He was now chewing noisily, with a healthy bite of toast and sausage distorting his answer.

"Maybe I should have rung later, when I could actually understand a bloody word you just said." Amber sighed, with more than a hint of exasperation in her voice.

George swallowed noisily. "Now-now, play nicely— I basically meant that my research was panning out better than expected."

He repressed apprehensive thoughts and continued with his weak explanation hoping she would fall for his explanation.

"However Amber dearest, there are still a few loose ends to filter out. Especially before I can start stitching the facts together— please be patient," George asked pleadingly.

"George Walsh— did I just hear you say the words please and be patient in the same sentence?" Amber sighed heavily.

"I seem to remember, in the past I was continually hearing those words. Plus a well-intentioned sorry to boot, when I was your Fiancé— didn't I?" Amber was beginning to get both angry and exasperated, at the same time.

George attempted to explain the way he had treated her. "Look, I am sorry about what happened in the past— really sorry, if you must know. But, it just didn't seem to be the right time in my life.

With two successful novels to my name, I thought it would be sensible to concentrate on the next one. I reckoned if I was to keep the ball rolling, I needed to ignore everything else going on.

Sadly I had deduced that work was far more important than us— Maybe things could have been different, but..." George's voice trailed off, as he heard short breaths of distress.

Amber was softly sobbing, at the other end of the phone. Realising George had stopped talking, she now remained silent herself, whilst choking back the tears.

Finally, steeling herself and trying to resume her professional stance, she replied sternly. "Okay, it happened, but you are not dismissing me so lightly— When I say it is time to get back to business, I mean it.

So, let me get this straight— from the last action plan you updated me with.

It would appear, you are now going to try persuading this woman, Kim— To trust you..."

She paused, "Good luck with that one. Although I have to admit, you are the consummate charmer. But, and it's a big but. You will fail— sooner or later," Amber concluded harshly.

"Look Amber, have I ever let you down?" Realising he had left himself open to further harassment, George quickly changed the subject. "How are sales doing, is there any sign of them slowing down?"

"They will do— if you don't have the promise of a new mystery thriller, in the can by Christmas.

As you say you are making progress, I suppose I don't really have any other option than to believe you." She asked her Employee, stroke Business Partner imploringly.

Her voice broke up slightly and raised a touch higher in volume. "Right then George, I will let you crack on. But you can expect another phone call sooner than later— Bye."

George realised she was still on the line, waiting for something else to be said. "Okay— Bye, Amber, speak soon," he said softly. Hearing the click, as the phone was immediately put down.

He put another cold piece of toast and meat into his mouth and began to seriously contemplate his next move.

✳✳✳

Maria placed her full coffee cup at the side of her computer table and pulled the comfy office chair in nearer. Swivelling slightly, she switched on the mains electric socket to supply the computer with power. She completed the action by depressing the computer on/off switch to boot it up.

Maria heard the staccato sound of the chattering hard disk. Just as the monitor burst into life, with the ubiquitous words 'PLEASE WAIT' displayed on the centre of the screen.

The computer recognised her identity, after examining her face using the built-in camera, and sped past the login screen.

Finally, the main desktop appeared at the same time as the sound of a welcoming trumpet. Maria clicked on the Chrome browser button, to display the Google homepage.

She began to type rapidly on the keyboard, readying sentences and terms to begin her daunting search. "Okay, Mister George Walsh— who the hell are you?" Maria said out loud to herself, while scanning the numerous pages of results.

Ninety minutes and two more coffees later, without even a sniff at revealing his identity. Her eyes tiredly flicked top left, and noticed the search statistics.

[About 94,300,000 results (0.54 second)], Maria sighed deeply.

Realising that the chance of finding him, while examining each page Google suggested. Would likely end up taking a lifetime— Unless she was very, very lucky.

Maria momentarily paused her search. Rubbing her tired eyes. She took a final long drink, from her latest coffee cup.

She frowned heavily, while trying to contemplate an easier strategy. "It would be easier to find a needle in a haystack, and then only if it jumped out and bit me."

Suddenly experiencing a 'Eureka Moment', Maria exclaimed out loud, "That's what I have been doing wrong. C'mon Lockyer— get your act together, you stupid girl!"

Clasping her hands together, interlinking the fingers and then pushing backwards— Until she heard a satisfying click, as pockets of gas burst.

"Right Mr Walsh, we resume battle— You will not hide from me," She said enthusiastically. Gripping the mouse and changing the search group from [All] to [Images] instead.

Pressing the search button again. Maria was rewarded by a sea of faces, on the resultant page. Feeling far happier, just scanning one page at a time for George.

"Must be far more efficient, and easier on the eyes and brain." Maria concluded.

Scouring the displayed results, for a handsome face. Finding she was actually looking forward to seeing him again, spurred her on.

Again, after yet another hour. Maria was again starting to feel despondent.

After screening visage after visage. She was about to go and get herself yet another coffee, when something caught her eye.

Excitement began building in her heart. Maria double-clicked on the potential image. Expanding it to full size allowing her to examine it closer.

"Jackpot! Got you Mr George Walsh— Author?"

She looked again doubtfully at the blurb shown below his smiling portrait. Almost as if she couldn't quite believe what she had discovered was true.

Newton Abbot Herald— Arts Section. 14/10/2019

Newton Abbot branch of The Bookshop was treated this week to a visit, by celebrated local author George Walsh.

George was in town to attend a book signing event, for the release of his latest book: 'Did She or Didn't She?'

The fourth Mystery Novel to be penned by the popular writer, was only released fourteen days ago. To rapturous acclaim by critics and his fans alike.

Sales are rumoured to have outstripped supply. But luckily George had managed to source a large amount of Hardbacks, enough to satisfy his loyal fans eager for a signed copy.

"Okay, he is a Novelist— I have now found out that much. But what is he doing hanging around Kim, like a bad smell?"

Intrigued, Maria checked the local Library opening hours. Armed with the intention of asking Mister George Walsh— A few insightful questions.

"Damn," she cursed out loud. "They are closed all day Monday, for an urgent plumbing repair. What about Tuesday?"

She pulled the mouse further down the page, past the Monday closure notice. Tuesday was normal hours— 08:30 to 19:00, "Perfect." Maria proudly thought to herself.

She now felt a lot happier and was herself in a better place. Now feeling an insatiable appetite inside. Hungry and primed to be able to make more progress, in her quest for more information on Mr George Walsh.

Maria sat thoughtfully, while planning her next moves in the hunt for George. She explored possible time management slots— wondering when she had any free time for the rest of her day.

"I don't start my shift until 10:00 and will be finished by 17:00. So if I don't find him before work starts. I should get a second stab at it, after work."

Now feeling a little giddy. As the mixture of excitement and a bucket full of strong coffee, were beginning to take effect.

Maria looked out of the window, to see whether the rain had finally stopped. Apart from occasional droplets of water falling from the branches on the tree out front. The sky actually looked hopeful. Quite clear and bright, minus the dark clouds.

Making up her mind, Maria felt she needed to get outside. Hoping a brisk walk would clear any cobwebs from her head. She snatched a woolly hat and coat from out of the cupboard, and finished dressing in front of the hallway mirror.

Maria considered the weather, and tugged on a cute and distinctive pair of pink wellington boots, nestling near the back door.

"Park or local shops?" She wondered. With the park coming out strongly ahead. After deciding, it would mean having her hands free, to keep warm in her pockets the entire journey. The decision was made.

Target now firmly set in her sights.

The expedition outdoors, had almost failed after only thirty seconds. After encountering a false start— Where she had to return after a few short yards, realising she had forgotten to pick up her mobile phone. Maria now began briskly heading south, already dreaming of George Walsh— Author.

✳✳✳

Having checked Roger had water and a meal available. Kim climbed into her car and placed the folder onto the passenger seat.

Adjusting the mirror and peering at herself, to check that her hair and makeup would pass muster. She pulled out of the drive and began heading towards Mum and Dads home.

Kim considered her habit of forever examining herself in the mirror. Reminded her of the times. When Mum had always taught her, that she should always look her best.

Constantly drumming into her, that she would never know until it was too late. Who she might meet, when out and about— Especially if the nice man might take a considered interest in her.

Kim began feeling angry with herself.

"Why bother— when there are so many rats hiding under stones everywhere, and you never really know whether you have just hooked up with one— until badly bitten, and it's inevitably too late to do anything about it, from mauling you some more."

Her run-in last night with Andy, came to the forefront of her mind. "I can't believe what he was up to— It beggars belief. Someone would solely marry for money, and not for the sake of sharing their united love.

She played back the scene last night at Ari's. Her recollection somehow seemed sharper in her head than the actual incident itself. "Who was that woman? What exactly was she supposed to be doing, with the man that Andy referred to?

If I remember correctly, she is probably his dream type. Blonde, quite tall and very curvy. The one thing that was out of character for Andy, though— she was at least ten years older!"

Kim grimaced, as the car dipped down with a thump. Into yet another hole in the tarmac.

The South Western local councils. Are now receiving an unsustainable income, from the United Kingdom Government.

The current political party has taken the word 'austerity'— To a whole new level.

Money to repair road surfaces, was no longer mandated as an essential. So— More and more pits and crevasses in the road surface, at various depths were inevitable.

Kim began slowing down. As a double-decker bus began pulling nearer to the kerb, preparing to pick up passengers.

The potential travellers were unaware of the large volume of water, nestling near to the gutter. While they innocently and patiently waited, in the safety of the bus shelter.

As the bus ploughed through the body of fluid Kim noticed a resultant wave of water was created, rapidly building like a micro-Tsunami.

Its kinetic energy finally dispersed, as it ended its short journey— by splashing heavily against the passenger refuge.

A random memory popped into her head— of Andy standing in front of her, ready to deflect a similar wave, bringing tears to her eyes— "Bastard," she spat vehemently, realising his false chivalry had hidden an alternative purpose.

Seeing a gap in the oncoming traffic. Kim decided to flick on her indicator and pulled around the bulk of the stationary bus.

Now possessing a clear view of the fairly open road now revealed to her. She depressed the accelerator further, allowing the car to easily reach the national speed limit.

Now travelling on the straight stretch, flying past the Park on her left, she instantly recognised a pair of distinctive pink wellingtons walking towards her.

Checking her rear mirror, before she pulled over to greet Maria. Kim was aware of a grubby car accelerating rapidly towards her from behind.

"Mad Bastard," she exclaimed. Angry, as the vehicle shot past her at considerable speed. Then just as quickly pulling back into the left-hand side of the road— Closely missing her car's bonnet.

As his front wheel dropped into another lengthy puddle, located at the edge of the pavement. With a loud bang from the protesting tyre, the driver appeared to totally lose control. As the vehicle violently mounted the concrete kerb— Heading straight for innocent Maria.

The inevitable happened, as the car hit her friend at high speed. Flinging her body— twisting uncontrollably, high into the unresisting air.

Maria crashed back down noisily, lying broken and bleeding against the unforgiving Park fence.

The driver began slowing down, as if about to halt and help. Apparently changing their mind, the car accelerated again, rapidly flying away at speed— disappearing into the distance.

Concerned for Maria's welfare. She screeched to a halt and flew out the car to kneel by her friend's side.

Maria's leg was twisted at an obtuse angle below the knee. Thick blood dripped from her nose and her hair was a shade of matted red, obviously from a head injury.

Although unconscious, Maria was making a coughing and gurgling noise at the back of her throat.

"Oh my god," exclaimed Kim, afraid to move her in case of causing further injury.

Rifling through her small bag, she pulled out her mobile phone. Immediately dialling the emergency services.

"Ambulance please, my friend has just been run over by a maniac in a car," Kim said. Shaking her head in disbelief.

After describing Maria's apparent symptoms and her physical location. Kim hung up the call to keep a vigil on her friend's condition, until professional help arrived.

Holding her friend's hand firmly, attempting to comfort both herself and Maria.

Kim noticed other concerned drivers pulling up behind her car, and flinging their doors open, quickly joining her at her side.

She felt her knees beginning to ache and dropped to sit on the wet floor instead— still gripping Maria's unmoving hand.

People were gathered around mumbling words of encouragement, and asking pointless questions. To Kim, they were just white noise in her ears, now focusing on hearing just one sound— Ambulance sirens.

Finally, she was rewarded, as an ambulance flew down the street. It finally came to a standstill upon reaching the crowd. Soaking them with another tidal wave, born from the fluid replenished gutter.

A paramedic's estate car joined the affray. Joining the queue of vehicles as it pulled up from behind. A concerned looking male exited the vehicle, pulling an aluminium case from the rear seat. He made his way to examine Maria, who was already being supported by the Ambulance team.

Apart from diagnosing an obvious broken leg and possible concussion, he gave the okay to move her onto a stretcher, and into the rear of the waiting Ambulance.

Kim turned towards the Paramedic, as he was about to climb back into his car, "Do you know which hospital she will be taken to? Maria is my friend, and she doesn't have any family.

I would really like to be around— when she regains consciousness, as I am sure she will be frightened. If I put myself into Maria's shoes, I don't think I would want to be lying there in a hospital bed, and not knowing anyone at all."

He reached onto the dashboard and picked up a microphone, asking someone if they knew her destination. After just a short conversation, he ended the call. Informing Kim that Maria would be taken to nearby Saint Richards Accident and Emergency. In a concerned voice and almost as an afterthought— the Paramedic asked if she was okay herself.

"Just shook up and worried to death— I will be okay thanks for asking."

Without waiting for a further reply. Kim climbed back into her car still shaking with shock and headed immediately towards the Hospital and her friend.

The roads were unusually busy, as the traffic passed through the centre of the town. Kim rapidly became more agitated with the hold-ups, only starting to become a little less frustrated— when the Hospital came into sight forty-five minutes later.

As usual, the hospital car park was almost full, with only the occasional space available.

Drawing into the first gap she could find, she paid in advance by waving her phone over the sensor behind. Completing the transaction as she carefully typed in her car registration, onto her mobile's touch sensitive screen.

Noticing there were already many other ambulances, stacked around a set of open doors. Multiple groups of hospital staff, gathered beside each vehicle. In no time at all they were ferrying stretchers inside, others were carrying saline drips beside them— trying to keep up.

Kim mentally shrugged her shoulders. Deciding to make her way instead, into the nearby Public A&E entrance. Handily endowed with automatic sliding doors, to keep out the now persistent downpour of rain.

Once inside, Kim looked around frantically for a reception desk, to inquire about Maria and her present location.

An elderly pair of ladies with matching grey hair, sat zombie-like at a desk underneath a sign announcing A&E inquiries.

They both looked up in tandem as Kim approached their desk. "How can we help?" They both announced in unison.

The woman on the right let the one on the left continue, by filling Kim's ears with further advice— given in a boring monotone voice. "There is currently a two-hour wait for Triage to complete— due to an incident at the local rail station less than an hour ago."

Further words trickled off her practiced tongue as if released by a metronome. "The emergency services are now overstretched, and it is impacting an inordinate amount of our resources." She concluded breathlessly.

The pair of officials waited for Kim to respond for a few seconds' more and were instantly distracted away— by a man dragging behind him a woman, smothered from head to toe in splashes of blood.

Transferring their professional attention to assist the distressed man and the woman. The receptionists stood up and began fussing over the obviously badly injured female.

Kim overheard the man, as he uttered a few words, "It flew off the rails..." He then became speechless with shock.

Kim walked further away, deciding it was unlikely she would get any valid information— anytime soon, from the pair of receptionists.

Glancing around the packed waiting room, she still couldn't see any sign of Maria. So she supposed the ambulance crew had got her inside and somehow managed to get her booked in— before all hell had been let loose around them.

Noticing a pair of heavy swing doors, labelled with one simple word 'Triage.' Kim strode purposefully past them, emerging into a room, with curtained booths fitted around the edges.

Behind each one poured out the sounds of distress or agonising pain.

Nurses clutching clipboards laden with notes, flitted in and out of booths, with requests for a myriad of tests made by the diagnosing registrars.

They ignored Kim. Probably assuming she was a family member, urgently called in for spurious reasons— regarding one of the unfortunate victims of circumstance.

Deliberately choosing areas within the room which seemed relatively quiet, she pulled back the curtains one by one. Peering inside each, hoping to reveal her friend was safe and well.

Kim was shocked a couple of times, by observing obvious disfiguring injuries. Thankfully it wasn't long before she finally discovered Maria half-awake, with her leg suspended by a pulley and stirrup mechanism— firmly attached to the ceiling.

"Some people would do anything to get a few weeks off work." Kim called out, while already closing the curtain behind her. She marched inside, to stand beside the small bedside cupboard next to the bed.

Maria looked up returning a crooked smile, "Must be easier ways to get an audience with a friend?" She initially laughed, then visibly cringed, as a stabbing pain in her leg burst through the haze of the strong painkillers.

"They are supposed to be putting on a plaster cast, but every time they pick up the casting tool— Someone else screams for help," Maria reflected with a sigh. She looked implorably at Kim— with a desperate question reflected in her eyes.

"What actually happened to me Kim? It's all still a bit foggy in my mind. Every time I try recalling what actually occurred— it's like a shutter is dropping, to block my view." Maria asked in a low voice.

Suddenly—Maria raised her eyebrows upwards in shock.

"Oh my God, I just remembered! It was Miles— Miles Quinn. He was staring at me through the windscreen, with a manic grin on his face..." Maria's words trailed off, with the realisation her ex-boyfriend had recently tried to kill her.

She remained quiet for a short while.

Distressed with the vivid memory, when she had flown through the air and struck the park fence— everything went blank after that.

Kim couldn't quite comprehend what she had just heard. "Miles— your Miles?"

She ignored the daggers, flying from Maria's acid look, at the mere mention of his name— still belonging to her.

Kim considered the statement farther out loud.

"Miles in a clapped out car?— that's never been a sentence, I thought I would utter in my lifetime. It just doesn't ring true.

Both you and I, have never ever seen him in any car less than twenty-eight thousand pounds— New or old!"

Maria nodded in agreement, Miles was definitely the consummate car snob.

"You have to tell the police," insisted Kim. "I must have caught the moment on my car's dashboard cam. I'm sure if I break hard or have a bump. The camera automatically saves and locks two minutes before, and two minutes after I came to a standstill."

Kim resolved to offer the camera's memory card to the police as evidence, as soon as she could.

They were suddenly disturbed by the swish of heavy curtains, as a nurse swept in with the Plastering trolley in tow.

Kim felt the hostile stare the nurse aimed in her direction, indicating she wanted Kim out of her sight.

Taking the hint, she kissed Maria on the cheek and squeezed her hand.

"I will pop in later to see how you are," Kim offered— still feeling the steely glare of the nurse, roasting the back of her head.

"See you soon Maria," Kim called out behind her. Already pulling back the curtain, and making her way towards the Hospital café, hoping for a stimulating coffee and a sweet cake.

As she turned the corridor corner, to enter the franchised café. Kim suddenly stood stock still. Finding herself frozen— in a state of shock.

Calmly sitting and reading a newspaper with a coffee cup in hand.

Was— George...

✳✳✳

#5   Sunday Ten AM

May 4th 2021

George hadn't spotted her yet, and Kim was feeling mixed emotions inside.

Every turn she made, there he was— appearing beside or in front of her. It was uncanny unless he was actually stalking her. In which case, it would kind of make sense.

He must have felt her nearness.

Looking up from behind his paper, George smiled in recognition. As he noticed Kim standing there, looking a little lost in the cafeteria doorway.

Waving her over towards him, still with a grin on his face. He asked, "Are you stalking me?"

Kim laughed out loud, and began to giggle uncontrollably.

Acting surprised— George asked her, "Did I say something funny?" With a serious look on his face and eyebrows raised.

Sitting down on the opposite side of his table. She placed her bag on her lap, after taking out a tissue to wipe the tears from her eyes. "Sorry," Kim apologised— still silently chuckling inside.

Eyebrows still aloft, George shrugged his shoulders carelessly. Secretly pretending, to wait for a lucid reason for the unprovoked outburst of laughter.

"I'm sorry, I really am— You asked me if I was stalking you. Where two seconds previously, I was thinking exactly the same question." She explained and was also pleasantly surprised. As George began to giggle too, after seeing the reason for her outburst.

Kim began to chuckle again— triggered by his unmanly laughter, until they were interrupted by a female member of the cafeteria staff.

"Everything Okay, Mr Walsh— Can I get you and your guest another cup of coffee?" The woman looked at Kim expectantly, waiting for her choice of coffee.

"I'll have an Americano please," Kim replied, while rummaging through her purse for a couple of pound coins, to make payment for her beverage.

George waved her money away and continued making an order before Kim could object.

"Add it to my tab please Anita. Could I also have three or four hot toasted buns, with jam and butter for elevenses please?"

He looked at Kim sitting opposite, with eyebrows raised. "A couple of plates and knives as well if you don't mind," he added.

As Anita walked back towards the kitchens, George transferred his attention to the attractive woman sitting opposite him.

"Okay, what brings you here— coincidentally, the same time as me?" He smirked, while waiting again for an answer.

She wasn't sure whether he was being cynical, but she decided to answer anyway.

"When you met my friends yesterday in the library, do you remember the girl with jet-black hair?"

George simply nodded, the smirk annoyingly still present.

"Well, some maniac ran her down, so I followed the ambulance here. She is in the Accident and Emergency Department at the mo'— awaiting a plaster cast to be put on by the look of it." George gave her a fleeting look. The smirk vanished, as he showed concern for Maria's welfare.

Biting the bullet Kim came straight out with it, "Why are you here then?" She said accusingly— with a little more venom than intended.

Ignoring her apparent disdain, he answered her truthfully. "Well, believe it or not; I also have friends." He paused momentarily, to see whether she was going to make an acerbic comment. Seeing no reaction, he continued.

"My best friend was badly injured in the train crash that occurred earlier this morning. Paul had planned to visit me." George coughed nervously.

"We had arranged to meet at the station, before I would have driven the both of us, to the local swimming baths."

Kim looked a little ashamed, and asked how long had they been friends.

He swallowed deeply, before he answered with a catch in his voice.

"When we were young— maybe ten or eleven. A gang of us had made our way down, to play by the little beach by the river.

We had taken with us a coil of rope that little Willy Perkins had found abandoned behind a post office van."

George looked down at the table for a moment— He looked slightly lost, but continued. "Anyway, by consensus, we decided to make a raft.

I remember us congratulating ourselves. Initially not having any more materials to hand. But, we had finally finished completing the build, after finding a load of loose fencing at the edge of the beach car park.

Only three out of the gang couldn't swim. Me, Paul and little Willy. Had to patiently sit on the bank, after the raft had been successfully launched.

We ended up feeling a bit jealous, watching others having fun— so we waited, until the others headed home for their evening meals.

Then as soon as they had disappeared from sight. The three of us dragged the raft to the edge of the bank and sat on it pretending to be sailing like pirates."

He took a swig from his almost empty cup and checked he still had Kim giving him her full attention.

George pursed his lips, "I don't know how it happened, but us jumping up and down— had somehow dislodged the raft from the bank. It began floating into deeper water, with

69

the undercurrent tugging it quickly, the raft started to speedily head downstream.

Panicked and scared— Paul and I jumped off. We tried attempting the doggy paddle, as our feet were barely able to touch the bottom.

Willy, however, was still on the raft. Totally scared to jump into the water, after realising he was now out of his depth.

He caught his foot on an insecure knot, and the raft began unravelling. By now, Paul and I had just about managed to struggle to the bank. Watching in horror— as Willy slipped between the untethered rafters, disappearing from sight as he sank underwater.

He came back up gasping, clawing at the air. His head twisted frantically left and right, as Willy looked for any suitable wood to hang onto.

Unfortunately, Willy was hit forcibly in the back of his head, by one of the logs— and disappeared for good..."

George stared gloomily into the distance for a second time, and eventually resumed telling the tale again. This time, in a slightly brighter tone of voice.

"I remember the both of us, thinking it was totally unfair. Getting a loud bollocking, for being unable to rescue our drowning friend.

So we resolved that we would learn to swim— as soon as we could.

Every time Paul visits now, we always visit the swimming baths, to remind ourselves how poor Willy died.

Always regretting— if we had only learned to swim, before that terrible accident happened."

A single hot tear dropped from an eye, and slid down his cheek, coming to a rest on George's chin.

Observing Kim, George noticed an identical trail of tears, shed in empathy for his sad tale.

Kim broke the taut silence, while shaking her head to try and bury the graphic image, grimly displayed in her mind.

"My god, that was tragic. I take it you also followed the ambulance here, to be with your friend?— I hope he will be okay George."

She suddenly realised, she had used his first name in his presence for the first time. Kim blushed slightly, hoping he hadn't noticed.

Luckily at that moment, George was distracted. As the coffee and steaming buns arrived and placed on the table in front of him.

Pushing across the table, a cup of coffee and a small jug of hot milk. George began slicing the buns into two.

Scattering dried fruit from the innards, as the ragged knife pulled roughly through.

"Butter and jam on top?" He inquired. Beginning to wipe cold butter across the eight halves, and watching it melt and soak in.

George piled four halves on a plate for Kim and handed it to her. "Is that enough?" He probed.

Without waiting for a reply, George politely offered Kim a couple of pots of fruit jam. "Help yourself as much as you like, especially if you fancy a sugar rush."

71

"There is rather a lot," she half-heartedly complained, already smearing raspberry Jam onto her bun, and taking a healthy sized bite. "Yummy," was her only intelligible word of thanks heard, while enthusiastically chewing her food.

Feeling a tap on her shoulder, she turned and saw the grumpy nurse that had been attending to Maria in the Triage Ward. "Kim Chapman?" She queried.

Kim began feeling cold— fearing what the nurse was about to say and nodded to confirm her identity.

"I'm sorry to be the bearer of bad news. I have been looking everywhere for you— to tell you your friend Maria has taken a turn for the worse. We have no idea who her next of kin is, so had I hoped you would still be in the hospital grounds and able to help?" The Nurse asked respectfully. And waited patiently for Kim's answer.

Kim explained regretfully, and wringing her hands nervously. "Maria's family are all dead, everyone died in a car crash last Christmas.

There is no-one really, she lives on her own. I do have a key to her house though, I'm sure she wouldn't mind me looking for any relations. They are probably hidden, somewhere inside her diaries— if needed, that is..." Kim offered brightly.

The nurse took a deep intake of breath, "I'm afraid it's a bit more urgent than that. I hope you don't mind, I will explain the situation, on the way to her assigned ward."

Kim began following, while beginning to panic inside.

She looked at George, and for some stupid reason mouthed 'I'm sorry.'

Kim fully understood he wouldn't be able to follow, as his own friend would be his current concern.

The nurse pointed to her name badge, and quickly informed Kim verbally. Her name is Norma Gubbins, and her position is 'Staff Nurse.'

Kim couldn't contain herself, "What about Maria, you said it was an urgent situation, are you going to tell me anytime soon— What other reason would you need my help?"

Norma came to a standstill, and turned towards Kim, looking her directly in the eyes. "Look, we got off to a bad start — shall we reset and start again in the interest of my patient and your friend?" She smiled.

Kim relented by returning the smile, and nodded her head. Sealing the agreement to the truce in full.

Norma began her explanation, of the situation in hand.

"We had noticed she had contusions to the head and was concerned that she may have fractured her skull during the incident.

After sending her for a routine MRI, the specialist discovered Maria had an intracranial aneurysm. Do you know what an aneurysm is Kim?"

Kim shook her head negatively, "Not really— if the truth be told, I have heard them mentioned. But, I never exactly knew that they were, for sure…"

"Okay, I will try keeping it simple," replied Nancy. "An aneurysm is a bulge in a blood vessel— caused by a weakness in the blood vessel wall, usually where it branches.

As blood passes through the weakened vascular

vessel, the blood pressure causes a small area to bulge outwards, like a balloon. With me so far?"

Kim nodded, and Norma continued.

"Most aneurysms don't rupture, so treatment is only carried out, if the risk of a rupture is particularly high. The MRI showed there is a potential for it to rupture, and become a subarachnoid haemorrhage instead."

Norma paused as they waited for the lift to clear. A couple of porters pushed out an empty bed trolley, allowing her and Kim to step into the space inside.

"Is that bad, and can it be fixed?" Kim asked, concerned, lowering her voice.

"Not good— That's for sure," confirmed Norma. "About three out of five people will die within two weeks, half of the survivors— well put it this way; their lives will be changed forever."

Kim was shocked at the statistics, "The fix though, is it easy to perform?"

The lift doors opened into a busy corridor, with NHS staff of all careers, heading somewhere with a purpose.

Norma truthfully answered Kim's final question, and shrugged her shoulders. "No procedure is totally without risk. In this case— this usually involves inserting tiny coils, or fitting a metal clip externally. Whatever the consultant thinks most suitable.

Ahh, we're here." She announced. Pushing open a split pair of doors, leading into a ward filled with windowed private rooms, and smelling of disinfectant.

Kim followed Norma into a nondescript room. Immediately noticing her friend propped up in bed, with her leg in plaster and supported by a sling and winch apparatus.

A beaming smile on Maria's face lit up the room, with the recognition of her friend standing worried before her.

"I'm sorry Kim, that I got you dragged in here, but to be honest I am shaking inside. I'm totally petrified with the thought of having any operation."

Kim held Maria's hand tightly, giving it a reassuring squeeze. "You daft sausage, If I had known where you were settled in— I would've been up here like a shot, to be at your side."

Maria looked down at her hands. "I've already had a visit from the surgeon and anaesthetist, while Norma was looking for you. Apparently they are just waiting for one of two beds in the main theatre to be cleared, and I will be on my way."

As if on cue, two jolly looking porters marched in, and began preparing her bed for transport to the operating theatre.

Maria looked guiltily at her friend, "I know I have never mentioned it before, but my only living relative is my real mum's sister.

Auntie Shirley had moved to Spain before mum died. Anyway, I will tell you the full story another time, but could you do me a small favour?"

Kim nodded and waited for the request.

"Would you mind calling at my house, and bringing in the photo-album leaning against the wall, on top of the sideboard please?

Aunt Shirley, used to send me the occasional postcard to inquire how I was. I'm sure she sent her phone number on one of them— I suppose she had better know the situation, One way or the other." Her voice dropped with a small sniffle, and the porters whisked her away.

With a feeling of déjà vu— Kim agreed to her request, and waved her off with misty eyes clouding her vision.

Norma put a hand on Kim's shoulder and advised her that the operation was normally quite extensive. So, she probably wouldn't be able to visit again, until sometime tomorrow morning.

Kim pushed up her bottom lip, tight against her top row of teeth, now lost in thought— without saying a further word, she left the ward wondering what to do next and habitually made her way back towards the Hospital cafeteria via the lift.

✳✳✳

Kim looked at her watch, It's only half past eleven— "I wonder if George is still here?" She thought hopefully.

She hurried into the café, as soon as having exited the lift and looked around for his handsome face.

Feeling slightly silly, as she stood still twisting her head left and right, hoping to catch a glimpse of George. "I must

76

look like a flipping Meerkat," she said a little louder than intended, and other customers began glancing her way.

Disappointed that George was not there, Kim decided that just standing about, was not going to be particularly productive. Thinking to herself, she may just as well make her way home instead.

Climbing into her car after paying the parking ticket fee, Kim placed her mobile phone into the hands free cradle.

She dialled each of her other two friends, one after another. Advising them of Maria's accident and pending operation.

Kim ended the conversations, promising to maybe meet up this evening at the café. Intending to give them both a blow-by-blow account of the hospital visit. Plus even more details of how she had already spent her Sunday.

Kim was about to switch off the mobile phone, when she received a text. She picked it back up from the cradle, and tapped through the menus to enable the message to be read.

The text was from her Mum.

It was rare for her to use the texting system to converse. Always preferring verbal contact, rather than written.

Mum's last attempt at texting a message to Kim, had left her in hysterics.

The automatic spell checker had altered whatever she had written, and it ended up totally incoherent.

Kim found that she could actually read this one. Surprised by the lucid content, she read it once more.

From: Mums Mobile.
Subject: Sunday Meal

Hi Kim,

Just a quick reminder in case you had forgotten!
The food will be on the table at 2 p.m. sharp.
Don't forget, or the moggie won't get any leftover meat.

LOL
Mum.

Kim tapped a couple of spots on the screen and quickly replied. Telling her Mum that she wouldn't want to face a miserable Roger, and would be there as planned.

Once again— she started placing the handset back into the cradle, when a sharp tap on her car window made her jump with fright.

Kim looked outside and saw George standing there, with an innocent look on his face. Pressing the button to wind down the electrically operated window. All she could manage herself, was to vacantly stare at him.

George was getting used to her, giving him strange expressions. "Err, sorry if I made you jump. I just wanted to know how your friend is— and you actually…"

Kim perked up, now listening closer as George continued.

"I was just having a walk in the Hospital gardens. Hoping to get some fresh air and I spotted you getting into your car— I'm starting to go stir crazy sitting in that café," he explained.

Pulling out a notebook from an inside pocket, he held it open— revealing a list of complicated medical terms.

Kim gazed blankly and was about to tell George that she had no idea what they meant.

George continued with an understanding smile on his face.

"By the look of you— it's gobbledygook to you as well. I asked the Consultant what was wrong with Paul, as he finished his rounds.

I didn't understand a single word he said and asked the Nurse if she wouldn't mind writing it down for me. I'm hoping to look it up on-line later."

Kim filled in George with what was happening with Maria and explained she had felt awful about going home. Leaving her friend, who would end up feeling all alone— as soon as she came around, after the operation.

"To be honest, I have got so much personal stuff going on at the moment." Kim said— hoping her face hadn't revealed how she was feeling inside.

She tried validating why she was leaving. "It sounds pathetic I know. But, I really have to visit my Mum today, to try sorting out a burning question.

It Involves a total mystery that I appear to have been drawn into." Kim said, carefully masking the actual reason. She turned the key in the ignition, and the car burst into life.

Pressing the control to close up the window. Kim stopped its motion, after thinking about her actions twice.

It began to reverse and was again heading downward — into it's storage area inside the door.

Kim called out to George, as he started ambling away.

"I hope Paul will be okay— George. If you could pop in to Maria with any news about him, you can bet your bottom dollar, it will reach me pretty soon afterwards."

She saw George in her rear mirror, waving and saying something unheard.

Exiting the hospital roadway, she filtered left and headed back home to check on Roger, and get ready to go to Mums...

✳✳✳

#6   Sunday One-Fifteen PM

May 4th 2021

Kirstie looked hard at Dave standing in front of a mirror. He had just walked out of the changing rooms inside the local branch of Primark, wearing a pair of new Chinos. He raised his eyebrows, waiting for her judgement on his choice of clothing. "Well, what's the verdict then Sis.' Will the prince be going to the ball next week?— or not?" He chuckled.

She continued looking him up and down, like a clothing mannequin on parade at the local barracks. Spoiling the image, Dave stood with his hands on his hips, and twirled like a ballerina.

Kirstie couldn't keep a straight face any more and exhaled loudly, "For God's sake Dave, I'm trying to be serious— for your sake. While you are flouncing around like Rudolf Nureyev, how am I supposed to confirm they look okay?"

"Rudolph?" Teased Dave, "Is that a yes or a no? Does that mean I am allowed to head back to the changing room now?"

Kirstie sighed, "Well considering, every pair has been the same size. Just a different colour separating them. I will say for the fifth time in the last thirty minutes— Dave, they look fine…"

Her brother smiled like a naughty boy, "I'm a man Kirstie, what else would you expect? I suppose I will have that pair as well." He flounced back through the opening into the changing area, leaving her wondering whether there were any more colours left hanging on the display rack.

Adjusting a distinctive orange handbag that Kim had given her yesterday, after explaining Andy had given it to her, and she wanted it out of her sight. Something caught her eye.

Picking up a chiffon headscarf strategically placed on a stand nearby. Kirstie wrapped it round her neck and turned towards the mirror to admire herself wearing the pastel colours.

She started as a large hand gripped her shoulder tightly, pulling her to face in the opposite direction. Surprise replaced the frightened look on her face.

"Andy— Would you mind taking your hand off me?" Kirstie asked firmly, pushing Andy away from her, angry at him violently invading her space— with no explanation.

For a moment Andy looked as surprised as she was, he immediately recovered with a contrite look on his face. "Err sorry Kirstie, I thought you were Kim— what with the red hair and..." His voice dropped away with embarrassment.

Anger still burned inside Kirstie, how dare he? "Tell me — Andy, if it had actually been Kim, would that still give you the right to be so rough handling someone?"

Taking one step farther backwards, Andy again felt in control.

"It might, if Kim had done something to deserve it," he said darkly, a smirk beginning to grow across his face.

"In fact I feel a burning need to talk to her real soon," he said cryptically, while slowly rubbing his lower abdomen.

Kirstie was confused, "I only spoke to Kim yesterday, and she told me that you two had split up. I didn't realise it was so acrimonious between you."

"Yeah? Well, it looks like I might have had a few expectations, which Kim didn't see eye to eye about..." Andy drawled, while pulling himself up straight— ready to switch to the charm offensive. "I don't suppose you know where Kim is today, would you? I really need to put to bed a recent conversation we had."

Suspicion grew in Kirstie's eyes, "You still have her mobile number, why don't you ask her yourself?"

Andy slanted his eyes and viciously spat an answer, "I asked a simple question— answer it before I get really annoyed— please." He felt a tap on his shoulder blade.

As he turned to see who had the temerity to disturb him, an open hand hit him in his thigh. Andy briefly saw a man crouched down in a martial arts position, with one leg out behind him for balance. Before he fell backwards from the impact and the intense pain.

Dave stood over Andy— Who was writhing with agony. "Hiya mate, I'm sorry there will not be any bruises for you to use as evidence— So I wouldn't try to make anything of my little love tap." Dave advised, "Next time you are disrespectful to my sister playing the big gangster, I won't avoid the kidneys and other considerably more painful areas. Do you understand?"

"Yes," hissed Andy through gritted teeth. "Only if I see you lurking around though," he silently advised himself.

Dave reached down and hauled Andy to his feet, "You need to be standing to allow the blood flow to get past the pressure-point," he advised. Putting an arm round Andy's shoulder, giving him a gentle disarming hug. "There, I told you so, the pain is melting away already— isn't it mate?" Dave said, looking coldly into Andy's eyes.

Andy was about to say something retaliatory, but quickly changed his mind and swiftly turned, hobbling towards the store exit.

Kirstie stood beside the store trolley full of Chino's. That Dave had been pushing as he came out of the changing rooms. "Are you okay?— or not, Dave?" She simply asked.

Dave inflated his chest and posed like a bodybuilder. "Me? Yeah I am fine, Army training and all that." He pirouetted once again, making her laugh.

"C'mon then you idiot, I suppose we should pay for this lot. Have you got your wallet ready?" Kirstie asked.

Dave started patting his pockets with a concerned look on his face, then he laughed at Kirstie's expression. "Of course I have 'frosty face', do you take me for an idiot?" He received a thump on the shoulder for his tomfoolery and a smile from his sister, as they joined the payment queue with Dave's multi-colour purchases.

✳✳✳

Pulling into the drive, Kim could see Dad peeking out from behind the curtains. She laughed to herself, as she remembered the time he had asked her whether she had seen him looking out to spot visitors.

Kim had sworn she hadn't, that there was no way she had realised he was peering at her when she had pulled up in her car. She had teased him further by insisting he must be like a chameleon, able to melt into the background.

Mum had nearly wet herself listening to Kim telling Dad her little white lie, and had played along with his invisible window snooping.

Kim saw him disappear and knew he was heading to the front door to surprise his daughter by opening the door, the moment she rang the doorbell.

Lo and behold, she placed a finger on the doorbell push and the door swung quickly open. Holding back a snigger— She pretended as usual to be shocked. "Good God Dad— how do you do it?" Kim was pleased when he reacted as usual, by preening himself while uttering "A trade secret."

As he always did, with a finger held on the side of his nose. Walking past her father she asked him, "Where's Mum?"

He pointed towards the study with one hand and fiddled with the door key in the other.

Satisfied the house was again secured, he made his way towards the kitchen to put the kettle on. "Coffee anyone," he hollered and began pulling out mugs as they both shouted back "Please".

After just a couple of minutes, he had prepared the beverages and placed numerous chocolate digestive biscuits onto a small plate. Popping the drinks and snacks onto a large tray, complete with another small empty plate. He carried it carefully into the study, where he found his wife and daughter, flipping through an old family album.

Pamela had heard her daughter's car door slam when she arrived and was already placing an album onto the wooden table, as Kim walked through the study door.

Nodding her head towards the photo Album, indicating to Kim to start having a look at the content inside.

Kim looked at her mother and asked. "Where did you say you got this from Mum? I don't remember seeing it lying around anywhere— before today."

Pamela flicked over another page before answering, "To be honest, I hadn't seen any of these. Until I had found it at your Nan's, when we were clearing it out after she died."

Kim raised her eyebrows, "How many other things did you take, before I inherited her cottage?"

She saw her mother also raise her eyebrows at her daughter's question, and quickly apologised. "Sorry Mum, I didn't mean to be rude, but— I want to see anything to do with Nan, I loved her too."

Her bottom lip began trembling slightly, and she felt herself welling up at the thought of her Nan no longer being there to cuddle her.

Pamela recognised Kim's distress and changed the subject quickly, "I'll have two Chocolate biscuits please— David, darling."

Her husband added a third onto a plate and passed it to his wife. Pamela smiled, David knew she would always ask for another anyway.

Kim sighed, her Mum and Dad were always showing each other affection in little ways. She hoped she would meet her soulmate one day as well, but she hadn't had a good record with men so far...

Her reverie was disturbed by the sound of coughing, she looked up to see her Mum wiping her lips. "Sorry about that, the biscuit went down the wrong way," she said, clearing her throat one last time.

Pamela pulled the album closer and began flicking through looking for a particular set of photographs. She paused and nodded her head to herself in satisfaction. "Here we are," She announced, "Helen."

Kim perked up and almost snatched the album from her Mum's hands in her eagerness to see more images of the mystery woman in her life.

Pamela stood up and stood behind her daughter. They were looking at a photo with two teenage girls standing outside what appeared to be a church door.

She pointed to a tall girl on the left wearing flared jeans and a striped tank top and announced with a smile, "That's me. I always tried dressing conservatively— but keeping with the fashion of my peers, as close as I could. The tarty looking girl on the right is Helen."

Kim examined the photo closer, "She is gorgeous, though. Helen has the legs to do the hot pants justice, and that large collar blouse is inspirational." She pursed her lips, being not quite sure about the six-inch heels, and murmured "overkill— maybe?"

"She always had the boys twisted round her little finger. Not only was she beautiful, she was incredibly smart. Combined with the fact that she was a formidable athlete as well." Pamela paused for breath.

"I remember she once went on a school holiday to an adventure centre. Shocking all the instructors, with how quickly she had picked up every challenge they presented to her. I believe she still holds the record for scaling Devils Pike in under one hour— without the aid of ropes."

Kim idly began turning the pages again, various holiday photographs passed by— some with Nan, some without. An unknown man stood slightly in the background of one image.

Kim turned to query who he was.

Pamela answered, "That was my dad, your grandpa— he didn't really like having his picture taken so that photo is a bit of a rarity."

The theme of the photographs now appeared to be when Pamela and Helen were older, maybe in their mid-twenties. Helen was dressed in a smart trouser suit, holding aloft a new briefcase while posing at the bottom of an aircraft stairway.

"She had just got a job with the Civil Service, where she spent all of her time travelling. One day she would be in an office on the banks of the Thames, another time she would be somewhere like Spain or Morocco," explained Pamela.

Pamela recalled her own youth. "I managed to get a job, selling nuts and bolts at Simmons hardware store. That's where I met Dave— your Dad. He was always there, buying tools and stuff, and had finally plucked up the courage to ask me out."

She added, "Your Dad always reckoned she was a red-headed spy or something, so I asked her outright one day if it was true. All she managed was to laugh out loud. Helen had thoroughly denied the possibility of being a joke, as it would be too much like hard work. Plus she didn't want to ruin her nails— fighting off assassins and suchlike."

"When did you last see or hear from Helen?" asked Kim brimming with questions coming to the surface.

Pamela lifted her cup and thoughtfully sipped her coffee, while trying to recall the last time she had contact with her sister.

Only one of many times she had spoken to Helen, came to the forefront of her mind. Pamela decided to use that as a reference point for Kim, as some later times they had spoken were painful. She didn't really want to bring those back into her life.

"The last time I both saw and spoke to Helen, was the day before you were born," she said calmly biting back the bile rising in her throat, and ignoring the moisture emerging from a tear duct.

Kim could see the memory had invoked her Mum's distress and decided to change the direction of the questions. "I know you said how beautiful and clever she was, but if you could sum her up with just one word, what would it be?"

Without hesitation, Pamela uttered one word, "Bravery".

David walked across the room and grasped his wife's hand. Tenderly giving it a squeeze, as she began to softly sob.

Confused and embarrassed, Kim couldn't think of what to say other than a simple sorry for bringing up the subject.

David broke the heavy mood by announcing dinner must be just about ready, and exited the room to make his way into the kitchen— leaving mother and daughter facing each other.

"I hope you are feeling hungry? I made extra to make sure the moggie had some dinner as well. Although it looks like we could actually feed a cat's home, as I have slightly over compensated." Said Pamela brightly and made her way towards the kitchen, leaving Kim to mull over what she had just discovered.

Resolving to pop around to Nancy's home later on to discuss her findings, she picked up the album and slid it into her carrier bag. The birth certificate and other papers still sat there. She didn't plan to ask her Mum any more questions about them today, as she is obviously upset.

The aroma of roasted chicken and vegetables made her stomach rumble with hunger, as she made her way into the kitchen. Dad had laid the table complete with a large bottle of Liebfraumilch keeping cool in the ice bucket.

Dave noticed her glancing towards the bottle of wine. He explained it wouldn't actually fit in the fridge, and you can't drink a sweet white wine at room temperature.

He lifted the bottle and twisted hard on the metal cap on the top. A slight hiss escaped as the bottle balanced with the room pressure. Pouring Kim a large glass full to the brim. David handed it to her, then continued filling the two other empty glasses for Pamela and himself.

He raised his glass to the air and announced he was going to offer a toast. Waiting until they both had glasses in their hands, he lifted the one held in his hand.

"To families— May they remain close and safe. If they have to travel, let lady luck watch over their journey— Raise your glasses and give your thanks for Family. There is nothing else quite like it."

They clinked glasses together, and each of them took a refreshing sip of cool wine.

Pamela laid the chicken onto the spiked carving dish, and Dave began to slice it into steaming slices. Kim asked her Mum a question while she appeared to be preoccupied dishing up the vegetables.

"Mum, would you mind if I borrowed the album please?" She said, not admitting she had already packed it into the bag anyway. Pamela was still distracted and just nodded her head in agreement.

Kim picked up her knife and fork, and proceeded to devour her dinner— while thinking to herself that today might be okay after all.

✳✳✳

#7   Sunday Four PM

May 4th 2021

George pulled up his motorbike onto its heavy-duty stand, turned off the ignition and put the key in his top pocket.

He pushed the helmet onto the integrated locking clip and made his way towards the hospital entrance.

Ambulances pulsing blue lights, stood in a row outside the Accident and Emergency Department. It was incredible they still appeared to be pulling survivors out of the earlier train wreck, he silently hoped they would survive their injuries.

He had been told via email and text earlier today that if he came into the ward around five, they might have some news regarding his friend Paul.

They had asked him to immediately sign an attached mandatory form in the email— that would allow him to represent Paul's next of kin. Paul's mother died when he was young, and his father had recently been accidentally killed, by a conman pretending to work as a gas employee.

Paul had told George, the man had informed Paul's elderly father John Carter, that someone had reported a gas leak. Urging John, it would be best if he waited outside while he investigated the claim.

John may have been elderly, but he was no fool and began to smell a rat when he couldn't see an official gas van parked in the road.

Making his way around the house via the side gate, he gripped the back door handle and carefully pushed it slowly down to release the door catch.

As the door swung back on its hinges, there was no sign of the fake gas man. Reaching behind the door he unhooked a heavy broom, with the intention of scaring the man to leave his home.

Fate was a cruel mistress to John that day. He poked his head into the hallway and was instantly spotted by the criminal as he came down the stairs. With arms full of valuables, the man roughly pushed past John in haste, trying to effect his escape.

Losing his balance the inevitable happened, and John fell onto the corner of the solid wood coffee table, cutting deeply into his head.

John had lain frozen with shock on the living room floor, slowly bleeding out for a little over an hour. Before the postman found him, after spotting his pool of blood through the open front door.

An ambulance was called, and he was swiftly transferred to a local hospital where his wound was attended to. Having lost a significant amount of blood, plus the inherent shock of the intruder, had sadly weakened his resolve to survive.

After barely managing to give the Police enough information to incriminate the criminal and saying his

93

goodbyes to a tearful son— John had died peacefully in his sleep, joining his beloved wife at the gates of Heaven.

***

George waited for the lift doors to open and stepped inside. Pressing the button for the fifth level, a robotic voice announced the doors were closing, and the lift began to smoothly rise.

Finally, after a short journey. The voice advised he had reached the fifth floor, and the doors were about to open.

With a muted ping the doors split apart, and George walked the short distance down the corridor to Malvern Ward.

Normally only available to private health insurance clients, the prevailing emergency, had caused the hospital to use every available bed. The smell of a coffee machine combined with the soft muzak playing in the background, shouted comfort and relaxation.

He reached into his pocket and pulled out an envelope containing the form that he had printed and signed earlier. George walked over to the Ward receptionist, busily typing on a computer keyboard.

She looked up and smiled, "Hi, my name is Mandy— Can I help you, or do you know which side-room you are visiting?" The smart young lady, cheerily inquired.

George handed her the envelope, and explained the email and text he had received earlier today. Mandy pulled the form from the envelope and quickly read its contents. She turned to the computer screen and tapped a few keys on the keyboard, resulting in more information being displayed.

"Firstly, may I apologise that you did not receive an initial phone call? We are trialling a new Artificial Intelligence system, 'supposedly' designed to communicate with patients and their families. Unfortunately, it would appear that the extraordinary number of admissions has shown a few cracks in the programming— Anyway, you are here now Mr Walsh," she consulted the screen again.

"And, you are here for a meeting with Mr Gupta, our resident neurologist regarding the patient— Paul Carter."

George continued standing beside Mandy's desk, feeling a little lost and not knowing what to do next.

Mandy looked up and raised her eyebrows, "Sorry, I forgot you hadn't visited this private ward before. Help yourself to a mug of coffee and make yourself comfortable with a magazine or newspaper. If you are feeling peckish, there are chocolate bars and sandwiches in the fridge. Mr Gupta will meet you in a while; he is still with another client, I'll call you when he is here." She went back to studying her computer screen.

Realising he had just been politely dismissed, he walked into the adjacent lounge and inserted an Americano pod into the expensive looking coffee machine. Mug-filled, and a copy of the Daily Mail gripped on the other hand.

George lowered himself into a comfy soft leather seat, to patiently wait for Mr Gupta to arrive.

After thirty minutes George glanced at his watch and noticed the receptionist appeared to be trying to obtain his attention. Mandy waved a hand towards him in a come-hither motion.

He put down the newspaper and ambled over to her desk. George raised his eyebrows, "Is there a problem, Mandy?" He asked with a nervous smile.

She looked up and pursed her lips, "Well there is a problem, and I don't think you are going to like it."

George placed his hands on the desk and raised his eyebrows. "Well, I suppose you had better spit it out then. I'm already on edge worrying about my best friend, plus the inability to leave and get back to urgent research isn't helping."

She averted her eyes away from George, unable to face him directly. Mandy clicked her mouse over a section on the screen and the laser printer whirred into life. Wordlessly she lifted the sheets out of the hopper and handed them to George.

He took the papers from her and began to read the text printed on them.

Mandy nervously watched his eyes scan left to right. The sheer intensity of the glare mushrooming across his face, revealed the true story of his withheld emotions.

George carefully placed the sheets back down onto her desk and simply stated, "There must be a mistake."

"I'm sorry Mr Walsh; the hospital security department has deemed you an unsuitable person, to spend any time on this ward," Mandy nervously advised.

George nearly swore, but managed to keep his cool. "It wasn't Mandy's fault, and she was only doing her job" he thought.

"Okay, how do you suggest I fix this issue then Mandy? This is either a case of mistaken identity, or someone is obtaining false information from somewhere." George waited patiently for her to respond.

"I suppose the first thing you will need to do is talk to security themselves." She glanced briefly at the screen for further information and swallowed deeply. "Please don't shout at me, George, but they shut down for the weekend at sixteen hundred. They only work the same hours as retail stores. I know it's madness, but their main customers are not the NHS."

"What time do they open tomorrow then?" he asked, his voice becoming more strained, as he tried remaining civil to the girl in front of him.

Mandy responded quickly and efficiently informed him; the security department would be available for comment— after eight a.m. Monday morning.

"I don't suppose there is an emergency number available?" George asked on the off chance of being able to sort this out sooner.

"I'm afraid not, the NHS always takes the cheaper option if they can. I presume out of hours is a chargeable option. The company I work for is privately run, and we only hire this ward for our own private use." Her voice trailed away on the last word, too embarrassed to continue the conversation.

"I suppose I had better leave then," he stated.

Mandy lent forward and signalled for him to come a little closer. "I can give you a juicy bit of information though George," she whispered, while pointing to the computer screen.

"Paul had earlier been partially conscious, but is now recovering from an operation on his knee. The Anaesthetic has taken him deeper than intended, and it is anticipated he should regain consciousness sometime in the night. We will allow him to sleep until early morning, as he has other remedial procedures to be processed during the rest of the day."

She looked up and gave him a friendly smile. "I hope you can get this sorted out— for Paul's sake. Otherwise, he will be a lonely man while he is spending time with us..."

George returned the smile and turned towards the exit, without saying another word.

He waited for the lift and stepped inside. As the doors slid shut, he leant against the wall, wondering what to do with himself for the rest of the day.

Inspiration struck, and he stabbed the button to stop the lift at the next floor. "I know what I can do," he said under his breath. "I will go and see if that girl Kim had come visiting is awake yet"— "What was her name?" he asked himself—

"Ahh Maria— that was it." Satisfied with his plan, he made his way towards the private ward that she had been assigned.

✳✳✳

Kim turned the ignition key to start her compact Honda car engine, turning on the windscreen wipers and the demisting heater.

Mum had finally gone back into the house after waving her goodbye. Just in time, to get out of the impending rain starting to show its hand. Dad had teased the curtains slightly to one side, so he could make sure that Kim got away okay as well.

Putting her mobile phone into its cradle, she initiated a call to Nancy just before she moved off. Turning onto the main road she heard the phone still ringing out. Then suddenly the sound of a loud click and a tentative "Hello" called out, confirming she had contacted her best friend Nancy.

"Hi there Nancy, are you up to anything at the moment?" Kim inquired.

"To be honest I am really busy," teased Nancy.

"I've already managed to sort out my long socks into pairs and am just about to start on the short ones— Why?" She chuckled, waiting to see how long it would take Kim to retort.

Kim decided to play the same game, "What sort of friend are you then, sorting socks is more important than me coming around for a chin-wag is it? Just wait until you want something." She couldn't hold back an emerging snigger— quickly followed by a snort of laughter.

"Where are you then?" Inquired Nancy, "Will I have time to finish these socks?"

"Socks and knickers as well if you want, I'm just leaving mum and dad's and should be there in ten minutes or so." Kim loved the banter they had together and hoped they would always remain friends.

Fifteen short minutes later, Kim pulled into Nancy's drive, switched off the car engine and pulled on the handbrake.

She walked up to the front door and found it was ajar. "Come in, the door is open," Nancy called as Kim pushed the door to.

"Hiya Nancy, I am already indoors, where are you?" Kim replied. Admiring the beautiful flowers in the vase by the mirror in the hall, she pressed her nose up against a mass of petals and inhaled the sweet scent.

She sensed movement behind her and turned to see Nancy with a cup of steaming coffee in each hand.

"I'm sorry, but I have come to bend your ears again." Kim apologised, taking the coffee from her friend and sitting down on an offered comfy chair.

"Tell me all about everything, I am all ears," sympathised Nancy. Kim commenced to update her with Sundays trials and tribulations. It was over two hours later, when she finally put her fourth empty coffee cup on Nancy's draining board.

"Look," said Nancy, "It might all appear to be confusing at the moment. But it's odds on favourite, that everything will seem to be more in perspective in the morning."

Nancy looked at Kim's tired eyes, "Especially after you have slept on it."

Kim felt doubtful that was going to be the case, but didn't feel she should dwell on it. Deciding she would just have to see what tomorrow will bring instead.

Nancy stood beside her, to give her friend a peck on the cheek to say goodbye. "I'm serious Kim, if you have to talk some more, even if it's the middle of the night— don't hesitate to ring."

Kim returned the kiss and simply nodded a yes. She took out her keys and headed towards her parked car. She thought to herself, "Don't worry Nancy— you will hear from me soon, that's a promise."

✳✳✳

George paused, before speaking to the nurse sitting on the ward admissions desk, she was busy looking at her computer screen and hadn't yet seen him approach.

Debating with himself whether this was really a good idea, to ask if he could sit with a girl he didn't know. How would he be able to explain to the nursing staff that he was worried she would feel alone when she woke up?

He knew what that was like, having experienced the same thing himself two short months ago. George had been intent on making sure Paul didn't experience loneliness either, but the damned hospital had put the clamps on that happening— any time soon.

"Damn it— since when have I been a coward, and shied away from something I thought important?" Sometimes he despised himself for trying to take the easy way out of life's dilemmas. "Not today, though!"

George coughed lightly to attract the duty nurse's attention. "Sorry to bother you, is there any chance I could sit with my fiancé until she wakes up?" He lied fluently and studied the chalk board behind her head, to get Maria's full name and room number.

"My name is George Warner, and her name is Maria Lockyer in room 4A."

The nurse consulted the notes on her screen, and looked up to notice the warm smile on his handsome face.

"Shouldn't be a problem Mister Warner, the doctor has just authorised the removal of the sedative from her drip. She should wake up in half an hour if you want to wait?"

George's smile managed to stretch a little more expansively, "I would and I will, thank you very much..." He looked at her apprehensively, prompting her for her name.

"It's Judith," she offered, returning his smile.

George continued, "Thank you, Judith— If you could point me in the right direction please."

The nurse stood up from behind her counter and pointed to the corridor to her right, "Second door down on the left," Judith advised as George left her side.

Looking through the window outside Maria's room he could see her lying in bed with her leg suspended in a sling. Drips and other medical equipment were attached to her arms, and he heard the steady beeping of the monitors as George entered the room.

He took a wooden chair at the side of her bed and sat down, looking at her breathing slowly while still asleep.

George smiled and gently took her tiny hand into his, stroking her knuckles softly with his middle finger. He felt happy, he had managed to comfort at least one lonely person today.

***

#8   Monday Seven-Forty-Five AM

May 5th 2021

Kim yawned and put her hand to her mouth. "Roger, I have to confess I am exhausted this morning. But you will be glad to know— I've remembered to leave some milk in your bowl today,"

Roger looked up from his food bowl in acknowledgement and crunched on a fish-shaped cat biscuit.

"At least you can get back to sleep. I have got to go out to work later, thankfully the first isn't until ten o'clock," she sighed. Kim absent-mindedly found herself running her finger down the list in her appointment diary, to confirm who she needed to visit first.

She spotted a name that perked her up. "Betty Warburton, that's handy. She might be just the person who can give me some answers to a couple of burning questions, I have in the back of my head."

Kim popped the diary into her work bag and headed off to visit Maria before she had to be at Betty's.

***

104

"This is becoming a habit," Kim told herself, impatiently waiting for the lift doors to open on the hospital restaurant floor. A ping from the lift speaker announced that the lift was inching into position— readying itself for the doors to open. With a hiss of hydraulics, Kim was released and walked the short distance down the corridor to enter the restaurant.

Standing by the tray collection trolley, she started looking around the seating area for any sign of George. She jumped— as someone tapped her on the shoulder.

"Hello young lady, are you looking for that nice Mr Walsh, by any chance?"

Kim turned to face the woman George had referred to as Anita, who had served them both with coffee and buns, the last time she was here.

Slightly embarrassed, Kim nodded her head, "I just wondered whether he was here today?" She felt her face begin to flush.

Anita Milan chuckled softly, "Don't worry dear, we have all been there. He is rather dishy, and if I was ten years younger..."

"So he isn't here then?" Kim said rather brusquely and quickly apologised. "I'm sorry, I didn't mean to be rude— I am rather tired," She unconsciously wiped the sleep from her eyes.

"That's okay sweetheart, worrying can cause sleepless nights," replied Anita already walking towards the serving area. "I will let him know you were asking," she called behind.

Disappointed, Kim made her way back to the lift, to investigate whether Maria was awake yet.

Walking into Maria's ward, she asked the on-duty nurse sitting at the reception desk. "Is Maria Lockyer awake yet?"

The nurse looked up without consulting her computer display, "I believe she is, I've heard her talking to her fiancé for the last couple of hours— lovely couple," she offered.

Raised eyebrows, all Kim could reply with was "hmm. She walked purposefully towards Maria's bedroom, and the sound of male and female laughter.

She peered through the corridor window before knocking— George was sitting next to Maria, talking and smiling with a coffee in his hand.

Kim opened the door and knocked it briefly as she passed, already half-way into the room. "Morning— both." she said brightly, noticing the slightly surprised expression on their faces.

"Kim— what a lovely surprise, I thought you would be at work this morning and wouldn't be visiting until this afternoon?" Maria gushed, holding out her arms for a cuddle.

Kim caught her eye, questionably flicking her own eyes quickly towards George, and back.

Catching her drift, Maria tried to explain George's presence. "George has been keeping me company. He had waited until I woke up, and we have been talking non-stop ever since. George said he had for some reason, to go and see an internal department in a short while. So, this is good timing— arriving as you did."

George responded by standing up and throwing his empty plastic coffee cup into a bin. "Yeah, George has got to go and sort out why he— still— can't visit Paul." He spoke sarcastically. "Paul, the poor sod, he must be feeling scared and lonely, I know I would."

He took Maria's hand and kissed it lightly. "Hope you feel better, and I will try to pop in when I can. Work for me as well, today I am afraid." He nodded with a smile towards Kim and left the room.

Kim waited until George was out of earshot and dragged his chair closer to Maria. "Fiancé?" She half sputtered, half laughed.

Maria smiled and feigned innocence. "If only," she mumbled under her breath. Explaining George used that fact as a ruse, as he wasn't really direct family.

Kim replied with a non-committal, "Okay," She looked at the fresh flowers on the bedside table, wondering whether a gift from George.

Maria tapped Kim's hand, "You will never guess what I have found out, and he doesn't know I know."

Kim ignored the slightly confusing comment, encouraging Maria to continue with a simple smile.

Maria gushed excitedly, "He is an author, a famous mystery author, with four published novels to his name as well. He is really quite intelligent and knowledgeable, we have had a lovely conversation, since I finally woke up."

Kim looked thoughtful, "Ahh, the library must be where he works, researching his next novel. Mr. Walsh's lifestyle was starting to make sense now, Maria." Kim had one of her eureka moments, "He is a mystery writer, a bit of a detective— I wonder if he would mind giving me a hand?" She was also now as excited as Maria. "Would you mind if I asked him?" Kim said with mild concern in her voice.

Maria stared at Kim and stuttered, "What do you mean, would I mind? We are not going out or anything you know."

"He is your fiancé after all," Kim teased.

A strange look remained on Maria's face, "I wonder," she thought.

"Maria?" Kim asked.

"Yes Kim?" Maria said apprehensively.

"Do you fancy George or something? You perk up every time his name is mentioned." Challenged Kim.

Maria took a deep breath before answering. "I might be," she said in a hesitant voice. "Is that going to be a problem if I do?"

Kim could see her friend was still holding her breath— while waiting for her answer. She kept her expression blank and shook her head. "Not a problem Maria, fill your boots sweetheart," she offered kindly. Noting Maria was slowly exhaling in relief.

Kim spent the next hour bringing Maria up to speed, before announcing she had better make a move, as Mrs Warburton was a stickler for time keeping.

She hugged Maria again and kissed her on the cheek, promising to call again later today. She picked up her bag and headed sharply towards the lift.

✳✳✳

#9   Monday Ten-Thirty-Eight AM

May 5th 2021

George made his way down a dirty corridor in the depths of the hospital. "*What a joke*," he thought to himself.

Everybody seemed to have heard about the security department, who were apparently quick to poke their nose into anyone's business. The annoying thing was that no-one upstairs seemed to know exactly where the office was located on the grounds.

That was until George had met with a friendly policeman. Who was in the process of investigating an outpatient recently arrested, while causing a violent scene in the Accident and Emergency Department.

He was on his way to the mysterious security department as well, hoping to obtain video evidence of the attack and had offered to lead George there as well.

Luckily, the officer had overheard him. Frustratedly asking a member of the nursing staff, for the elusive location.

The policeman stopped outside an unmarked door, the only clue to its possible origin was the steel security plate bolted to the outside.

"Anybody would think they are the damn SAS or Special Branch the way they act," the policeman said, with a little acid in his voice. He opened an innocuous-looking

109

mailbox to one side of the door and pushed a hidden doorbell push button inside.

Also, located in the box was a small camera and speaker. A red LED lit up by the camera, and a distorted voice uttered from the speaker, "What do you want?

The policeman shuffled slightly to one side, so that the inquirer could see his uniform and face. He held up his warrant card to complete his identification and explained, "I rang earlier, videotape impound request— remember?" He was answered with the sound of a door lock release snapping apart and pushed George ahead of him through the open armoured door.

They stood in a constricting small area, with a glass-windowed booth at the farthest end.

There was no illumination inside, shadows from the lighting above their heads made the booth look intimidating.

A sliver of light emerged from within, as another door opened inside. Its creation was quickly followed by a fluorescent light flickering on.

The luminescence revealed a man dressed in an intimidating carbonide jacket, and wearing a visored helmet with an action camera affixed on the top.

George could tell this was the person who had answered the intercom when he repeated his question of "What do you want?"

Realising he was now addressing him, rather than the policeman, George stepped forward to the booth and slid under the glass portal the denial of access letter that he had been given last night onto the counter.

The visored guard took a brief look and placed it back onto the counter. Declaring a simple "So?" He stared moodily back at George.

George drew himself to his full height to return the intimidation, "Who the hell is George S Walsh?" He asked accusingly.

The man looked down at the paper again, "Seeing as you gave it to me, you are mate." George hissed, "You do realise I could sue for defamation of character? I'm sure your company would appreciate that, when my friends working for The Daily Reflection get a hold of this situation."

The man displayed both worried and slightly confused expressions on his rugged face. "What do you mean, it says here you are a serial rapist out on bail awaiting conviction?"

"Can you identify me personally without any doubt?" George asked accusingly. "Or does that mean any male named George Walsh aged sixteen to sixty will be accused of the same crime? Oh, and by the way my middle name is Mark, and there is no S in Mark." He was now in full flow, the policeman watched with interest.

George reached inside his jacket pocket and pulled out a wallet. "What would you like?— business card, driving licence maybe even a passport?"

He flung the wallet under the partition, "Help yourself, and have a look at the photo identification and say for certain that I am George S Walsh— Please."

The man did not say a word and just pressed a button underneath the counter. A suited male slid inside, and the original uniformed security man whispered words into his ear.

The suited guard nodded and left the booth. After a few silent moments, he returned with a slip of printer paper in his hand and handed it to the uniformed man.

After a few minutes of examination, he turned back to face George. "Apologies— Mr Walsh, it would appear that we have made a clerical error after re-checking your identification online." He said contritely, "My colleague is adjusting the security bulletin as we speak, I believe you will no longer have any access issues forthwith."

The policeman nudged George with his elbow and congratulated him with a simple "Nice one mate— That told them." Without waiting for a further response he pushed past

George, and announced he wanted some videotapes — please.

Taking the opportunity to leave, he slid out of the still open armoured door and began to head immediately towards Paul in his private ward.

✳✳✳

Reaching into the rear of the car, she grabbed a hold of what she called her tool bag. Originally starting life as a frozen food box, it was quickly commandeered when she first qualified as a hairdresser. Now covered completely with hairdressing product stickers, its original identity is hidden from inquiring eyes.

Noticing her reflection on the glass porch outside Betty Warburton's large, four-bedroomed house. "My hair positively looks like a right mess," she thought to herself; it had been left to its own devices since the break-up with Andy.

She pushed the ornate bell push and smiled as she heard the loud sound of a musical ditty, jauntily being played somewhere inside to announce her arrival.

The shrill yapping of the small dog ensured her presence was confirmed.

Noticing three large clunks as heavy bolts were drawn back, Kim stepped back expecting the usual canine tsunami to rapidly fly towards her.

As expected, when the door was pulled back, she heard a scrabble of claws trying to gain purchase on an internal wooden floor.

The gap between the door and its frame reaching the optimal space for an exit, allowed a short-legged dog to explode outside into the glass porch.

The door opened completely, allowing a portly woman in her seventies to exit the house as well. Scooping up the little dog with one hand, she opened the outside door with the other.

"Come in Kim, ignore Keeley, she just thinks you are here to make a fuss of her. She will soon give up and go back to her bed," advised Betty.

Kim smiled and followed Mrs Warburton through a long hallway, then through a door on the right into the kitchen. Mrs Warburton said chirpily, "I've already rolled up the mats and got a chair ready— would you like a cup of coffee or tea?"

Kim smiled and nodded her head, "I would love one Betty, you get the kettle on while I get the scissors and brushes out."

As she rummaged through her bag for the required tools, she looked around the familiar kitchen. Nothing had changed since she had started visiting Grandma Angela, every Saturday morning— without fail.

Angela Taylor and Betty Warburton had been childhood friends and had been inseparable.

Together, even though the examinations and studies when attending scientific lectures at Oxford University.

Holding each other's hands when being interviewed by a government department as civil service specialists.

Speaking soothing words at the hospital, when either was giving birth.

After travelling the world together for work, and finally settling down to get married and have children. They continued their friendship until the saddest day when Angela had mysteriously died somewhere in the hillsides of Spain.

"One cuppa— milk, no sugar," announced Betty. While thoughtfully putting a mug of coffee on top of a coaster, to protect her highly polished Welsh Dresser.

She sat down on the pre-prepared chair and allowed Kim to draw a protective hairdressing shawl around her shoulders. "How's the lovely boyfriend then my dear?" Betty innocently asked. "What was his name again?"

Kim had started lifting Betty's hair ready to drop a section between the blades of her scissors, she paused momentarily. "You mean Andy; we aren't together any more," she replied. Then squeezed the handles together— tightly.

"Oh," said Betty, realising she had just managed to find a sensitive subject to start their conversation with. "I will just come right out with it then, what the heck happened? You and— Andy, he seemed like such a nice boy."

"Seemed— being the operative word Betty, all he wanted was half of the cottage once he had sealed the knot. I can imagine right now, what an arse he would be to ensure a quickie divorce straight after the happy day..." sighed Kim, feeling a little angry and sad at the same time.

"But— your grandma left that cottage for you in her will. She loved you to pieces, and it had your name on it on the day that you were born." Betty stopped short as she realised that Kim had just taken a sharp intake of breath behind her.

Betty apologised. "Sorry Kim, I do remember the hassle Angela's will had caused— the moment it was read out. I am sure she didn't realise how uncharitable your family would be when you were declared the main beneficiary of her estate."

"Mum and dad had said it should have gone to Mike, my older brother. I remember the fuss they had made when they found it impossible to force it into probate. Grandma had already employed those hard-boiled lawyers, to ensure that I got the lot— no matter what." recalled Kim.

"How are things now with your mum, dad and Mike? Inquired Betty instinctively changing the subject.

"Mike still hasn't spoken a word; he never seems to be about when I visit mum and dad. I think he is deliberately avoiding me— his loss," Kim reflected, more than annoyed with her brother.

She took a belated sip of her cooling coffee, and asked a loaded question. "Who was Helen, then Betty?"

Mrs Warburton pretended she hadn't heard Kim's interrogative sentence.

"Would you believe it. Clara Neumann has taken up ballroom dancing, and she is ninety if not older? She said something about a woman dancing, attracting a better-looking man. Or, was it the other way around? I don't quite..."

"Betty, are you avoiding my question? You normally hear a butterfly cough at five hundred yards," Kim accused, holding her scissors high in the air.

Betty sighed, "Rumbled, where did you come across that name? I haven't heard it mentioned for a long, long time." She stood up and looked softly into Kim's eyes, waiting for her answer.

Kim explained about the mysterious folder and Mum's admission that Helen had existed. Betty put the kettle on for another hot beverage, while Kim has bought her up to date with what she knew.

Betty finished her own drink and sat back down on the chair, while remaining mute until Kim finished trimming her hair.

Kim walked in front of Betty and raised a mirror for her to check she was happy with the cut.

Betty spoke softly, while looking at the floor, "It's more complicated than you could ever imagine Kim."

"Complicated. Just how complicated can revealing more details about Mum's mysterious sister— be?" Kim's voice was steadily rising in volume.

Betty held up a hand and showed the palm to Kim. "Hold it right there young lady, I might be the same age as your Grandma, but I am not too old to put you over my knee..." She was suddenly aware Kim was noisily sobbing into her hands.

Standing back up, she put her arm around Kim's shoulders to try to comfort her and waited until the flow of tears began to abate. "Kim, I am really sorry, I didn't mean to tell you off or mention Angela. Sit down instead, and I will do my best to tell you— what I can."

Kim looked up as well and admitted she was sorry as well, and hadn't meant to raise her voice. "I couldn't help noticing the short pause in that last sentence before you said what I can." she said questionably.

"Definitely Angela's granddaughter, spotting that hesitation on my behalf," Betty smiled genuinely, "I will reiterate that last sentence, and yes there is an emphasis on what I can."

She began explaining. "I will start with a little history lesson to try to set the context to what I am about to reveal. After World War Two, the free world entered into an unseen war instead. It was known as the Cold War, and sort of petered out nineteen-eighty-nine, nineteen-ninety or thereabouts.

You can read all about the boring details in various places on the web if you want, but I digress. You will need to know a bit more in detail about Angela and little old me and how we helped fight the war."

She held up a finger, noticing Kim was beginning to mouth a question. "In a bit Kim, let me continue please, while I have lowered my guard." Unladylike Betty hoisted herself up to sit on the work surface, and wriggled a little until she was comfortable.

"Okay, where was I? Oh yes, Angela and Betty the English spies," she gave a little laugh. "Spies that's a lie, more like a pair of nosey women, spending a lot of time at foreign house parties."

Kim wordlessly raised one eyebrow questionably.

Betty continued her tale. "We were approached the same way hundreds of other potential agents of the empire were. if you'd shown any aptitude and intelligence at university, you could expect a request for an interview with intelligence— sooner rather than later.

Angela and I had the knack of making friends with people in high places. Especially important people in certain positions, spending time travelling to and from the eastern bloc— including Russia.

Anyway, it was mostly the same thing day in day out. Listening carefully to important wives and husbands, telling tales of who did what and when, then reporting it to our masters in London."

She stopped and smiled— "And— then there was Helen..."

***

#10   Monday Three PM

May 5th 2021

After spending a sleepless night, Kim felt surprisingly upbeat. She visited Maria late in the afternoon and spent a couple of hours chatting with her and the other girls. Who, had turned up brandishing chocolates and packets of cheese and onion crisps.

Maria admitted she hoped that George would be paying her another visit, and at that, the rest of them had ribbed her mercilessly.

Kim had unburdened herself from the conversations she had with Betty and her mum and dad. But she had deliberately not mentioned that Angela's mysterious daughter, Helen, was probably also a successful spy.

With a plan already inside her mind, she finally excused herself by saying she had things that she wanted to check out at the library. Giving each of the girls a quick peck on the cheek and a call to 'see you soon.' As she left the ward and headed towards the exit and her car.

She had decided— that now was the time to ask a professional for some help.

***

Arriving at the library, she parked her car and hastily walked inside, first stop— visiting the café.

She asked the lady standing behind the counter if she knew George Walsh and whether she had seen him today.

The woman eagerly admitted that she and the rest of the staff all knew exactly who George was, and she would like to get to know him better— personally as well.

As for seeing him today, she turned and nodded to prompt her elder colleague.

The older woman admitted she had served him coffee earlier this afternoon, and that he was now probably in his usual spot within the Library itself.

Kim asked if the library would allow drinks inside, and the woman behind the counter advised not normally. But, George had come to an agreement that he would automatically pay twice the value of any document that accidentally got damaged by a spilled drink. Although the woman had suspected, that permission was given by the assistant head librarian— because she fancied George herself.

"I'll bet Mr Walsh is getting ready for a caffeine fix, especially if he hasn't had one since early afternoon. If you could pour whatever he normally has please— I will pay for it and take it through to him." Kim said with a devious tone in her voice.

The lady behind the counter raised an eyebrow, wishing that she had thought of the simple ruse first.

Handing the coffee to Kim, she held up a hand when Kim offered to pay. "If it's for Mr Walsh, it's on the house. Just make sure you tell him that Carol in the café has sent it," she said with a slight hint of jealousy in her eyes.

After thanking Carol for her generosity, she twisted sharply on her heels and headed for the main library doors.

Kim could never understand why they built libraries with high ceilings and wooden floors. The acoustics from the hard surfaces magnified any whispers, sneezes or coughs. Let alone anyone who wanted to confer.

After a couple of false starts down book laden isles, she finally saw some half-hidden reading alcoves to her far left. Spotting George sitting alone while carefully examining an official-looking manuscript.

Initially worried he might be startled, if she announced she was standing there beside him.

An unwarranted coffee flying over his valuable documents would not necessarily leave him in a good mood.

So she stood back out of any waving arms range and spoke quietly, "One mug of coffee Mr Walsh, white, no sugar— just as you like it."

George surprised her by calmly twisting in his chair towards her and smiling in recognition.

"Why hello Kim with a K, have you got a job at the café or something?" He asked.

"No, I have brought it to you, to say thank you for keeping my friend Maria company at the hospital. Well, to be honest, a lady called Carol at the café gave it to me at no charge. I hope it was needed and am not wasting my time," confessed Kim, and placed the mug onto the edge of his workspace.

George nodded with gratitude. "Well, you have arrived at just the right moment, I was only thinking a couple of minutes ago that the caffeine was starting to lose its get up and go." He took a long sip and placed the mug onto a shelf built into the back of the research alcove.

Noticing that Kim was not making any signs of leaving his side— He looked her in the eye and asked her an embarrassing question. "I don't mean to be rude and ungrateful, but I am knee-deep in research for my next novel. Was there something else you wanted to talk about?"

Kim nervously played with the earring in her left ear. "I notice that the document you are scouring through appears to be in a foreign language, are you conversant in Spanish?" She asked, bending over slightly to get a better view.

George graciously leant back. To allow her to get a little nearer to the document. She could feel his hot breath on her naked arm, a shiver working its way up her spine finally manifesting itself physically.

"Cold?" George asked, and she shook her head in denial. "No, it must have been a draft blowing in." Kim changed the subject, "I notice you have a Spanish-to-English dictionary," she smiled spotting a potential way to garner his assistance. "I can speak and read Spanish— Fluently," she added with a smile.

"Really?" Answered George— his interest piqued.

"Gotcha!" Kim thought, silently pleased with herself, about spotting an opportunity and taking the initiative. "Can you? Or am I being rude, tell me if I am."

"I admit my Spanish is rudimentary at best. I work my way through very slowly with the aid of the dictionary, and sort of guess sometimes at the content." Confessed George taking a gulp of his coffee, "Do you want a job?" He asked lightly.

"*Hook line and sinker,*" Kim laughed and said, "Are you that desperate for a translator? I will have to check my diary to see whether I will be free."

She mocked counting down the fingers on her left hand. "One, I have finished my photography course for this term— Check. Two, Roger won't be expecting a meal for quite a few hours— check, Three, I want a favour from you, so I wouldn't need payment."

She saw he had a concerned look on his face and realised he probably had a question to ask of her. "Is there a problem with your end?— George."

"Roger?" George said sulkily, "I didn't realise you had someone else in your life?"

"Oh yes, Roger can be very demanding. He will probably be waiting at the window waiting for me to get home." Kim paused and decided she was enjoying teasing him just a little too much— maybe just one more go.

"When I finally get into the cottage, I will find him lying on the sofa— waiting for me to rub his tummy." She was almost fit to burst, watching his face fall downwards, further and further.

"Tummy?" He croaked, unable to say anything else, with the growing tightness in his throat.

"Roger is a cat!" Kim laughed out loud, the sound of shushing noises from around the library, rapidly brought her sobriety back. "Sorry," she apologised, "I couldn't resist that— the look on your face…"

George looked at her with a lopsided smile, "Okay I asked for that— but does that mean a yes, that you will help?"

Kim picked up the document and began to write down on the pad in front of George, the translated contents of the first paragraph and beyond. A few minutes later she leant back, for him to now view her work instead.

George flicked back a couple of pages of the pad and read what he had previously written there. He raised one eyebrow, "That paragraph took me just over an hour to translate using the dictionary— I am impressed, I accept your token of payment. How can I help you?"

Kim began telling George about the questions that she would like him to assist her with. A further barrage of shushing caused her to stop and suggest they change the venue to the café instead. George agreed and picked up his empty cup, notebook and pen, making his way towards the café with Kim in tow.

He turned to check that Kim was following and smiled inwardly to himself, "Gotcha Karen Taylor— Gotcha."

✳✳✳

George sat relaxing in his home office, his feet resting on the corner of his desk. He was deep in thought, whilst chewing on the end of a Biro pen.

The mobile telephone on the desk began to warble a high-pitched tune. Looking at the caller ID on the screen, George immediately recognised who was calling— Amber Prevett, his literary agent. Sighing deeply, he picked up the phone answering with "Hello Amber, how can I help?" His tongue was firmly in his cheek as he had uttered those words, knowing full well why she was calling today.

Amber quickly realised that he was teasing her and used a tone of voice that suggested she was deadly serious.

"Progress George has there been any, or have you been just dragging it all out again?"

"I could be hurt— But I am not," George continued light-heartedly. "Okay, let's play a game— do you want the bad news or the good news?"

"George, can't you ever be serious?" she sighed.

"Bad news or good news." he insisted.

"For Goodness' sake George, the bad news I suppose," she said exasperatedly.

"The novel you are waiting for me to write— won't be finished this year," he revealed.

He imagined he could hear steam spouting from her ears, with her blood pressure rising after his unexpected announcement.

Without waiting for her to rage obscenities into his ear, he continued, "But— I have found one of my earliest manuscripts, that I had never bothered to present to you.

Mainly, because I thought it wouldn't be good enough. I've had another look at it and with a few grammatical changes, I think you will have another winner on your hands."

George could sense she was calming down as she answered, "George, I know you are holding something back. That wasn't all the bad news, good news— was it?"

"Can you wait a minute or two I need to put the kettle on, I am parched," He teased her further— he moved away from the earpiece, as Amber bellowed in frustration "George!"

George laughed, "Keep your knickers on— I could always wind you up when we were together, couldn't I?" He imagined her silently fuming, "Right then, here we go— here is the good news first. I managed to finally get my source to trust me. She not only wants me to help her with 'my story', but is also working as an unpaid translator as well."

"And?" Hissed Amber.

"Oh yeah, the bad news. I am going to have to dig pretty deep into my research fund. My contact doesn't know it yet, but we are going to be spending some time in Spain together— real soon..."

He heard the sound of a phone being banged against a desk, followed by a dial tone in his ear. "There may be trouble ahead," he hummed the old Nat King Cole song to himself. "Let's face the music and ..."

✳✳✳

#11   Friday Nine AM

May 9th 2021

Rubbing her tired eyes and becoming slightly confused, after feeling around on the bedside table and finding her mobile phone missing.

Kim sighed deeply in mild annoyance, recalling that before going to bed last night, she had left the mobile out of reach on its charger in the kitchen.

She felt totally frustrated, as it had just finished ringing out-of-sight without being answered.

Any other time she could have remained warm and comfortable in her bed, as most people always rang her mobile.

The caller had since abandoned ringing the mobile and had quickly switched to calling the landline phone instead.

Casually pushing Roger off the bed with her foot, she swung the other to the floor.

"Typical," she thought to herself while wiping the sleep from her eyes. The first time she had managed to get a lie-in for three weeks, and some maniac wanted to talk to her.

Kim stamped down the stairs and hastily picked up the handset. "Hello?" she said with an edgy tone to her voice.

127

Her greeting was answered by a female voice, excitedly repeating one word, "Kim, Kim, Kim…"

She rolled her eyes, "Mum— it's me— What's up?"

"Kim, Kim…" Pamela repeated.

Now she was becoming exasperated, "Mum!" Kim said a little more forcibly than she had intended. Pamela silenced — sharply halfway through yet another utterance of the word 'Kim.'

"Whatever is the matter, Mum what is the urgency? You sound like that BBC comedy-video thing on the internet. When the Marmot shouts 'Alan, Alan— Alan' all the time." Kim said with concern in her voice.

"I have had some amazing news— We have won a three-week holiday for two. All-inclusive in Spain and it's over Christmas and the new year as well!" Pamela gushed.

Kim heard her dad David Chapman, shouting something unintelligible in the background.

"That's fantastic Mum; what competition did you enter?" Kim asked Pamela.

"Well that is the strangest thing," Her Mum replied. "I don't recognise the name of the company giving out the prize."

Kim heard her mother fiddling with something near the phone.

Pamela continued, "Anyway, I have checked with the holiday company, and it's official, and our names are booked to receive the tickets and stuff. All we have to do is take our passport's down to the TIH holiday shop in the town, and they will present the package tour to us on behalf of the mystery company."

"Do you mind if I come around?— and cast my eyes over it as well?" Kim offered, thinking how lucky they were to have won such a wonderful prize.

"Please Kim, if you wouldn't mind. Your dad and I are so excited, we would love for you to have a sensible look over the letter for us as well." Pamela urged, her voice raising in volume as she became more excited.

"I'm on my way over there now Mum, I haven't got anybody booked in for a hairdo today. I was going to have myself a 'lie-in', and tidy around the house a bit, before I went to the library to help George in translating some stuff again."

Before Pamela had a chance to comment; on how much time Kim appeared to be spending with this fellow

George and disappointedly hadn't brought him around to meet them yet.

The phone call suddenly ended— signalling that her daughter was definitely on her way. "Maybe later," she thought and placed her handset into the cradle as well.

✳✳✳

"It was going to be a flying visit," Kim had decided before arriving at her parent's house. Thinking about it a little, she realised it was really fun, and she was enjoying every minute helping George out.

After nearly four days, he had told her that he had finally managed to get in touch with someone associated with the home office. They had willingly agreed to assist, regarding any potential leads, for more information about Helen.

She pulled up outside Mum and Dad's, and knocked on the door impatiently.

David opened the door and smiled at his daughter fidgeting with the buttons on her coat. "Kim— Hello darling, come in. Your mum is waiting in the lounge— go straight in after taking off your shoes."

Before he could say another word, Kim had pushed past and was struggling to get the boots off her feet.

By the time he had closed the door and pulled across the night chain. Kim was already padding her way into the lounge, to be greeted by Pamela waving a sheet of paper.

Kim managed a quick "Hi Mum," and was already devouring the letter from top to bottom, and then from the top again.

She finally put the letter on the table and announced: "it certainly doesn't appear to be fake, especially if TIH says it's the real deal, what else can I say— but congratulations." She hugged Pamela to her chest. "Is Mike going with you as well?"

Before Pamela could reply, someone else answered instead. "Your brother Mike is staying here over Christmas, as I have a new lady friend to entertain instead," announced her skinny slightly older brother, emerging from the kitchen with a steaming cup of coffee in his hand. "Besides, there are only two places paid for, and I am kind of skint— let alone it being Christmas."

Kim's brother was glaring at her, making her feel distinctly uncomfortable.

She glanced at her watch and apologised. Announcing it was time to make a move, as she hadn't had time for breakfast. Adding as an afterthought, she wanted to make sure her tummy wasn't going to rumble— when she was working with George.

Hugging her dad before she left and offered her congratulations to him as well. Kim climbed into her car and began the journey towards the Library café.

✳✳✳

Walking through the entrance into the café, Kim immediately noticed Carol Peters. The pleasant lady who had served her coffee, the first time she had met George inside the library itself.

Carol had a smile on her face as usual, and was waving to her across the room.

Already heading to the counter for some breakfast anyway, Kim waved back whilst genuinely returning the smile herself.

She hadn't seen the café manageress for a couple of days, as Carol appeared to be normally working the early shift instead. Kim hadn't finished each day's hairdressing appointments— much before one pm.

"Hello, stranger, long-time no-see. I presume as it is a Friday you are here to serve our lordship? He got here extra early today, and— appeared to be rather pleased with himself for a change." Observed Carol already pouring two coffees into large red mugs, each with their name on.

Kim presented George with his yesterday. As a 'thank you' for agreeing to help her research Helen, while they worked together at the library.

She remembered that he had moaned that it wasn't his favourite colour blue. A swift and sly elbow in the ribs— had rapidly changed his opinion, and they had both laughed out loud.

Carol was 'spot-on' about George's demeanour being normally deadpan serious. Although when he had the right trigger, he would immediately switch to caring, charming or comical. But without fail he would eventually fall back to become 'Mr Serious' and continue with the job in hand.

With a coffee in each hand and her bag over her shoulder, she made her way into the library.

The Overall Head Librarian Harold had personally moved them both into a private reading chamber, normally reserved for visiting dignitaries.

There were two reasons for Harold authorising the change in location.

The first was practicality, Kim and George were continually conversing, plus the occasional incoming phone call was causing a little friction from other library users.

Not that he particularly cared, as Mr. Walsh did hold regular workshops for potential authors at no charge on behalf of the library.

The second reason was closer to home, where his wife Carol Peters the café Manageress, had verbally insisted that he should give them a bit more privacy. She also reminded her husband of the fact, that the last dignitary that had used the facility, was in nineteen thirty-nine.

Kim tapped the door with the toe of her shoe and waited for George to twist the handle for her, to allow entry into the small office. By the time she had placed the cups onto their respective positions on the desk, George was quizzically examining an email on his laptop screen.

He turned to Kim to ask her opinion of the content and noticed that she seemed both happy and distracted. Raising an eyebrow, George asked, "Am I missing something Kim— has something happened to one of your friends?"

He reflected for a moment on his comment, and continued, "Sorry, I am being stupid— you are smiling, so something good then?"

"Mum and dad have won a mysterious prize for an all-inclusive holiday over the Christmas period," Kim gushed. "They are so lucky, I wish I was going..."

George immediately answered in a positive voice. "Why not Kim, the family, are important at Christmas."

Kim rolled her eyes, "Duh, I am only a mere hairdresser, and I know it is hard to believe."

"But— I am not receiving much in the way of company dividends, to be able to afford a holiday at one of the peak periods of the year." She replied sarcastically.

As George watched her face, he could see an 'and' approaching.

Kim didn't disappoint. "Plus there is my pal Roger, who would look after him? Not forgetting the girls, I haven't missed spending some time at Christmas with them for the past four years— no holiday for Kim I am afraid." She took a deep breath and sighed.

George cupped a hand underneath his chin, appearing to be deep in thought. He was mentally congratulating himself for promoting this conversation, by purchasing and sending the mysterious holiday tickets to her parents.

He did feel really guilty. About the fact that he was getting Kim to unintentionally get him access to— the information he still needed to complete his planned novel.

Still, that would depend on completely, whether the next part of the plan went smoothly or not.

"Well, as you have worked so hard without any pay, plus we haven't discussed a wage. If you promise to continue helping as often as you can, I will also pay for you to take the same holidays as your mum and dad." He said generously, now waiting a few seconds for that to sink in.

George saw a dubious look appear on her face, so he continued to try to 'seal the deal'. "I will also pay seventy-five percent off the same package, for any friends you may wish to bring as well."

Kim laughed out loud in surprise, "George I know you are successful and all that, but that would cost you a bundle?"

He held up a hand to signify her to wait. "Kim I am serious, but there is a method in my madness." He held one finger over another in his hidden other hand.

"George?" Kim stood with her hands on her hips waiting for an explanation.

"I thought it would be more sensible if sometime we transferred our investigation to Spain. I was just about to tell you about a phone call I had, from that contact in the Home Office.

I was going to suggest we both went out there when convenient, and follow up on the fresh information given to me." George admitted.

Kim made one more vain attempt to refuse, "But, what about Roger?"

George countered with, "What about your brother Mike? I am sure your Mum will be able to talk him into looking after him. Especially if I sweeten him with a cat-sitting reward. He can't hold a grudge forever— can he?"

Defeated, Kim could only give him a silly grin and a kiss on his cheek. "George Walsh, there really is a heart of gold under that gruff exterior," she said tongue in cheek.

George could only pretend to be offended for a few seconds before laughing out loud, and teased her by uttering, "Cow— back to work woman, before I change my mind..."

✳✳✳

Kim was feeling rather pleased with herself. Today had been in just one word— GOOD, and she was now on her way to visit Maria at the hospital.

She had just texted her main friends, and asked if they could be there at the same time as her. Ignoring text replies of why, she climbed into her car after feeding and watering Roger, and headed once more towards the hospital.

As usual the route was jammed packed with traffic, due to the ever-present roadworks and diversions. Kim was now arriving into the hospital car park twenty minutes later than she had hoped. She had already decided to call into the hospital shop, to pick up a bunch of flowers for Maria, as an apology for being late.

Rustling through the small choice of wrapped bouquets available, she chose one with a beautiful mix of red and yellow roses, and after paying she made her way towards Maria's ward.

Waving to Norma Gubbins, the on duty reception nurse as she passed the desk. Kim made her way through the door leading into Maria's private room.

Nancy and the girls had drawn their chairs around the bottom of the bed and were currently giggling. Kirstie held up for Kim to see a very short nightie with the words 'If you want to snuggle— I promise I won't struggle.'

136

Kim smiled and turned towards Maria to present her with the bouquet, and almost tripped over her own feet. Once again, George Walsh was sitting next to the bed.

Noticing the surprise on her face, George stood and showed her the palm of his hand. "Don't mind me, I was here early today to visit Paul, and I thought I would just give Maria some company for a bit. It was only a couple of minutes later when the girls had invaded the room."

He looked at Kim and slyly winked. "I'm sure you have loads of things to discuss with your friends, so I will take my leave and make my way to see Paul." He started heading for the room exit, waved and disappeared into the corridor beyond.

Kim found four pairs of eyes staring questionably towards her. "What?" She teased.

"We don't know, you called us here to tell us something according to your text," Kirstie said with an impish look on her face. "Unless we are all going to now meditate while you update us telepathically, spill the beans sister…"

Everyone laughed, but remained focussed on Kim.

"Okay, Okay I get the message, here's mine to you— does anybody fancy a three-week Christmas party? All-inclusive in a four-star hotel?" Kim paused for effect.

"Offered at seventy-five percent off the already discounted price, as seen in the twenty-twenty-one TIH catalogue, Winter edition." Kim curtsied and awaited their reaction.

The gang simply continued to stare, until Nancy asked with a slightly disappointed look in her eyes, "Seriously Kim, what did you really ask us to meet here for?" Nancy rejoined the others in their communal gaze.

"I am being serious," Kim replied and began to tell them about her mum and dad's competition win, concluding her story with George's generous offer.

The resultant bedlam caused by the screams of joy and loud talking as they all agreed to go, caused Norma to show her stern face at the door. "Believe it or not this is a hospital, whatever is causing you to display this uncharacteristic noise?"

Maria looked up from her bed and announced, "We are all going on holiday together— spending Christmas in Spain."

The noise level began rising again. As everyone began to excitedly tell Norma about George's promise, to subsidise the cost of a holiday for the entire group of friends.

Kim noticed that Norma's face was beginning to show she was losing her patience.

"Okay everyone, I know we are all excited and cannot wait for December to arrive. Let's think of the others here in the hospital that aren't so lucky as us and begin talking quietly once more— so they can have a chance to rest and get better."

Norma smiled and left the room, as they quietly discussed whether it would be warm enough for a bikini or not.

Finally, Kim looked at her watch and remembered that she needed to go to the local supermarket to buy some fresh cat litter for Roger.

Giving each of her friends a kiss on the cheek and a promise that she would speak soon.

She was just about to leave the room when she saw a familiar woman pass by in the corridor.

Putting her hand to her mouth in shock, all she could say was "My god; it's her."— She had just seen the mystery woman, who was sitting with Andy in Ari's Indian restaurant, the night she dropped the soup into Andy's lap.

Before she had time to react further, the woman had unfortunately disappeared out of sight.

Leaving Kim thinking to herself, "What the hell was she doing here, and who the heck is she?"

✳✳✳

#12   Sunday Six Forty AM

December 19th 2021

"Remember five minutes to six you must tickle his tummy, and just after that, you can plonk his bowl in front of him.

Miss out the tummy tickle and you will have trouble on your hands— He will not eat or drink anything until you have performed tickle duty.

I swear he would starve if you didn't do it." Kim tried thinking if there was anything else that Mike should know before he was left in charge of her beloved cat.

Mike was staring with glazed eyes at his sister and was nodding just out of politeness.

How hard could it be to feed and water a cat for god's sake? Still, as he had been promised the money from George, he was now stuck with becoming Rogers' slave for the next three weeks.

He was secretly relieved they were talking again and the animosity from the past was now swept under the carpet.

It was a good job that to date, he still hadn't admitted he actually loved his sister to pieces.

Mike wouldn't even do anything like this for his new girlfriend, if she ever asked. He had to maintain his 'Street Credibility' somehow.

He suddenly became aware Kim was staring at him expectantly. Mike suspected she had just imparted some useful information and was now expecting an answer.

"Sorry Kim, can you tell me that again, as I want everything to sink in?— I don't want a wild cat on my hands." He self-congratulated himself for that smart excuse. As Kim once again pointed out the locations of biscuits and cat litter.

"Phew close," he thought. "The poor cat could have been using cat biscuits as litter, and cat litter rather than biscuits." He gave an involuntary chuckle at the idea.

Kim showed she suspected his thoughts were more spice than sugar, by giving him a stern look.

She was quickly distracted by Roger rubbing her legs whilst meowing lightly. "You know I am leaving you, don't you? No need to worry, Uncle Mike will make sure you are fed and watered."

Her mobile phone bleeped an alarm, so Kim gripped the handle of her cabin luggage-on-wheels and began wheeling it towards the outside.

"I take it that's a signal that you want to make a move then Sis'?" Mike asked, already dragging a heavy suitcase nearer to the door.

Kim nodded in agreement, "Mum will have a blue fit if we are late checking in. She has watched too many of those cheap airline reality programs and their strict policies, to think any other Airline might be a bit more lenient." She patted Roger for the last time, before making her way outside towards the car.

Mike heaved the suitcase and bag into the boot, grunting from the weight and exclaimed. "I hope for the airline's sake that the others don't pack as much, or nobody will be taking off at all."

Kim simply gave him the 'evil eye,' making sure he kept mute until they arrived at Pamela and David's home.

Their main luggage was already sitting on the drive waiting for it to be stowed. Mike just about managed to lift them into the car and noticed the rear of the car drop significantly.

He raised his eyebrows— after realising his mock prediction may just come true.

Pamela spoke firmly to her son while hugging him tightly, "Love you and see you soon Mike, just make sure you look after the house and yourself."

She paused slightly noticing Kim raising her eyebrows, and amended her advice slightly.

"Also, do not— I repeat, do not forget to feed that smelly old moggie, or your sister will make sure your girlfriend will not be a happy bunny. Get my drift..."

It took him a few seconds to realise what she had alluded to and then smirked. "Okay, okay I've got the picture— have a nice time and be careful yourselves."

Mike stepped away from behind Kim's car, and watched her reverse out onto the road. With a slight grinding noise, as she put it into first gear, his family finally drove smoothly away— towards Heathrow airport.

***

"Kirstie Hanson, for god's sake, can you explain why there are five cases sat in the middle of the living room?" Shouted Kirstie's brother Dave— Feeling totally exasperated.

He had just fetched their car from the agreed parking spot on Mrs Walker's drive.

Mrs Walker had kindly offered the space for free, after Dave had carried her shopping home from Mr Ranjak's corner store. When she found out he had just left the Armed Forces, they quickly sealed the deal on the spot.

A couple of minutes later, Kirstie emerged from her bedroom dragging yet another suitcase:

"What did you say?" she puffed, arranging the powder blue case next to the others, and looked up at Dave.

By now Dave was almost speechless, and just about managed to sputter "Suitcases?"

He coughed and recovered slightly, by pointing at the 'Elephant' in the centre of the room.

"I will need to go out to Carry-it and hire a van for them. There is— no way that lot will fit in the car, plus whatever suitcase Nancy brings as well..." Dave sighed deeply for effect.

"I can tell you are not a woman," Kirstie answered cryptically.

She looked her brother in the eye, noticing that his expression shouted 'Confused man looking for Help.' "Look— it's very simple, what do you see?"

"Six suitcases," he easily replied.

"A little more?" Kirstie encouraged. She waited for a moment or two and stated the obvious. "They are all different colours..."

Dave continued with the blank look across his face, "Okay, they are all different colours— so?"

"I will give you a clue," she smiled smugly, "What can you see dangling on the hangers over the door jamb?"

He was now beginning to enjoy this game, "Clothes." he replied.

Kirstie corrected him, "Not clothes— those are outfits Dave, and how many are there?"

Dave wrinkled his nose, still baffled, wondering where this example of female logic was taking him. He walked over to the door and counted each one. "Six," he announced.

"And?" she prompted.

Dave took a step backwards and then stated the obvious, "They are all different colours." The penny had dropped, and he confirmed his thoughts by turning towards the cases in the centre of the room.

"I hadn't decided which outfit to travel in yet and wanted to make sure I was going to be colour coordinated.

The other five cases are still empty, and I had just decided I fancied my powder-blue outfit to wear.

I had already dragged the matching coloured suitcase into the bedroom— where I was in the process of filling it up just as you walked in through the door." Kirstie explained, as if the whole situation was obvious.

Dave put a flat hand up to his forehead in mock surprise, "Yeah, silly me— I should have known better. Anyway, have you finished packing?

Nancy will be wondering where the hell we have got to — Unless she is staring at six empty cases as well..." He laughed out loud, grabbed hold of the newly populated suitcase, and began dragging it out to the car.

Kirstie rummaged in her handbag for her phone and began to compose a text to Nancy.

To: Nancy Myers
Subject: On our Way

Hi Hun,
Hope you have chosen which outfit and matching suitcase you are using.
His highness might not see the funny side. LOL.
Be there in twenty min'.
Xxx Kirstie.

Smiling to herself, she twisted the latch to lock and slammed the door tightly shut.

※※※

The doorbell was ringing, and she hadn't finished getting ready yet, pulling her new yellow polo-neck sweater over her head, she fought her way past her luggage in the hallway and opened the door.

"Hi George, come-in, I'm sorry I am not quite ready, wardrobe failures and all that," Maria rambled nervously—directing him into the living room.

George smiled and nodded his head, "Not a problem Maria, we are okay for time so far," he said with a hopeful look on his face.

"Thanks for picking me up, I would have taken the coach if you hadn't offered," Maria began brushing her hair in the mirror, to make repairs after pulling the sweater over her head.

George leaned against the door frame. "Not a problem, I only live half-a-mile down the road, and I knew the others already each had a full car. It made sense for me to make sure we all arrived at roughly the same time."

George had continued visiting her occasionally, after both Maria and Paul had left the hospital. He told everyone it was a habit he had got into, and simply enjoyed her company.

Maria secretly wished that he was picking her up because of other reasons— For example, he was only here because he was infatuated and it was Maria he wanted to travel with.

"*Still, beggars can't be choosers. At least I will be sitting next to him for the next hour or so.*" Maria thought, while giving her hair a final flick.

She picked up an atomiser filled to the brim with her favourite perfume and sprayed her wrists and neck with two short bursts.

Maria opened her handbag, dropped the perfume in, and swung the bag over her shoulder. "Okay, I'm ready," she announced smiling.

George made a point of slowly looking at his watch, "I'm impressed— I expected at least a couple of 'won't be long', and just a smidgen of 'nearly ready.' Before announcing we are going to be on our way," he teased.

"Cheeky sod," Maria laughed and hooked her arm under his, leading him firmly towards his car.

"Aren't you forgetting anything?" he asked, while opening the boot of his car.

Maria looked puzzled, "I have got my passport, money and tickets…" The penny dropped. "Shit— my luggage, sorry George, would you mind?"

Already back indoors, George rapidly re-emerged through the front door, pulling behind a large wheeled suitcase and swinging a leather cabin bag over his shoulder.

He threw them into the back seat of the car, with his cases already filling the boot.

They had only got a couple of miles down the road, when George's hands-free phone began to warble loudly.

Pressing the answer key conveniently located on the steering wheel, he answered, "George Walsh how can I…"

He glanced at the caller ID and gulped heavily, "Amber, and what can I do for my favourite literary agent today— you do realise I am on my way to Spain today, with— friends."

"Yes, I do realise— that's why I am ringing." She answered softly.

George found his hands involuntarily gripping the wheel a little tighter, acutely aware that Maria was intently listening to another woman dripping affection on the phone.

"George dearest, you will be careful, won't you? You know how much I worry about you— even now," Amber oozed.

George's jaw was beginning to ache with tension, "Please god, I pray Amber doesn't mention the master plan with Maria in the car," he thought nervously.

He heard a snuffle and realised that Amber was starting to cry.

"Amber," uttered George as he was just about to begin comforting her distress. When she tremulously announced she had to go, as she had just received an alert that someone was on the other line.

George suspected she was obviously lying, so that she didn't have to expand on her emotional feelings as Amber hung up a couple of seconds later— leaving an uncomfortable silence in the car.

He noticed that Maria's bottom lip was pushing petulantly outwards with obvious jealousy. "Are you okay?" George asked in a concerned voice.

Immediately she appeared to perk up at the sound of George's husky voice addressing her, instead of the mysterious voice on the phone.

Now encouraged, she snuggled closer to George. "I'm feeling terrific George, absolutely fine," she smiled contentedly, not caring a jot, about the traffic they were heading towards on the M25 Motorway.

✳✳✳

"Right, is that everything?" asked Dave and gave his sister an affectionate hug followed by a peck on the forehead.

"I would stop and have a coffee with you, but I can see a bunch of females, and a couple of blokes waving like lunatics at you." He sighed after waving back, and turned towards the airport exit.

"He hates goodbyes," disclosed Kirstie to Nancy, wondering why Dave had made excuses and left as they finally arrived. "You should have seen the tears when he had to go to the annual scout meeting as a young boy. You would never believe he had been in the Army." She laughed at the thought.

Nancy smiled, "I think it's really nice— I wish I had met someone like him before I got together with that idiot Brett last year. That relationship was doomed as soon as it started. I should have realised, when he first told me I wasn't dressing in the right clothes. The final clue was when he informed me he had some clothes in his wardrobe— and I could borrow them any time I wanted..." She finished, shuddering slightly.

Kirstie looked at her friend wondering if she had heard correctly that Nancy liked the thought of being with Dave— her brother. She chuckled involuntarily at the thought, wondering if she should reveal some of his less wholesome habits. Noticing that Nancy was now dragging her wheeled suitcase in the direction of her friends, she gave chase.

***

After checking in and making their way through the custom's area, they finally managed to sit together in the departure lounge.

George stood up and asked everyone if they fancied a drink, offering to pay and fetch it for them.

Maria quickly pulled a small notebook out of her handbag and offered to write down who wanted what. She then dutifully followed George to the café, located at the other end of the hall.

Nancy turned to the others, "Is it me— or does Maria seem to be infatuated with George. I mean, don't get me wrong. I don't blame her. He is rich, clever and best of all— decidedly hunky too."

Everyone gave their verbal agreement apart from Kim, who simply nodded, whilst secretly believing she wasn't sure that Maria was right for George.

"What the hell am I thinking, I only work with George every day. It's not as if I am dating him or anything," she thought— slightly shocked that such ideas were floating around in her mind?

The problem was, Kim felt uneasy now, with her mental denial of any feelings for George Walsh washing around in her head. She shook her head imperceptibly and listened to the excited conversations of her family and friends, already planning a picnic on a sun soaked beach.

Kim didn't intend spending much time with that sort of activity. She was far more interested in the investigation of Helen Taylor and her secrets, to waste precious time on such frivolous things.

✳✳✳

#13   Sunday One Thirty PM

December 19th 2021

"I can see the ground below again, I think we must be coming around to land," Kim observed while peering intently through the slightly misted porthole. The aircraft continued to bank around sharply with it's wing facing downward.

Kim was sitting near the window next to George and Maria by the aisle.

George leaned forward and peered past Kim's shoulder. "Looks nice and sunny here, I hope it will stay like that for the next few weeks. I'm glad you took up the offer; I would have missed you over the Christmas period otherwise."

Maria had a glint of jealousy in her eyes, "Would you have missed me as well, George? Because; I would rather miss you as well."

Diplomatically George replied, "I would miss all you crazy women. I don't doubt I wouldn't have missed the incessant jabber, though," he laughed.

Simultaneously he felt an elbow jab on his ribs from either side.

"Hey come on, play fair, at least pick on someone your own size." He giggled childlike while tickling both of the girls' waists, making them wriggle and squeal inside the safety belts, unable to escape.

The obsolete no smoking and fasten your seat belt signs, flashed on together— accompanied by a loud chime from the overhead speakers.

"Ladies and gentlemen, please fasten your seat belt. Captain Stannard has just received clearance for us to land, and we will soon be beginning our descent. Please don't remove your belts until the plane has come to a standstill on the runway. Thank you for flying with TIH airways and all the crew wish you a very Merry Christmas." Kim smiled at her mum and dad as the steward finished his announcement, and gave them both a thumbs up.

Kirstie quietly began singing the lyrics of 'The Sun Has Got His Hat On' and was quickly accompanied by other passengers in the cabin. In an attempt to ease their nerves, as the plane began to steeply drop altitude, causing multiple eardrums to pop.

Maria's hand wrapped smoothly around George's, and was disappointed when she noticed he was now also sliding his other towards Kim. She quickly forgot his friendliness towards her friend, as he firmly squeezed her hand after a period of heavy turbulence rapidly abated.

The rumble of powerful motors announced the extension of the landing gear, readying the passengers for the final bump as they landed on Terra firma.

A crescendo of clapping ensued as they zoomed along the runway towards the terminals of Alicante Airport. Before finally coming to rest, awaiting the arrival of the passenger buses.

As they queued in the gangway, they felt the unseasonably ferocious heat soaking in via the open cabin doorway. Whether caused by changes due to global warming or the expected global flip of the magnetic poles. The projected good weather for Christmas was causing unprecedented levels of holiday bookings Europe-wide.

The whole group thanked their lucky stars for being able to book early. As, it was unlikely they would have been able to get such a fantastic hotel with the now inflated prices.

As people were completely happy to pay a premium to escape the typical cold English weather— elsewhere.

One by one they clambered down the stairs at the front of the plane and stood in an orderly queue on the tarmac. Patiently waiting to be allowed access to the transfer coach.

With standing-room-only in the interior of the vehicle, they were grateful for the air-conditioning within. The journey was mercifully short, as they had been swaying from side to side. Passengers were grumbling, the driver appeared to have been attempting a new speed record.

After collecting their luggage from the carousel room, they made their way outside. They needed to find their holiday representative, and the coach to take them to their hotel. They saw an officiously dressed woman, beside a makeshift TIH billboard, located halfway up the coach park outside.

While the women and George were deciding, whether the uniformed woman was likely to be 'Their Rep'— David

Chapman was already marching up the melting pavement, to investigate for himself.

A number of people had already gathered around a double-decker modern coach, and the holiday representative standing nearby was checking off names on an iPad.

After a quick conversation, he had confirmed this was the coach they were all booked on. He put two fingers into his mouth and blew an ear-shattering whistle to attach his group's attention.

Like a pack of huskies their ears pricked up, and each began dragging a suitcase in place of a sledge towards David. Now frantically waving like a mime artist directing traffic, beckoning them towards him.

Almost breaking into a canter, they speedily reached David and the Rep' who introduced herself as Kiki Leigh. After swiftly logging them in, their luggage was quickly stowed into the bowels of the coach.

As soon as the full complement of passengers was reached, the coach began the long journey to drop them off.

The journey time was enhanced as the coach stopped numerous times. Expelling passengers and their luggage, when they reached whichever accommodation they had booked.

✳✳✳

Their destination was the renowned Hotel Los Naranjeros in Moraira located between Alicante and Valencia.

The spectacular views over the sand and sea from the panoramic balconies were deemed to be a memorable feature of their own. Let alone the five-star facilities of the hotel property itself.

Well tanned and Happy holiday-makers, thronged around the scorched gardens, as the coach squealed to a halt outside the lobby entrance.

With a hiss of compressed air, the doors swung open and the temperature within immediately began to rise.

After patiently queueing outside the coach for their baggage to be unloaded, the passengers made their way to queue again at reception, ready to book in.

The group then took some time in their individual rooms to unpack clothing, and wind down after today's journey. Once rested, they all met outside and sat in a group near the poolside bar.

George made his way towards their table, with two large jugs of Sangria dangling from each of his powerful hands. He was followed by Evandro, the poolside waiter, with a large tray of iced glasses in his arms.

George waited until each of the group had filled their glass to the top, before making an announcement. "Friends Romans and others gathered around this table; I would like to make a toast."

Evandro raised his eyebrows. Deciding this was probably an opportune moment to leave them to it, and made his way back towards the bar.

George watched him scuttle away and continued his speech. "First, I would like to mention the lucky competition winners. Where, if they hadn't received such good fortune— would we all be here today?" The group all took a sip of their cooling drink, and gave a short cheer of thanks.

"Next, I would like to propose a toast to my glamorous assistant Kim. Who as you all will know by now, has been helping me with difficult translations and other editorial duties — like fetching my coffee and putting the waste paper into the bin."

Everyone laughed out loud— while Kim gave him the 'death stare', until she couldn't keep a straight face any longer and began to giggle uncontrollably.

George waited until she had quietened down and raised both hands palms outward. "Of course we mustn't forget the members of Kim's gang, for agreeing to chaperone Kim. While she would be spending untold hours lying on the sun-soaked beaches— Saving a small fortune, by not using tanning beds or any other artificial means of stimulating melanin."

Nancy and Kirstie clapped loudly, although Maria was slightly less enthusiastic. No-one else seemed to have noticed though, and everyone raised the glasses once more for the final toast followed by a tremendous hurrah.

As the relaxed mood set, George raised his arm as a signal for Evandro to bring a tray of delicious Spanish Tapas. The waiter placed them onto an adjoining table. Then made additional room for a second tray, already heading that direction via another colleague. The whole group began to dive in, determined to enjoy the snacks— raising the partying spirit.

Other holiday-makers naturally migrated towards the sound of fun, and George responded by providing even more drinks and nibbles for them to consume as well.

Eventually, as things started to quieten down. Kim's dad announced that as he hadn't drunk too much, he was going to make his way over to the Car Hire centre located in the town. Hoping to hire a large SUV to be able to ferry everyone around.

George interrupted, by explaining he would need a separate vehicle for him and Kim to use as well— for work purposes. David nodded in agreement, "Makes sense. I will just get my licence from the safe, and we can go together."

George apologised to the girls for leaving the party so soon, and made his way to reception to wait for David to join him again.

They were soon walking the short distance to the harbour, where the car hire centre was located on the site of the old fish cannery.

They walked into the reception area where a smartly dressed man was already attending to a middle-aged woman.

From behind a water dispenser a tall Spanish girl walked towards them with her hand held out, offering them a greeting. David took her hand first, and she asked his name and how she could help.

While she was attending to David's needs, George wandered around the rest of the small office and began browsing leaflets. Advising tourists about the locations of the best restaurants through to nearby Aqua Parks to spend your valuable holiday time.

George overheard the nearby smartly dressed salesman announce that he was popping out to get the salesgirl and himself an ice cream. As the man left, he noticed the tinkle of the overdoor bell shortly after.

George looked up and noticed the woman who had been hiring a car was now staring at him. As soon as she realised her actions had been observed, instead of turning away she purposely strode in his direction.

She looked at George quizzically and asked him outright, "You look familiar, aren't you an author or something?"

George raised an eyebrow and tongue in cheek he replied, "Author yes— something well that depends on your point of view. I'm George Walsh, and you are?"

The woman spoke to him in an accent he couldn't quite recognise, "Nadine Spencer— If I am right, I seem to remember you writing thrillers. I think I might have read a couple of your paperbacks previously." She smiled disarmingly and asked, "Are you here on business Mr Walsh?"

George furrowed his eyebrows then answered slowly. "As it happens, I am here researching for a future novel based around the time of the Cold War."

Nadine wiped a bead of sweat from her brow, "Cold War eh? Well, you have come to the right place to warm up." She smiled briefly, and just as quickly, again became serious. "I noticed you had walked in talking to someone else, a member of your research team perhaps?"

George knew when he was being pumped for information and decided to play along, "Yes, I thought I would treat the whole group to an early Christmas bonus. The other European teams will be arriving sometime within the next week or so," he lied with a convincing smile.

He looked at her directly in the eyes, and countered with a question himself. "What about you Nadine? I observed you have rented an expensive Mercedes-Benz, with the keys dangling just inside your open purse."

Nadine looked down immediately towards her handbag and wondered when he had identified them. She was totally surprised. Only the metallic part of the key appeared to be exposed, with the rubberised handgrip emblazoned with the Mercedes-Benz symbol, buried deep inside.

"I am impressed with your detecting skills, Mr Walsh," she reflected, skilfully deflecting George's first question asking why she was also on the Spanish mainland.

Undeterred, George repeated the question a little more directly, "And— why are you in Spain Nadine? Visiting friends, or possibly for business reasons?"

Nadine pursed her thin lips tightly, before answering. "That's rather a personal question George; I wouldn't have expected a gentleman like yourself to be asking questions of a lady— but of course, that is your profession, isn't it?"

Without waiting for an answer, she turned sharply on her heels and walked swiftly towards the exit.

George stepped quickly to the window and mentally took note of her car number plate. He detected that the saleswoman had finished with David and was cheerfully waving him over to her desk, with a beaming smile on her face.

George had already chosen an open-top Toyota Rav 4 from a leaflet on a desk, and the hire transaction was swiftly completed. David and George were introduced to their vehicles in the car lot and were now exiting onto the main road to head towards the hotel.

They didn't notice sitting in a side alleyway, a metallic silver Mercedes-Benz coupe facing towards the main road.

In the comfort of the plush leather seats, Nadine Spencer observed them through expensive sunshades leaving the Car Hire outlet, in the comfort of plush leather seats.

Taking a small tube of sunblock from her bag, she put a small amount on the tip of her sculpted nose, and slowly rubbed it into the pores.

She mused out loud to herself, "Well Mr Walsh, if you want to associate yourself with someone who has caused me to lose an important contact— That is your problem now as well. If you don't give me and my colleague your secrets willingly, I suppose I will have to play hard ball now instead."

Nadine gloatingly smiled to herself. "Kim Chapman, you will soon rue the day that you decided to have a curry on that rainy day in May, and saw Andy King talking to me. You thought your life had changed then, but that is nothing compared to what awaits you in the future..."

She put the expensive automatic motor car into drive and began to stealthily follow the two vehicles that had just passed her.

Nadine carefully stayed out of their rear and side mirrors and had only once lost them in a busy town. With impromptu market stalls erected at the side of the road. An elderly man pushing a cart of caged live chickens, walked in front of her car. Causing her to sharply brake and lose sight of the cars, she had been tracking.

Ignoring her shaking fist and hurling obscenities, he remained ambling at a pace set by his elderly health, only reaching the other side when he wanted to— not dictated by anyone else.

Nadine finally caught up with them, just as they were turning into the driveway of the hotel property where they were staying. She drove past at speed, allowing herself a slight glance to notice and record the name of the hotel.

***

Kim was fuming, and it wasn't long before her friends noticed her mood. They had agreed to meet at the poolside again that evening, as the advertised magician and hypnotist really took everyone's fancy. They reasoned the best seats would obviously disappear quickly near the outdoor stage. So they had all arrived a good hour before the show was due to start.

"Okay, spill the beans sister, what's with the glum face?" Nancy asked Kim the obvious question while standing with her hands on her hips.

Kim sighed loudly, "George." she simply exclaimed. "He has gone out somewhere on an investigation, and just apologised saying he wasn't taking me— before driving off into the ruddy sunset…" She sighed again, pouting slightly in annoyance.

Evandro the waiter was on duty once again. It appeared that he had taken a liking to the group and headed straight towards their table to take their drinks order. "Ola— Signora, Señoritas and Signor Chapman, have you had a good day enjoying the Spanish sun?" He asked, directing a smouldering smile towards the younger girls in particular.

Nancy blushed after imagining spending an evening being romanced by the handsome Spaniard. She shook her head briskly to clear the thoughts, "Yes thank you Evandro, did you?"

Evandro gave her an incredulous look and laughed out loud. "I spend every day in the sun; it was okay I suppose, I live here— remember?" A sea of smiles from the heavily female group agreed with the statement, while Nancy blushed an even deeper shade of red.

The waiter took their requirements and quickly returned holding a tray with glasses and the almost obligatory Sangria pitchers. He was followed by a colleague, who was also carrying a second large silver tray with the remainder of their drinks ordered.

An hour later, surrounded by poolside gas heaters to stave off the cool air, they were being entertained and astounded by the amazing first act. Known simply as 'Harry' and sporting a silver false scar on his temple. The magician swirled his cape to reveal once more another fluttering dove from out of thin air.

The act continued along the same lines to its conclusion, where things were either disappearing or appearing out of thin air at a rapid pace, to tumultuous applause.

Another hotel guest sitting at the next table leant over to speak to the group, and advised that the Magician act was always on a Sunday. He added that sometimes it was Harry, and other times a random magician flew in from elsewhere in Europe. The man explained he would normally spend the entire winter months at this hotel, to escape the cold days and nights prevalent in the United Kingdom.

Nancy turned to Kim and stated the obvious, "Still no sign of our benefactor then?"

Kim looked at the watch on her wrist, "I would have thought George would have returned from his mysterious journey by now. Still, he is a grown man and should be able to look after himself by now."

Maria heard every word that Nancy and Kim had uttered, but made no reaction apart from momentary biting her lower lip in concern. The others, meanwhile, were now laughing out loud at a rude joke that David had just told. While keeping a straight face right up until the punchline itself

— Where he gave way to an attack of giggles, whilst sputtering out the last part of the joke.

Standing up, Maria announced that she was going back to her hotel room to get a shawl, as she was feeling a little cold. Before she could leave the table, Kim stood up and added that she was also getting cold and was going to collect her poncho as well.

Following each other to their respective rooms to collect warm clothing, they began to descend the stairs to go back to the poolside theatre— when Maria held up her hand. "Are you thinking, what I am thinking?" Kim just nodded, and they began making their way to Georges holiday cottage located in the hotel grounds.

They held each other's hands, as they walked down the sparsely lit path to an area devoted to a holiday village. They finally stood outside his stark white cottage.

"There aren't any lights on inside, maybe he has fallen asleep?" offered Kim.

Maria started hammering on the door and noticed Kim staring at her questionably.

"It's okay, I'm sure he will be grateful for us waking him up. He wouldn't want to miss sharing drinks, on our first night at the hotel." She explained, while now adding an occasional kick to the bottom of the door, making enough noise to wake the dead, let alone a tired young man.

Kim peered through the bedroom window— brightly lit by a nearby light pole and her vision inside aided with the curtains undrawn. "No sign of him in bed, he must still be out somewhere else," she concluded disappointedly.

Maria looked through the window herself to concur that George was indeed absent.

They both turned silently, to return to the evening entertainment with the same thought in mind, "I hope George is okay..."

***

#14   Monday Seven AM

December 20th 2021

"Fantastic breakfast," announced David Chapman, who had only just come back from refilling his plate from various tubs at the heated counter. Stabbing his fork into an enormous six-inch-long sausage, and dipping it into the runny yolk of one of the many fried eggs on the plate.

"Any sign of George yet?" asked his wife Pamela, placing a piece of sliced pineapple onto her large spoon and savouring its tangy juiciness.

Nobody appeared to have seen him today, and Maria had already scoured the car-park and surrounding roads for any sign of his car earlier this morning.

"I know from working with him, that he can be a bit of a loose cannon when it comes to following up a lead. But, to be honest, I am getting more than a little worried that something grave may have happened to him." Admitted Kim drinking the last of her strong coffee, and placing the empty mug onto the large round table.

Kirstie stretched and performed an enormous yawn, "Sorry, I don't know about everyone else, but I came away to relax and enjoy myself." She sighed deeply while pushing her chair back, so she could stand.

"So— until we find out what the hell has happened to George,— his fans..." Kirstie paused and looked accusingly towards Kim and Maria. "Will only drag the rest of us down with their mithering and worrying.

Therefore, I reckon the only way we are going to get back into the happy zone, is to find mister bloody George Walsh. I'm really not in the mood for all this latent misery."

Everyone but Kim and Maria laughed out loud, but they both eventually had to see the funny side and each woman nodded to Kirstie with a lopsided grin.

Kirstie swung her handbag over her shoulder and began to amble in the direction of the hotel reception. "Alright then gang, let's find out where George is and whether he is okay..."

Everyone, apart from David still gorging his food pushed their chairs back, making a horrible cacophony with the scraping sound. As one, they formed a pack and followed Kirstie towards Reception.

✳✳✳

José Martinez nearly fled the counter when he saw a determined-looking horde of females heading towards the reception desk.

Señores Phillips, the English manager of the hotel. Had advised him he would experience no problems looking after the front desk. In his absence— while he visited the dentist.

Frantically looking around the room for backup. He realised with a sinking heart that all on duty hotel staff had appeared to sense his panic— and evaporated from the room.

Resigned to his potential fate. José spread his arms wide and almost bellowed the words, "Welcome, Welcome my English friends. On behalf of the Hotel Los Naranjeros. How may I help this beautiful winter morning?"

He wasn't sure whether their steely-eyed gazes were due to anger or concern.

Kim had decided as he was her employer, it was probably her responsibility to report that George was missing. "Mister George Walsh that has a room in one of the Holiday village cottages, didn't turn up at breakfast today," she explained.

José felt the weight of concern sliding off his shoulders like a block of melting fat. He chuckled to himself.

"Signorina, If I had a Euro for every guest that did not come out of their room, for breakfast early in the morning. I would probably now own this glorious hotel where you are standing." He said in a pretentious tone, combined with a condescending smile.

Kim stood her ground, "So if a guest died in their accommodation, you would just assume they were inebriated for the rest of the holiday." She glared at José.

Kim could feel anger rising, while she asked sensible expectations. "Wouldn't you send a member of staff to simply check? What if they left the premises the previous evening and had not parked the rental in the allocated hotel parking bay by the following morning?"

She paused for breath and continued in a stern voice. "George mentioned the hotel had shared responsibility for the car hire, under some obtuse Spanish law."

Once again, José felt the weight of responsibility return, combined with a cold feeling rising upwards from his nether regions.

He rustled under the counter and pulled out an almost pristine folder. On the front printed in large red letters were the words 'OFFICE PRACTICE— what to do in uncertain situations.'

Señores Philips had insisted everyone knew of its existence, as he wouldn't always be available for advice. José decided this was one of those times and flicked rapidly through the pages, trying frantically to spot anything that may be relevant.

"There." he exclaimed aloud after spotting a helpful section labelled Missing Persons. The gang looked at him, waiting expectantly for him to take some form of action.

"Okay, as it is only one night that he has been missing, I am advised not to ring the police. However, the notes in the folder do recommend that I ring around various medical institutions. To see whether there have been any reports of the missing person being admitted to their care."

Encouraged, José looked up and spotted Sofia Vasquez, the person in charge of the hotel entertainment. "Sofia," he called out to her, before she disappeared into her office.

Sofia smiled and walked over to the reception desk in response to his call. "José , I was just about to update the timetables— so you have saved me from a totally boring job, how can I help?"

José sighed in relief. "Thank you, Sofia, I have a little emergency to deal with for these customers. Could you possibly look after the clients that have since arrived, while I continue dealing with these Señoritas?" He gave Sofia a pleading smile. "That will then allow me to make necessary phone calls."

Sofia nodded her head in agreement, and José started to ring around the hospitals, to check if anyone had admitted George overnight.

Hitting the jackpot on the second call, and thanking whoever was on the other end of the phone. José excitedly turned to the girls with a wide grin across his face and proudly announced, "Señores Walsh has been found."

"Where is he, so we can go and visit him?— If he is in a hospital that is..." said Maria nervously, already in mild trepidation that he may be badly hurt.

"He is no longer in hospital and has been discharged from their care around one hour ago," explained José. "Mister Walsh appears to have been the victim of an automotive accident and had been transferred by ambulance. To check for signs of hidden medical problems— just to be on the safe side, you understand?"

Before they had the chance to interrogate José further, they heard the hiss of the automatic doors into reception and through the gap walked George.

"George," they excitedly squealed in unison and stampeded towards him.

George looked momentarily shocked, but he held his ground. He realised it was pointless trying to get a word in, between the constant barrages of questions.

He noticed Kim looking him up and down, as if she was looking for something. "What is wrong Kim, is there a problem?" George queried in a concerned voice.

"That is just what I was thinking," Kim cryptically replied.

"I am sorry, am I missing something?" He asked, now becoming rather confused.

Again Kim replied mysteriously, "I don't know George, are you?"

George began losing his temper, surprising the girls so much they became instantly silent. They waited in suspense, to see how George was going to now respond.

"For god's sake Kim, you know you are wasting your time talking to me with female logic or whatever they call it. What the hell have I done?" He asked in an exasperated voice.

Quietly contemplating George for a few more seconds, Kim then calmly replied, "Bravo, George that is the question we have all been asking ourselves. Where have you been, what happened?"

Kim pointed directly at him, "And the biggie is— Why is there just a single sticking plaster stuck on the centre of your forehead?" She couldn't completely suppress a snigger following her last question.

George lifted a hand and lightly touched the plaster as if to confirm there was one there. "Oh— that," he replied.

"Come on, let's stop blocking the walkway and sit down on the comfortable leather settees instead." He played the 'wounded soldier and pretended to limp.

He looked at the girls and explained, "I'm sorry for walking so slowly. After all— I am injured and will need to rest while I tell you my story." George chuckled, as his tongue nestled in his cheek.

They all sat down on comfortable leather settees, arranged in a half circle at the far side of the reception area.

The open side of the semicircle was next to a waterfall. Cool liquid was noisily flowing, from a metal shelf incorporated into the stone faced wall. The aquatic feature was endowed with animated lighting effects, complete with obscuring mist sitting on top of the small decorative pool below.

Evandro the waiter appeared from a side room and was now passing through the reception area. When he heard familiar voices.

He made his way over to George and the ladies. "Hot or cold," he asked simply.

Everyone agreed it was much too early for alcohol, and chose by consensus 'hot.'

Evandro had already memorised their preferences for hot beverages from the previous day, and without a word strode off towards the internal bar for coffees.

George felt slightly uncomfortable as they all stared at him, waiting for him to explain his night in the hospital.

"First, I would prefer putting your mind at rest. I am fine apart from sporting a small cut hidden under the plaster on my forehead." Again he unconsciously touched the wound.

"I had received a phone call from my friend, that procures me information from the home office. She had discovered in the records, an address that had not been completely redacted." George noticed by Maria's face, that she had not missed the word 'She' in his explanation.

Ignoring her stare he resumed his story, "I remembered from the translations that Kim and I had been working on. The name Town supplied— coincided with the same area that we were already focusing on, looking for more information regarding Kim's investigation."

Pamela Chapman piped up, "Kim's investigation?"

Realising that Kim had obviously not told her mother, all of her aspirations to find her missing sister. He chose to ignore her and carried on moving forward with his tale.

Making sure he changed the subject, before she could ask any awkward questions. He offered an explanation, "I began making my way further inland towards the place of interest, and that's when I had my accident," said George with an innocent expression on his face.

Kim's eyes flashed in recognition of him defending her by dismissing her mum. She nodded in silence, "Thank you, George."

"How did you crash your car George?" Nancy keenly asked. Noticing George appeared to be slyly trying to evade Pamela from asking any more awkward questions.

George nodded. "I was following the Satnav, down a dirt track that barely passed any definition as a road.

Unusually for Spain, the sides of the road were obscured by bushes and trees— As if the field behind had been neglected and overgrown for a long time." He replied.

George paused momentarily, as Evandro had returned. He placed his coffee in front of him, steaming a gorgeous aroma on the marble table.

"It was my own fault really, and to be fair I had got the sound system up pretty loud.

So loud in fact. That I didn't hear the almost tortured sound, of one of those weird looking three wheeled tractors. The Spanish insist on using them for some reason, instead of the family estate car.

Anyway, It had been dragging a trailer behind loaded with potatoes or something, and had just got over the brow of a hill. It was beginning to pick up speed, towards the corner I was also approaching— But, from the opposite direction.

All I saw before I hit the tractor, was a Spaniard leaping into the air. He sailed from the tractor saddle into the bushes on the side of the road.— Then I heard a bang.

I must have been unconscious for quite a while. As when I came around, I saw a police car and a paramedic's car blocking the road. My four-wheel drive looked like a right-off— As the tractor's engine was interlocking with the car's radiator block." He took a sip of his Americano.

"The policeman had taken my details, and the paramedic took me straight to the nearest hospital for an overnight stay."

175

George waved his arms dramatically, "And here I am—back with the gang." He grinned and took another gulp of the strong smelling coffee.

Kim stood and sidled over to where George was sat, nudging him over, so she could sit next to him.

"I suppose we had better get going then George?" She said.

Appreciating from his blank look, George still hadn't quite got the hang of understanding female abbreviated conversation.

Kim repeated the sentence, modified slightly to assist him. "We need to get another car, if we are going to check out this address together."

George noticed the pronounced words of we and together and rapidly realised that he wasn't going to be doing any investigating without Kim this time.

He nodded and agreed that this time they should get something bigger instead. Both laughed in amusement, as they headed back towards the car hire centre for a replacement vehicle.

✳✳✳

#15   Monday Three PM

December 20th 2021

Kim climbed up the single chromed step, unlocked the heavy door and slid into the leather clad driver's seat.

After a brief but predetermined argument, about whom was going to drive the Toyota Land Cruiser. It was evident the driver was going to be Kim.

Primarily, because the hire centre had been totally reluctant to hire George anything ever again— Even a moped, after his accident the night before.

This was regardless of George's Insurance Company having already generously reconciled the repair bill. Mysteriously before it had barely been anywhere near a garage.

George suspected Amber's intuition had already presumed, he was likely to experience an accident sooner or later. She had obviously already primed their insurance company. To add a down payment, to the only hire company in the nearby area to the hotel.

With the premise, that there would be hidden additional cover against any vehicle that George rented from them.

Kim started the mighty engine, and waited for the chill of the air conditioning, to begin cooling her legs before pulling away. George was already affixing his Garmin Satnav to his side of the front window, with the intention of taking on the unspoken role of Navigator.

"So— how far away is this village that you want us to visit, and how long will it take to get there?" Asked Kim, carefully following the road. Looking out for obstacles, like a hawk.

"Benimaurell is the village that we are heading for, and it will require fifty minutes to an hour— dependent on any traffic," advised George observing the Satnav route details.

"Plus tractors," laughed Kim— Having a playful dig at George's previous misfortune.

As predicted, the journey taken was a leisurely one hour to reach their destination. George directed Kim to pull over. Arriving at an area of scrub, masquerading as a car-park for a nearby taverna on the opposite side of the road.

Today was a market day, and the parking was a little difficult to achieve.

Combined with the haphazard placement of the busy stalls and dodging their customers wandering from booth to kiosk. They eventually managed to squeeze behind a large Luton van.

Taking advantage of the shade given, they parked the car. George and Kim wandered over to the taverna, hoping for a welcome cold drink.

They sat under the shade of an extendable canopy, sheltered from anyone's direct view by a sturdy cactus-like plant. George ordered a couple of cold Spanish beers and patiently waited. He was looking for an opportunity to question any visiting locals, about their previous neighbours.

"I love watching people," admitted Kim, "And, this is 'people watching' on steroids."

George chuckled, "I don't mind people watching myself, but we came here hoping to talk to anyone that knew Adam Bridges or Helen Taylor. The only problem is, I haven't seen anybody that remotely looks like a local sitting here in the Taverna."

"Well it's early yet, I'm sure we will find someone to ask sooner than later— Oh shit." Kim exclaimed, as a Mercedes-Benz pulled out of a side road. The driver was turning carefully into the Market car-park. "Not her, for God's sake."

George had also recognised the driver, as being the woman from the car hire centre. "Nadine Spencer, how do you know her Kim?"

"You know her as well?" Asked Kim incredulously, after initially ignoring the fact that George had asked first.

"Sorry George, I didn't know who she was until you just announced her name. Do you remember the time I told you about finding my so-called boyfriend with another woman?"

George nodded his head to indicate he did recall.

"Well that Nadine woman or whatever she is called. Sat with him bold as brass, discussing what sounded like a con that she was operating— As well as my ex', trying to fleece me out of half my cottage"

George raised his eyebrows in mild surprise, "Are you sure it was her?"

Kim's face looked like he had just accused her of a crime. "I am more than sure, that horrible night is emblazoned in my memory as one of the worst times in my life."

She now looked accusingly at George. "How the hell do you also know her and remember her name as well? Is there something you are not telling me— George Walsh?— I thought I could trust you…"

He lifted his hand and showed her the palm, "Hang on one minute Kim Chapman, what exactly are you accusing me of? I innocently met the woman in the hire centre, when I went with your dad.

She said she knew me as an author, and the only thing that happened, involved having a quick chat. Then she disappeared into the sunset at the wheel of a hire car.

That was the first and last time I have ever spoken to Nadine Spencer," he stated, noting she was now looking at him doubtfully.

Her accusations were temporarily forgotten, as a Spanish couple sat down at the table next to theirs. The Taverna owner appeared to immediately recognise them. So

George suspected they were probably locals, who regularly visited the establishment.

Winking conspiratorially towards Kim, he coughed lightly and said to the woman. "Excuse me, I hope you don't think I'm rude, but do you live locally?"

"Si, I am sorry but I do not speak the English very well," she replied in a friendly voice.

George looked at Kim and suggested she interpret his English, so that the woman would feel more comfortable chatting.

Kim introduced herself and George in Spanish and came straight out with her first question. "Thank you for talking to us, I have a bit of a vague question. Have you ever happened to have met, either Helen Taylor or Adam Bridges?

We are family from England and are trying to locate them. The last place we knew they had been living— was in this area." She looked at the woman expectantly.

"What did you say their names were again? My name is Martina Ramirez, and this is my husband Pablo.

Having lived in the village since childhood, we would expect to know just about anyone who lived here for more than a year." The woman looked at her husband with love in her eyes.

Kim repeated the two names and Martina's eyes lit up, "Ah Helen and Adam, I remember them well. What a wonderful couple they were, always willing to help anyone in need."

Kim looked thoughtful, "You used the word 'were', does that mean they are no longer here?"

Pablo raised a finger and stated simply, "They disappeared earlier this year, around March or April I think." He looked at his wife who simply nodded to affirm his statement.

Martina took over the conversation, "Both Adam and Helen were always working away. I don't know what they did for a living, but I suspect whatever it was— paid a lot of money."

Kim excitedly updated George with the gist of the conversation so far and turned back to Martina. "Why did you think they were blessed with cash?"

Pablo replied, "The house they lived in must have cost many millions of euros, and they were always having work done there. The security was amazing with high walls, razor wire fences and closed-circuit television monitoring the grounds. We supposed it was because they were very aware, even in this day and age, bandits are still in the hills of rural Spain."

"So how does anyone know, that they are not just away somewhere working?" Kim asked.

Martina looked at Pablo, "Because my husband is both the local vet and blacksmith," she explained.

After noticing Kim's apparent confusion, Martina tried to expand on her simple statement. "Pablo had a contract to look after their horses in the stables.

One day he received a panicked phone call from Maya, a local young girl who feeds, exercises and sees to all their needs.

She had initially tried to contact the missing couple, when one of the mares had fallen ill. Maya normally needed their permission, to call in Pablo to have investigated any problems. When she couldn't contact them on either of their mobiles, she rang Pablo directly for assistance regardless."

Pablo continued the story. "After attending a mare suffering from mild colic, I tried contacting them myself and left umpteen messages to ring me back.

This was totally out of character, and completely the opposite of their normal responsible behaviour. So I informed the police that they were missing— Maybe a couple of days later.

Police had swarmed onto the property and searched every nook and cranny for any clues. The buildings were numerous and large, and they were very thorough.

The rest of the village, and we tried to assist, but were discouraged by the Police— As they appeared to have found nothing at all. They had pottered on with the investigation for a couple of days, and then mysteriously abandoned the search— shrugged their shoulders and blamed it on the fact they were foreigners..." Pablo concluded.

Kim stared into space for a couple of seconds trying to comprehend what she had just been told. Then asked the obvious question, "Has anything ever been heard from them since?"

Martina shook her head side to side. "I am sorry, no-one has seen them at all, although the house is still there and standing empty— just in case..." She cast her eyes sadly towards the floor.

"Maya was struggling to feed and look after the horses. Pablo knew the wealthy people at the other local house with stable blocks, and they offered to house the horses for life if necessary. They were all finally moved last week, as a matter of fact."

"So the house is now completely empty?" Asked George winking surreptitiously towards Kim.

Martina looked at him exasperated, as if he was a little simple, "Apart from a few lizards maybe— of course it is empty apart from the furniture and fittings, I have just spent the last ten minutes explaining that."

Martina sighed and looked at her watch looking for an excuse to exit the conversation. "I am sorry, Pablo is a diabetic, he needs to get a meal inside him to make sure his sugars don't hit rock bottom."

She turned to the side and waved to the waiter for the bill. Rummaging in her handbag, she produced a piece of paper and a pen. Martina wrote quickly and folded the note before handing it to George. "Here is the address if you are interested, goodbye and have a pleasant day."

Recognising that they had just been dismissed, George thanked Pablo and his wife, and Kim followed through with the translation. Pablo simply nodded and smiled as they left.

George turned to Kim, "Are you thinking what I am thinking?" he asked.

"I am pretty sure I am," Kim smiled. "All we have to do now is get to the car, without that Spencer woman spotting us..."

"Leave that to me," offered George. As Kim stood, he took hold of her hand and began to lead her over the road towards the market.

Feeling the warmth of his hand lightly clutching hers, she felt a strange feeling spread across her face. "George..." Kim began to speak and quickly fell silent again.

George raised an eyebrow waiting for her to continue, and when nothing further came, he smiled knowingly towards her. "Come on Kim; we will need to be quick and silent to evade Nadine."

He looked again at Kim, noticing she had now gone a deep shade of red. "We can talk later," he explained softly and pulled her a little roughly behind a vehicle parked beside a stall.

George looked at Kim again and noticed this time she had now turned a pasty white colour.

Before George could even utter a single word of concern. Kim muttered, "I'm fine, George," and gave him a weak smile. "I just hadn't expected such an emotional roller coaster, when we climbed into the rental this morning."

Realising she was not just referring to Nadine Spencer's appearance, he rapidly changed the subject back to the issue at hand. "Okay, I saw her just go in between the stalls on the other side of the car park.

It would appear that she is definitely looking for something, and it is most assuredly not knick-knacks for her fireplace mantle!

When I say, go— run as fast as you can behind these vehicles along the edge, until we reach our four-wheel car."

George continued carefully observing Nadine's movements. Until she finally wandered down the side of a large Ford articulated lorry, with a butcher selling meat from within the open sided trailer.

Recognising that this was probably the opportunity they had been waiting for. He gave the signal to Kim to begin running as fast as she could, while he followed close behind.

They both reached their car at roughly the same time and ducked quickly down beside the passenger door. The vehicle's bulk hiding them, from where they had last seen Nadine, orbiting purposefully around each stall.

It was almost like something out of a comedy sketch. As first, George slowly raised his head to window height. Quickly scanning the scene beyond and rapidly dropping back down again.

Kim repeated the routine and then sat there with her back against the car door. "What now then 007?" She shook—trying to contain her nervous giggles.

George did look unamused. "Might be an idea if I got in and laid down on the back seat, and you climb into the drivers side and get ready to move."

Without waiting for her to comment, he yanked the rear door open and slid inside. Finding that he couldn't pull the door shut with his feet. He hissed towards her, "Kim push the door closed for me, and then go for it yourself..."

Kim pushed the rear door to, and slowly pulled open the driver's door wide enough, to allow herself an entrance into the vehicle.

Sitting upright and fastening her safety belt, she looked into her rear mirror and tried to spot George. "Okay, I'm ready. But you never said whether we are going to make a break for it or go softly, softly— The only problem I can see with option one, is that someone is likely to get hurt.

My driving isn't that good either— sorry." She apologised and began revving the engine as if she was a getaway driver— getting ready to 'burn rubber.'

George laughed out loud behind her, "Err— that's a negative Stirling Moss; we want to disappear quietly. The idea is, Miss Spencer doesn't even realise we have even left.

Hopefully, we will get far enough away, so she doesn't pick up our trail, before we reach Finca Nunca Aquí— Well, It's the address on this piece of paper, so that's where we are heading Amigo."

Kim sounded concerned, "Okay smart arse, how do you suggest we get out of here without us driving past that Spencer woman— fly?" She said sarcastically.

She felt her headrest being pulled slightly back, as George pulled himself over and into the passenger seat. He snapped his seat belt clip into place and turned to face Kim.

"We're going that way," George pointed towards the back of the car park, surrounded partially by a wire fence. Twenty feet beyond, the ground dropped sharply.

Kim looked at him as if he had lost the plot. So he pointed down towards the automatic gear selection stick.

George suggested they select low ratio gearing, and then engage down hill assist.

She still looked confused, "It's a four wheel drive Kim, let's use that to our advantage." He waited for her to put it into low, and the car began crawling forward— without her even touching the accelerator.

"Okay now engage the turn assist feature as well, and head towards that gap in the fence at the rear of the car park." George suggested while pointing at the appropriate control button. Kim gripped the wheel tightly and began to steer the car to where George had just suggested.

"How do you know it's not a sheer drop?" Kim nervously asked. "Because I can see the tops of trees," calmly answered George.

Kim was unconvinced and began softly whimpering as they almost reached the edge, of what she believed was probably a precipice.

She let out a sigh of relief as she realised the car had breached the top. It was now heading downwards across scrub grass at an angle of thirty degrees. Safely under control by the downhill assist feature.

George undid his safety belt, so that he could twist fully around to face the back window. When he judged the car had descended enough, that the top of the car could no longer be seen. He pointed to his left and asked Kim to redirect towards a small cottage at the bottom of the hill.

As they changed direction and neared the valley below. Kim could see a rutted track heading towards the house, and to the right the road meandered farther down the hill.

"With a bit of luck, if we follow the trail in the opposite direction to the house, we will eventually meet up with a tarmacked road— I reckon," George hopefully surmised.

After another forty minutes of bouncing along the dried clay road, they slid to a halt on loose gravel at the path's exit onto a main road.

Kim deactivated all the off-road aids, and selected 'drive' as soon as George had entered into the Satnav, their new destination.

With a squeal as the tyres found a grip on the hot tarmac, they headed towards Finca Nunca Aquí at speed. Eager to investigate what may have been Kim's relation's home, and to look for any clues as to what may have caused their mysterious disappearance.

✳✳✳

#16   Monday Five PM

December 20th 2021

"You've got to be kidding me," exclaimed Kim. Staring at a pair of grandiose polished wooden gates, that hung from a massive stone wall disappearing into the distance in both directions.

They had just pulled up in front of the property, indicated on the Satnav as being the entrance to Helen and Adam's house.

George stretched and smiled as they got out of the car and walked across to stand in front of the gates. "Blimey Kim, I have to admit that this is a whole different level of ostentatiousness, to what I imagined we would find."

Kim nodded, ignoring his use of big words. "All that trawling through the records on the internet, didn't reveal that they were rich or anything." She looked at George for confirmation. "After reading the report you received— Neither did your contact in the home office suggest anything like this..."

Shrugging, George started to push the large button on the intercom speaker beside the entrance. "Let's see if there is anyone inside. We don't want to get caught wandering around, if there are security guards looking after the property or something."

They waited a few minutes without any reply. George this time held his hand on the button and finally released it after thirty seconds. He smiled in relief and nodded to Kim. "Looks like the chickens have all flown the nest."

Kim burst out laughing, "I'm not sure that saying is correct, but I get the gist. So how do we get in there then mastermind?

If you think I am climbing over that wall— you have another thing coming George Walsh."

"Probably easier than you think," he replied, already in motion heading towards the gap in between the gates.

Pulling towards him, a plate of metal with a recess at the bottom. He was rewarded with a loud clunk, and the doors parted slightly.

Kim raised an eyebrow in mild surprise.

"The police are probably the last people in the world to lock up after themselves, once they finished looking for any clues," George answered smugly.

Putting a shoulder against a door, he pushed hard on the opening. It swung inwards, creating a gap large enough for them to gain entrance into the grounds.

They slid through, and George pushed the gates closed again.

He ratified his last action: "The car sitting outside— 'might' attract some attention, but an open door definitely will."

Kim grinned, "Smart arse, let's see if you can find any clues that the police have missed. As soon as we get inside the house."

Looking up, her face dropped. "Err is it just me, but isn't this drive supposed to lead to the building itself? Where the heck is it?"

The nearby road was lined with palm trees, with antique road lamps interspersed between them every one hundred yards. It seemed to go on forever, heading towards a nearby valley in the distance.

George shook the cobwebs from his head, thinking hopefully the house would mysteriously appear. He sighed deeply and reflected, "I knew I should have viewed the property first on Google Maps. Sorry Kim, looks like we have a little walk in front of us."

Kim looked nervously around as if someone was closely watching their every move. Satisfied that they were truly on their own, she bravely hooked an arm around George's muscular frame. "Come on then big guy, I bet there will be a cooling glass of Prosecco waiting when we eventually arrive.

George swung an arm letting his hand noisily connect with her backside. "That's if there will be any left by the time you get there..."

He began jogging backwards down the fine gravel road, "C'mon slowcoach, last one there— clears the table off from any cockroach infestations," he teased.

Kim flew forward, and mischievously tripped George as he was still jogging backwards. He fell to the floor surprised.

Finding his balance, he pulled himself back up onto his feet— With taunts of "Who is the slowcoach now?" Ringing in both ears, as Kim trotted purposely ahead. Suspiciously

192

trailing a hand behind her, with her index finger raised for his benefit.

✳✳✳

George's eyes opened wide, as they finally approached the imposing group of buildings, That somehow comprised the living quarters of Finca Nunca Aquí.

A magnificent cobbled courtyard, with an inactive fountain stood at its centre. Surrounded by numerous single story stone clad buildings. Every structure was meticulously painted a traditional dazzling white. Masking the fact that under the stucco, they were all constructed using modern methods.

George whistled softly, hardly able to believe the opulent vista he faced. "Well whoever Helen and Adam were, they 'definitely' were not short of cash."

Kim agreed wholeheartedly— already heading towards the nearest doorway, set at the top of numerous wide stone steps. "If we are going to search every building, I guess it will take at least a couple of days. Each one that we can already see, has to be the size of a small school or something?"

George had noticed something else. "Interestingly. There doesn't seem to be many windows," he shrugged nonchalantly, before pushing open the first door of many more to come.

✷✷✷

Maria was sulking. She had been contemplating telling Kim outright, that she considered him to be hers. But of course he wasn't anything more than a good friend.

Or so he had told her every time, she had blatantly asked if they could become an item. Maria had seen the sly looks he gave towards Kim— every time he thought no-one else would notice.

A shadow fell over her, eclipsing the bright sun at the end of her poolside sunbed. "Bacardi and Coke— large," announced an effeminate Spanish male voice.

She looked up to see a muscular hunk dressed in a waiter's uniform, offering a tray containing a large frosted glass filled with an alcoholic drink.

"Shame," she thought to herself. "Just my luck, he probably bats for the other side."

Maria felt a heat wave of guilt fall over her. Thinking about her homophobic thoughts, and realising that they were only born in spite.

"Why can't I find my perfect man?" She said under her breath. Something caught her eye. Maria noticed there appeared to be a male limping slightly, heading straight towards her and Nancy's position at the side of the pool.

Nancy had also noticed, and nudged Maria to get her attention. "He looks familiar," Maria said.

"Quite tasty too…" Nancy observed, pulling herself up into a sitting position— to give herself a better view of the oncoming stranger.

He approached and spoke in a deep baritone voice. "Good afternoon ladies, I hope you don't mind me interrupting your tanning session?

But I'm looking for Maria Lockyer and was sent in this direction by the lady and man over there." The stranger pointed towards Pamela and her husband David, coyly waving towards them.

Maria twisted to the edge of the bed and stood to announce she was whom he had been looking for.

Before she could say a word, he stepped forward and thrust his hand towards her in greeting.

As she took his hand, he squeezed it slightly as they softly shook hands. "Hi Maria, I am really sorry I have arrived unannounced. However, you are as beautiful as the description I was given."

Maria now suspicious, raised an eyebrow. "Have we met before, or was that just a successful chat up line you use, when introduced to an interested female?"

He looked slightly confused by her comment, then realised that he hadn't mentioned who he was.

The hunk smiled with natural white teeth, "My name is Paul Carter," he announced.

Disappointment caused the smile to momentarily fade, when he realised she did not recognise his name.

Paul carried on regardless, "I know we haven't actually physically met. But I heard everything about you every day, for a month without fail.

Maria finally twigged. "Ah George's friend, you were in the hospital at the same time I was? She surmised. Now smiling warmly back, as she realised who he is.

Nancy spoke up, pointing out the elephant in the room. "Err, why are you here in Spain then? Did you come here especially looking for Maria?"

Paul laughed, "Not exactly, although I am really glad we finally have met. Amber Prevett— George's agent is the person responsible for me flying out here, to share the remainder of the holiday with all of you."

"That's very generous of this 'Amber' woman, does she do that for all of George's acquaintances?"

Paul felt a nervous tickle in his throat and began to cough guiltily as he answered. "I don't think so— She has sent me out here to keep an eye on George, I don't think she trusts he will reliably be working on his research.

I have to report back to the UK every couple of days with an update on his progress." He swallowed deeply, after he realised he had got away with the fib. Without revealing that they were all here, via money managed by Amber Prevett on behalf of George.

He swept his arms wide. "Nice hotel," stated Paul, making small talk, and changing the subject.

Maria pulled herself to her feet and bent over to pick up her glass. "Tell you what Paul Carter, seeing as you are the new boy here relatively speaking. Why don't I put my arm under yours and give you the two peseta tour— ah the two peseta tour you ask.

But, Spain hasn't got any of those pesetas now. If there are any, they must be pretty rare to find." She paused for breath and looked into his eyes, "Rare to find just like me, so let's go enjoy a tour together around the hotel."

Paul grinned, "Smooth— real smooth." He was heard muttering to Maria, as they waltzed away together arm in arm.

Nancy left her sun chair behind as she headed towards Pamela and David, to update them with gossip about the unfolding romance. Kirstie would be agog when she got back from the hairdressers and learned the news.

***

"What the hell?" George exclaimed as they entered what appeared to be a sports hall inside the first building.

The room itself was at least three times the length of the building outside. It may have been more expansive, but from where they stood— That was all they could currently see.

The moment they entered the building, they realised more had been hidden than they could ever believe. Now standing on what was a mezzanine floor, suspended over an enormous and deeply excavated area below.

At the point where the outside building finished at the rear. The ceiling of the lower space fell fifteen feet more,

197

below the bottom of the outside wall. Becoming a subterranean extension to the massive hall.

"Doctor Who, eat your heart out— the Tardis has gained a new interior," said an impressed Kim looking around at the surroundings below. "Is that a velodrome I can see down there, I can just imagine someone whizzing around there on a push cycle..."

"Not just bikes, I can see different types of motorcycles there as well." Observed George, raising a pair of bewildered eyebrows. Out of the corner of his eye, he could see Kim standing perilously close to the landing edge.

"One problem though, how the hell do you get down there? The police must have brought ropes and rappelled down to the lower level or something," Kim said. Already walking from one end of the mezzanine to the other, to hopefully find a hidden way down.

They spent together an unfruitful ten minutes staring at the floor and walls on the mezzanine. Neither could detect a hidden lift switch or anything that would help, and finally admitted defeat.

George looked at his watch and declared it would be getting dark soon, so they would have to return better equipped. Especially if all the surrounding buildings also hid unknown obstacles.

They strolled down the long drive. Becoming quite tired by the time, they casually opened the car doors and fitted their safety belts.

George sat for a few moments, silently contemplating tomorrow's adventure. With a plan in mind, he turned to Kim and mysteriously announced. "We are going to need a bigger car…"

Ignoring George's chuckle with his attempt at humour. Kim put her foot heavily on the accelerator, and powered away towards their hotel.

#17   Monday Seven Thirteen PM

December 20th 2021

After parking, the four-wheel drive in a nearby side street. Kim and George, closely walking together. Passed through the reception doors of their hotel. Extremely parched, the tired pair were heading to the bar for a refreshing drink.

Kim laughed as George had just finished telling her of the shenanigans caused, when he was visiting a nightclub in the Midlands with his best friend Paul. "C'mon George, I can't believe you and Paul got up to those antics without being arrested. I will have to ask the poor man, when you finally invite him to meet us all."

A male voice behind her interrupted, "It's all true, and I bet he hasn't even told you what happened afterwards— either..."

Kim spun around and was momentarily shocked when she spotted the tall and smiling, handsome hunk— loosely holding Maria's hand.

"Excuse me, we haven't been introduced," she answered icily.

She found herself looking at Maria questionably, as if to say 'Who the heck is this?' Fully expecting Maria to introduce her companion.

George totally surprised Kim by stepping forward, and giving the stranger a manly hug, before thoroughly shaking his hand.

George stood back slightly and loudly greeted his friend. "Paul— What the hell are you doing here?"

Paul Carter grinned and explained about Amber arranging for him to report back. Letting her know whether George was pulling his weight or not.

Rather than being annoyed, at Amber's blatant method of keeping tabs on him. George simply raised an unconcerned eyebrow.

"Typical— I was going to ring her tonight and give her an update." He laughed, slapping Paul on the back, "Now, I'll leave that up to you instead..."

Guiding his friend away by cupping his elbow, George and Paul sloped off towards the bar for a catch up.

Leaving Kim and Maria on their own, without even a 'Goodbye— See you both later.

Maria sniffed and muttered indignantly. "I don't know what I saw in him— I thought he was a gentleman."

"Hmm— Paul seemed quite polite to me," observed Kim.

"Not him— George! I've been mooning over him ever since the first time he held my hand in Hospital," Maria admitted and sighed. "I'd mistakenly thought he might get jealous, if he saw me with Paul..." Her voice wavered as she fell silent

"We've all seen the way you look at George," said Kim kindly.

"But let's face it, Maria, you have been acting almost desperately to hook up with someone else— Especially since that disaster of a relationship with Miles Quinn."

Kim looked sympathetically at her friend, noticing moisture in the corner of her eyes. "I'm sorry Maria, but if your best friend can't tell you the truth…"

Maria wiped her eyes with the back of her hand and sniffled slightly. "I know Kim and do appreciate you caring. It's just that every time I seem to find 'Mr Right', it all falls apart…"

Kim offered an unused paper tissue, pulled out from the sleeve of her cardigan.

Harbouring guilty feelings, meant she hadn't now got the courage to confide in Maria. How the hell does she now tell her close friend— Kim Chapman was becoming deeply enamoured with George Walsh as well.

In fact, she was only just coming to terms with the situation herself. Where until earlier today, he was only a friend and colleague— nothing else. Kim tactfully changed the subject.

"You know what— considering this is an all expenses paid holiday. Maybe it's about time we checked out the poolside bar.

I'm looking forward to seeing what exotic cocktails they recommend." Kim said brightly, trying to distract her friend from continuing the day in a morose mood.

Maria pulled her mobile phone from its zipped pocket in her bum bag. She unlocked it and began composing a text.

"Who's that to then— Paul?" Teased Kim.

Maria immediately replied with a smile, "Nope— Kirstie and Nancy actually, I've just challenged them to see who can drink three alcoholic cocktails the quickest."

Her phone bleeped a few seconds later, and she opened the received text straight away.

Maria laughed out loud after reading it. "It was your Mum, and she wants to know why she wasn't invited as well."

"That means she is already drinking with the girls," realised Kim. "We had better get round there, as soon as we can. Especially If they have already got a head start. Three more cocktails could get them out of the running, before we can even have a fair race."

They quickly left reception, after dodging a queue of new guests booking in to the hotel.

***

After requesting Evandro the waiter and his colleague. To drag a heavy third square table, to join onto the end of their current two. Paul pulled two extra chairs to its side, to allow Maria and himself to join the rest of the group.

All the females appeared to be a little inebriated, to say the least. The men looked at each other with knowing looks on their faces.

George took out the ladle from an almost empty jug of Sangria and tapped the glass gently on the side. The high-pitched ringing interrupted the incessant talking of the females, and they tried focusing on the source of the noise.

203

"Ladies," began George, trying not to laugh as he looked at the unfocussed eyes trying to concentrate.

He looked around the table, "And, Gentlemen. I apologise for interrupting your festivities."

"I call it getting drunk— actually..." Muttered Kirstie to herself.

George ignored the heckle, "I will need some help tomorrow." He noticed Kim's accusing glare and changed his sentence accordingly. "Okay, Kim and I will need some help tomorrow, and would any of you like to volunteer?"

"Depends on what it is," slurred Pamela, waving a glass a little close to her husband for his comfort. "Will there be drink involved?" She giggled drunkenly, as David took from her hand the glass still waving in all directions.

George sighed, "No alcohol I am afraid. However, there will be lots of excitement and action involved."

Pamela screwed up her nose, and the rest of the girls didn't look convinced either.

George looked at the men and winked. "Well I know for certain some pretty dishy guys will be there, and you will be the only girls attending— if that helps?"

Hand after hand flew up in acceptance, without even actually knowing what they were letting themselves in for.

"Okay, we will finalise who will be doing what, where and when after breakfast. We can meet on those comfy sofas in reception, and thrash out the details then." He added cheekily, "When you are sober."

The harsh sound of scraping chairs filled the air, as the group of inebriated women attempted to make their way back to their rooms. "Don't forget to set your alarms." George called, as he watched a ragtag group of females, staggering towards the hotel lifts.

"Fat chance"— George mumbled under his breath, "Or no chance, that is the question..."

✳✳✳

George, Paul and David made their way slowly up the stairs, leading towards their rooms on the fifth and sixth floors of the hotel.

Both of the lifts sat inert on the lower floor. Each with a sign taped to their doors, announcing in Spanish that they were 'fuera de servicio.' Which, when roughly translated to English— simply meant 'Out of Order.'

They suspected the damage may be attributed to 'The Girls.'

But they had no proof it was them, as they had all gone to bed a couple of hours earlier. Just before the men had spent time relaxing, with cigars and brandy on the warm patio.

George and Paul said goodnight to David on the fifth floor and carried on up the final flight of steps to reach the next landing.

Paul pushed open the glass door, leading out into the long corridor where their rooms were located. Both immediately noticed the poor lighting, as it appeared over two-thirds of the corridor was in total darkness.

205

They forged on— feeling their way, by holding the dado rail between hotel rooms.

George turned to Paul and contemplated, "Might be related to the broken lifts— I suppose?"

Paul shrugged, "I thought they had to have emergency lighting in place, for situations like this?"

They both cringed, at the sound of broken glass under their shoes. "Looks like the lights have probably failed for other reasons," George surmised sarcastically.

"Not the normal place, where you would expect to find youths venting drunken anger is it?"

"To be honest, I think our gang are definitely the youngest in this hotel. With the majority of the guests I've seen. Appear to be spending this winter, putting air miles onto their motability scooters..." observed Paul with a wry chuckle.

George was concerned. "Well, I hope the lights are on in our rooms.

Otherwise, we might find ourselves, walking straight out onto the balcony. You could easily end up— heading straight back down six floors, a heck of a lot quicker than using the lift."

He had been carefully counting rooms, as they navigated the gloom. Fairly convinced this was his stop.

George felt for the slot, located in the modified door handle. He inserted the electronic card to unlock the door.

George was rewarded with a brief glow of a green LED, and a slight clunk as the locking pin retracted, allowing him entry.

After a few seconds, the lighting automatically illuminated the contents of his room. George gasped, "Oh my gawd, what the hell has happened here?"

Paul had been taking advantage of the illumination from George's room. He had already almost reached his own, as he heard his friend's shocked voice. He found himself quickly turning around, and making the short journey back.

Paul found George still standing at the dimly lit threshold of his room, and he did not appear to be making any attempt to enter at all.

He stood beside George and looked towards the interior of the lodgings.

Paul's jaw momentarily dropped, before jokingly commenting. "Well, unless you had previously smuggled a raging bull elephant into your room. Before we went out for a drink— I would say you have been burgled, mate!"

They both walked inside, to better assess the mayhem within.

Staring at the end of his upturned bed. George swivelled to his left and then the right, trying to see what was obviously missing.

"I will tell you what Paul, I think this looks more like someone was looking for something— rather than old-fashioned, random and chaotic robbery." George muttered, nervously chewing on his bottom lip.

Paul continued to stare, at the drawers emptied out across the floor. "Blimey George, what have you managed to get yourself into?— this time..."

George didn't reply— Paul had already said out loud, exactly what he was currently thinking.

***

#18   Tuesday Six AM

December 21st 2021

George stretched out his arm to cancel his alarm clock before it went off. He flicked his hand round trying to find the clock a couple of times, before he remembered it was unlikely to be on a bedside table— He took a deep breath and sighed, It was more likely to be lying on the floor now.

He slowly opened one eye, to immediately be confronted by a new definition of 'one heck of a mess.' Stretching from one end of the room to the other, were clothes flung astrew and fragments of wood from broken bedroom furniture peppering the marbled floor.

He carefully swung his leg out, attempting to place his bare foot into an area he had cleared late the night before.

Standing up, he pulled on a pair of jeans perched on a chair at the bottom of his bed.

The beeping of his travel alarm caught his attention, he smiled to himself for no reason and pushed the cancel button to mute its unwanted calls.

Resisting the urge to begin tidying up, as he just recalled the tail end of the moments of drama last night.

After reporting the suspected break-in, reception had

advised him that the nearest police station was unfortunately in Alicante and is not fully staffed until early morning.

The duty manager came up a few minutes later to George's room, to survey the damage for insurance purposes.

He had offered to move George temporarily to another room, until the police had looked for any clues as to what the perpetrator might be after. He concluded by insinuating they would be pretty upset if he disturbed anything crucial.

George had refused the offer of the move, after explaining he really didn't want a second visit from his unknown visitor. Waiting for the manager to leave, he simply pulled the mattress back onto the frame. Removed his boots, then fell into an undisturbed sleep.

The sun was already streaming into the room; strange shadows drew shapes from the debris, giving the room an ethereal light.

Attracted by the bright light like a moth, he carefully made his way outside onto his ample balcony.

In the corner he found two steel chairs and a white plastic round table. George selected a random chair and drew it to one side, allowing him space to push his legs underneath the table and make himself comfortable.

Humming a catchy tune that he had heard playing in the local restaurants and cafés. His eyes roved over the well watered gardens, that stood out in the arid surroundings with their fresh and healthy colours.

He soon began getting bored with the view and looked at his watch for the umpteenth time.

George was disturbed by a thumping noise coming from the door. He was about to get up and see who was there when the door creaked open of its own accord. Nerves and muscles began tightening with tension, building quickly within George's body as he warily wondered who was entering his room unannounced.

His thoughts were soon answered— as Paul poked his head through the gap of the open door. "You awake yet? Sorry - but your door lock doesn't seem to have latched. You probably didn't need your card when we arrived last night after all?" Paul called out, already halfway across the room without waiting for an answer.

"Out here on the balcony— enjoying the early morning sun— waiting for the police to get here before having to leave for a siesta," replied George, expressing mild sarcasm.

"Good job I came prepared then," laughed Paul, while handing his best friend a styrofoam beaker filled with steaming Spanish coffee from the breakfast bar downstairs.

George pulled off the plastic lid and gulped down a healthy swig. He shook his head quickly, as soon as the high concentration of caffeine hurtled down his oesophagus and imparted a hit of energy boost.

"Wow, that touched places that were still fast asleep and are now firing on all cylinders," laughed George and took another deep draught of the beverage.

"Well, I am still waiting for a word of thanks to come out of your mouth. The damn lifts are still out of action, so I had to make the journey both ways via the stairs." Teased Paul 'Tongue-in-cheek', and trying to keep a straight face.

211

George turned to Paul, "You cheeky git, by the flab on you, it was…" His acerbic comment was interrupted by a gruff cough emanating from somewhere near the door.

Two large men wearing padded vests and swinging H&K submachine guns marched into the room. George winced as he watched the leading member of the Guardia nonchalantly kick debris and furniture from his path, as he stomped towards Paul and George.

Wordlessly they stared round the room. Singling out Paul, the leading policeman then stated the obvious. "Good morning Señores, I see you appear to have suffered some damage?" He paused for no reason, then continued, "Maybe it was a burglary?"

Paul almost snorted but managed to hold it in, "Good morning officers, I believe that you need to be talking to my friend here— as it is his room."

"I'm not sure, I was told not to touch anything as it might be evidence," said George emphasising 'anything.' He was feeling disgust at their apparent disregard to property, as they had entered his room.

Oblivious to his undisguised sarcasm, the leading officer drew a tatty looking notebook and pen from a voluminous utility pocket on his vest. He consulted an open page, "George Walsh, English— Yes?"

"If that is what it said on my booking details, then yes I am English," George insisted.

The policeman finally indicated by a stare, that he had recognised George was being facetious. "I am sorry Señores Walsh for any distress you may currently be experiencing. But, to be realistic tourist areas are like— How do you say?— honey pots for any criminals working in the area." Putting the notebook away the officer continued, "However, I will be honest with you." He sat down on George's vacated chair, leant back and lifted his legs up onto the table.

"My name is Diego Wilson Abad, and my quiet colleague here is Paco Feliz."

Paco simply nodded with a wooden expression on his face.

Diego looked up at George and Paul and sucked in his top lip in concentration. "I know what you are thinking, why has Diego got a middle name of Wilson? Not exactly your typical Spanish name eh?"

George chuckled, "Well now you mention it..." Paul just smirked.

"My father was an Englishman just like you two, and he loved my Spanish mother so much that he changed his surname from Wilson to my mother's— Abad.

He did this so that my mother as the last survivor of the family name— Was able to continue the heritage she had always wanted."

Diego steepled his fingers, then pushed until the knuckles cracked. "Anyway, the reason I am telling you this. Is because my father instilled honour and righteousness into my daily way of life— As would any Englishman. I am sure you will agree.

I will tell you the truth; we have not had a single robbery here in the Hotel Los Naranjeros in Moraira since the building was opened two years ago. We are sitting in the

213

middle of nowhere, and any crook, bad or otherwise, wouldn't make the mistake of coming here— rather than the rich pickings available at the major resorts not too far away."

Paul nodded his head in agreement, I thought as much— I had read a fair bit about the area on the internet," he noticed officer Abad looking at him curiously. Paul sidestepped any further questions by adding, "For holiday research purposes of course."

Diego Abad continued looking at Paul for a little while, then turned towards George. "The question is— Should I call in the forensics department for what would probably be a pointless exercise?" He paused thoughtfully, "Or— just sign the hotel managers insurance sheet, with police authority of closure to the case, so he can make a claim?

Of course if it is the latter, I will expect you and your friend to search the room. Looking for anything that appears to be missing and asking the manager nicely to add it to his form."

Diego Abad made his decision without waiting for an answer, by leaving his card on the table and silently pointing to the open door. He left with his colleague Paco without a further word.

It only took Paul and George ten minutes to ensure that nothing had actually been stolen. Paul muttered under his breath "If it wasn't money the intruder was after, what could they have been looking for?"

His thoughts were roughly disturbed by a healthy smack on his shoulder from George. Who exclaimed he was starving, and the gentle trot down the stairs to the restaurant would be all he needed to bring it to a peak.

Paul agreed it was a 'No-brainer' as they pulled the door to, without even attempting to operate the broken electronic lock and headed straight for the stairwell.

✳✳✳

By the time George and Paul reached the restaurant, there had already been a steady flow of hotel guests streaming through its doors. George looked at his watch and exclaimed, "Good god, it's already past seven, the others will already have found us a table." As he spoke, he noticed Kim waving to them, trying to indicate where the group was already sitting. Paul and George efficiently weaved their way past sitting guests to swiftly reach her and the rest of the gang.

Kim spoke first, after visibly looking George up and down and noticing his rumpled clothing, "Clothes that comfortable eh?"

George was momentarily confused by her statement—until he realised he hadn't let anyone know about his break-in last night. "Sorry, but I am not exactly sure where half of my change of clothes are. As I had an uninvited visitor in my room yesterday, and they have rearranged my wardrobe."

Noticing that now everyone appears in a state of confusion, caused by George's cryptic reply. Paul explained the break-in and visit from police earlier this morning.

215

Kim reached up to innocently adjust George's shirt at the rear, and he responded with a smile. The simple act of affection wasn't missed by Maria, who responded by clutching Paul's hand and guiding him to sit at the vacant seat beside her. Nancy and Kirstie looked knowingly towards each other.

David interrupted everyone else's thoughts. "Well folks, if you would excuse an old married man for interrupting the obvious mood, would you mind if I left the table and headed straight to the buffet?"

Pamela added, "Once you have been married as long as we have, you will realise a man's stomach takes precedence to any thoughts of romance."

Mistakenly taking the nodding heads of the females as a signal for assent to leave the table. David and the other men pushed back their chairs with a combined squeal, and almost broke into a trot, heading towards the awaiting sustenance.

Nancy sniggered after watching the men scrabble rapidly away. "I don't know about you, but I suspect we have just witnessed a good example of the old saying— 'The way to a man's heart is through his stomach.'

The only other lesson you will need to learn though, is— You just need to be able to keep up with their stampede to the food…"

Everyone laughed, before they realised their own stomachs were also expecting nourishment. Twisting their chairs to face outwards, to indicate the empty table was already occupied, they went hunting for food and drink themselves.

✳✳✳

Sated now that breakfast had been consumed. George arranged that they all meet outside just before nine with the two cars, and to bring walking shoes with them. He explained the place they were all going to be being located slightly off the main road.

As everyone else went to their rooms to get ready, George encouraged Paul to hold back by placing a hand on his shoulder. He leaned against the nearby wall and voiced the concern that had been bubbling in his mind, since Paul arrived unannounced yesterday. "Quick question Paul, before we get on the road. Do you think Amber knows what your current job is?"

"Not as far as I know, she said she wanted me to come as your best friend. Somehow she coerced me by insisting there was no-one else she trusted that would look after you."

Paul honestly answered, "Why?"

"Amber has other talents apart from being a damn good literary agent." George fell silent in reflection.

Paul took the bait, "Okay— I know you are itching to tell me, spill the bean's Sherlock..."

George replied mysteriously, "She used to work for the same company you did."

"But I have never worked at any other companies before the business I have now. I joined the Army at the age of sixteen and spent eleven years there. So how can she have worked at the same company?"

George still leaned comfortably against the wall, "Think about it." He said simply, waiting for his clue to be understood.

Paul mulled it over, mumbling softly "Company, company— what company?" He grinned, the penny had dropped. "She was in intelligence in the Army, where was she based?"

"Salisbury," informed George

"As you know I was based at Northwood, so unless there was a need we wouldn't have met at all— What a small world eh." Paul sighed, "So what does that mean?"

"It means Amber is my source of information and inspiration, as well as my agent. She was the one who came up with the fact that MI6 was investigating missing agents and gave me the documents that I initially gave to Kim posing as a courier. I'm betting she has known all the time about your new business, giving close protection services to the stars and celebrities, courtesy of professional training in the military."

Paul whistled softly, "Okay, looks like she has played us both."

"I suppose we had better start the trudge up to our rooms to attempt to get changed and put on some decent walking boots," groaned George as they made their way back to the staircase. As they turned the corner Paul and George's mood was immediately lifted with a welcome sight. The lift

218

engineers were just removing the work barriers and ripping the out-of-order sign off the lift doors.

"Yes— no more stairs for us," enthused Paul fist pumping the air above.

George stood back a little to avoid Paul's wild action. "Well, well— well," he grinned, stepping forward and tapping Paul's stomach. "Looks like you need a little exercise anyway."

As Paul bent over to examine his physique, George lifted his hand off Paul's stomach and tweaked his nose instead. "Still falling for the same trick after twenty years..." He roared and climbed into the lift as the doors hissed open.

#19   Tuesday Nine AM

December 21st 2021

David pulled the MPV into the welcome shade of the covered arch, while steadfastly ignoring the indignant stares of both hotel concierges.

George had already parked outside the modern building. As soon as they had properly finished breakfast, he'd instantly made his way into town with Paul. They visited the local builder's yard for what they termed 'essential expedition supplies.' Carefully preparing for their investigation of buildings within the extensive grounds of Finca Nunca Aquí.

He had deliberately not told Kim what he was up to, seeing as the car was only insured in her name. She had still given him the evil eye when he had returned, although no more had been said.

Pamela and Kirstie convinced the hotel catering staff that they would be out all day, and would undoubtedly require several packed lunches. The Kitchens excelled themselves, as now crammed into the rear of the vehicle were the following donations.

An insulated freezer box filled to the brim with cans of soft drinks and reusable bottles of refreshing water. There were also two other boxes stocked with fruit, plus a few hearty sandwiches and snacks.

Maria, Kim and Nancy leant comfortably up against a granite pillar supporting the archway outside the reception doors.

"Kim, I hope you don't mind me asking this?" Said Nancy with a devilish twinkle in her eager eyes. "Is there something going on with you and George? I know you have always insisted your relationship is purely Platonic— but, come on. His eyes are always flicking in your specific direction when he hears you speak. At the same time you are practically drooling in his presence..."

Before Kim had a chance to reply, Maria's eyes flashed in latent Jealousy. "Paul and I genuinely seem to hit it off, I think we look perfect together. If everyone else will grow a relationship while basking in the sun— So am I..."

Kim pursed her lips while glancing at Nancy, raising her eyebrows in mild surprise. Nancy simply nodded in silent acknowledgement of Maria's unwarranted outburst.

The bubble of growing silence burst as they heard a car horn insistently repeating a call for attention.

They looked across to the cars and saw Pamela gently waving at them. "C'mon let's get this show on the road," she hollered to the girls.

A pile of discarded backpacks sat at their feet were hastily collected as the girls made their way to stand at ease beside David's large people carrier.

"Plenty of room inside," David graciously offered. "Pile in." He climbed nimbly from the driver's seat and chivalrously opened a side door for them to scramble in.

Nancy bumped her way across the rear seat to leave room for the others to get in beside her. Kim and Maria remained firmly standing where they were.

"George's escapade the other evening means that I have to drive the other car. The Rental Company was very insistent I was the only one to sit in the driver's seat." Kim carefully explained, declining the offer of travelling in David's car.

Maria looked panic-stricken when she realised there was no explicit mention of where Paul would sit, although she realised it was most likely with his friend George. She looked up imploringly towards Kim. "Any chance I could cadge a lift in your car Kim?" She mouthed sorry towards Nancy, who smiled knowingly in return.

Kim invariably found it almost painful— hearing the pitiful tone in her dear friend's voice. "Sure thing, not a problem." She mutually agreed, while noticing Nancy surreptitiously whispering the apparent reason for Maria's change of venue, to a puzzled David.

Bending down to the passenger side front window, she spoke to her mother and explained without revealing whose home it was, the location of where they were going. Also, adding that the journey time was roughly an hour.

David overheard the address and began tapping it into the car's Satnav display. His free hand pointed in her direction, raising a thumb to his daughter in thanks for the information.

Maria flounced off in the chosen direction of Kim's car, brightly waving to Paul leaning against the car.

They all climbed in and Maria snuggled up against Paul in the rear seat.

Kim instantly started the motor, and they slowly pulled away. She observed the nose of her parents' car pulling nearer as David flashed his lights to signify 'they were following behind.'

***

Eventually, after an hour on the sparsely occupied roads. They pulled up in a cloud of dust, outside the imposing gates of Finca Nunca Aquí.

George told the occupants of the car, to him the structure looked almost mystical. He also wouldn't be surprised if happy dwarves watching over the group occupied them— waiting patiently for them to open the gates and explore inside the grounds beyond.

Kim looked at him, mystified, for a short moment before realising he was pulling her leg. "I thought the heat was getting to you or something," she laughed.

George attempted to keep a straight face, and feigned being hurt. "What do you mean? It was deadly serious. Look there is one over there…"

As Kim twisted towards where he was pointing, George held the bridge of her nose and flicked its tip, causing her to look at him astonished by his actions.

George burst out laughing uncontrollably— while Paul leant through the gap between the front seats and explained what had just happened.

"Congratulations, you are now one of the gang— When we were young, that was the initiation ritual of acceptance." Paul could hardly hold back the laughter after observing the look on Kim's face.

Kim rubbed the tip of her nose and silently looked at each person sitting in the vehicle. Suddenly a grin peeled her lips away from her perfect teeth, and a rumble appeared to be building from somewhere within her chest.

A tumultuous guffaw exploded from between her lips, and tears streamed uncontrollably from the corners of her eyes. "You sod," she squealed and collapsed in a fit of giggles against George's shoulder.

Maria offered Kim a paper hanky from her bum bag to clear her eyes and wiped tears of laughter from her own.

Finally, the laughter abated, and they climbed out of the air-conditioned car. A shroud of sweat instantly formed, as they felt the heat of early morning enveloping them.

George and Paul opened the boot of the car and extracted two enormous fisherman's barrows. Under the curious gaze of the surrounding group, they assembled the frames and installed onto each a pair of wide wheelbarrow wheels.

George, feeling the combined stare at his back, turned towards the group and raised his eyebrows awaiting the inevitable question.

"Err— what are those?" asked a puzzled Nancy.

"Okay, before I show you— did anyone organise some donkeys?" He responded with a smirk on his face.

Paul imagined at this moment— A bunch of dummies would have expressions more animated than his friends. Almost catatonic stares spear-headed towards his friend. "Here we go," he smiled to himself— having previously witnessed his best friend's method of dryly teasing others.

"No..." questioned Pamela in a querulous voice.

George wordlessly pointed towards the ever growing pile of things— They would need to transport for their adventure behind the closed gates.

Simultaneously, frozen faces melted back to reflect animated human beings, as the reason became obvious for the barrows.

Pulling out a pile of wide adjustable straps from the depths of the vehicle. George began securing a multitude of boxes onto the steel frames of the wheeled transport.

Eventually, they loaded up what appeared to be far too much for anyone to carry. With a deep breath and a heave upwards on the barrow handles, George and Paul started pushing the barrows the short distance over to the gate.

George placed his trolley back down onto its stubby legs and pulled the latch to open the door. "Okay everyone— Inside," he hissed.

Kim stood her ground. "Two questions Mister Walsh. One, why aren't we driving up to the house? Two, why the hell are you whispering?"

"Sorry, number two is from habit. Normally when I am, err accessing a property that I don't have permission for. It makes sense for me to be quiet." George explained with a disarming smile, already pushing on the heavy gate for them to gain access.

Kim took just a half-step forward and cocked her head at an angle. "Okay number two is understandable, but surely number one will not be a problem?"

George gave an exaggerated sigh. "Oh dear, and they say men have bad memories. Remember Mr and Mrs Ramirez at the Taverna near the market? They said that the security was amazing on the property, and were not wrong."

He pushed the barrow through the gated portal and doubled back minus the barrow to push shut the door.

"Believe it or not we were lucky, when we left the car behind on our previous visit." He walked a few yards forward and pointed to the tarmacked drive.

"See those lines going across the drive? Most people think they are just separate sections of the tarmac as it's laid. Everyone come and look at this." George walked to the edge of one line and knelt down.

He scraped sandy soil away with a bare hand, revealing a wire embedded in the joint and then heading farther underground.

George explained its purpose. "Believe it or not, these embedded cables are a familiar feature back home in England."

David piped up, "Are they the sensors they talk about, detecting traffic motion? I think I read somewhere they

226

operate by detecting the metal of a vehicle, then triggering something else to say a car or lorry has just gone over it?"

George gave David a small handclap. "Bravo David— Spot on. In this case they will trigger something a lot more daunting. Paul and I will push the tubular metal barrows round each of these sensors. Don't worry. Humans will not set anything off— so stay on the tarmac if you want."

Paul caught up in a few moments, striding quickly forward with his heavy load. After a few moments of reflection absorbing George's explanation, the group followed carefully in each other's steps.

✳✳✳

"Thank you for that and make sure you keep that drone overhead until I say otherwise..." Without waiting for further response, Major Nadine Spencer dropped the compact Satphone into its charger.

She reached down beside her and picked up her ruggedised mobile phone off the plush leather seat of her Mercedes rental. Stabbing the touch sensitive screen, she activated a Military grade application. Nadine was immediately rewarded by an overhead view of the expansive grounds of Finca Nunca Aquí.

The drone was held in a silenced orbit of the property, allowing her to observe the whole area in unsurpassed detail.

She spotted the group and smiled at the sight of them

comically approaching the complex, pushing loaded wheelbarrows.

A mask of concern then spread over her face. "Good luck guys, I hope one of you has the answer to obtain access to the fortress. My expert team has been unable to crack the code and bar a small nuclear device— no-one is going to gain entrance anytime soon."

Nadine continued observing the unfolding adventure and unconsciously crossed her fingers on their behalf.

✳✳✳

Kim heard the hiss of a can of lemonade being opened. "Hang on, we have only just arrived, and we are stopping for refreshments?"

"Speak for yourself, me and Paul have been hauling this lot, if you have even noticed…" observed George throwing Paul another can to quench his thirst as well.

Kim was trying hard to think of a suitable acerbic response, when Nancy asked an obvious question. "Why are we here?"

George slyly looked at Kim and winked. "I'm sorry everyone, Kim and myself have been so wrapped up in our dreams, we have forgotten to tell anyone what stage we are at."

"Oh come on George, just because we are female and not a genius author like you. Doesn't mean we can't spot 'BS' beginning to be fed to us." Spluttered Kirstie exasperated. "We know the reason Kim is here; it was to look for Karen Taylor."

Pamela lowered her eyes as if holding back to say something else. It wasn't missed by Kim who reached forward and held her hand. "Mum?" she asked.

Her mother fluttered her eyelids nervously before answering. "I know where we are; I've visited with Mum a couple of times."

A pin dropping at that point would have sounded like a peal of thunder to the friends.

David held up his hand, "Me too— at least once a year..."

Kim didn't have a clue what to say— she was speechless.

George broke the pregnant silence. "Anyone else had anything they would like to get off their chest?" He sighed deeply, "Well I have to be honest— I was not expecting that."

"Tell you what, Pam and I will reveal it all when we stop for some lunch. In the meantime what was the plan?" Offered David. Kim shook her head trying to help her think more clearly. "What the hell is going on?" she thought, "Mum, Dad and Nan had all been here before when? How?"

Looking at her mum and dad calmly waiting for George to reveal his plan, as if they were used to following orders, was freaking her out slightly.

George gathered everyone into a circle. "Okay everyone, the plan today is quite simple. Investigate in all the buildings clustered round us, looking for clues to help us find out what happened to Adam and Helen."

"What should we be looking for and where will we be hunting?" Nancy asked.

"Well the first thing we will need to do is split up into groups. Maybe Pamela or David each lead a group, and me and Paul another two as well. Before we started searching for anything that would help, and I admit I have no idea what that would be. I noticed on our last visit there don't appear to be any living quarters?" George looked anxiously towards Pamela and David for a possible lead.

David appreciated the gesture of encouragement and replied. "Sorry to be a disappointment, but we only ever used the Barracks. The Fortress, as it was known, was just a myth as far as we were concerned. Although we knew that was where Helen and Adam disappeared every evening."

Pamela piped up, "Your nan knew how to get in there, but it was above our clearance rating."

"And pay grade," David chipped in with a smile on his face.

Kim's head was spinning with multiple questions bursting to be given a chance to be let out. Before she could say anything, a coil of rope and some denim bags were thrust into her hands.

Paul looked round the group satisfied the contents of his barrow had been distributed fairly. George passed round the final items and held up his hand for attention. "Okay everyone, I think we should split up into a few groups as previously suggested." He waited for the announcement to sink in as Nancy listened to Maria moaning about a sore cuticle. They noticed that he had gone quiet, and both looked up, nodding their readiness.

"Maria with Paul.

Pamela and Nancy.

Kim with me.

Finally, Kirstie with David. I would have thought that would be a reasonable mix of experiences. Is everyone happy with that?" concluded George, showered with a sea of shrugs.

Paul took the conversation forward. "After previously conferring with George earlier. We thought it would be a good idea to check out the outer buildings first, and steadily make your way to congregate outside the large building over there." He pointed to the Multigym building located close by.

Each person joined up with their assigned partner and began to fan out round the complex.

✳✳✳

Kirstie nearly jumped out of her skin as a muffled voice suddenly shouted out something from inside her rucksack.

David turned and laughed at the haunted expression on her face. "Looks like George has sensibly managed to rustle up some walkie-talkies from somewhere."

She pulled the strap off her shoulder and swung the zipped opening towards her, so she could examine its contents. With a quick pull on the zip, she plunged her hand inside and pulled out a cigarette box-sized walkie-talkie.

231

David leant over and took it from her hand. "Hi, this is David and Kirstie, please repeat your message— over."

A male voice quickly answered. "David and Kirstie, this is George and Kim. Just checking everyone's radios are working. Sorry— I forgot to tell you they were in the rucksacks. — over and out."

"Well that was short and sweet…" said Kirstie wrinkling her nose. She gave David the radio, and he clipped it firmly onto his leather belt.

A few short seconds later they were standing in front of a padlocked steel door. David pulled the brass padlock towards him and examined it briefly, before letting it swing back against the door with a solid clunk.

"Looks new, I'm guessing the police had cut off the old and replaced it with fresh." He rubbed a finger against the door, "Yep, I can feel and indent where they had used a grind wheel instead of the usual chain cutter."

"Can you remember what was in here? Whenever it was, you last visited." Kirstie became quite excited with the prospect of entering their first building to explore.

David shook his head. "Nope, I can't remember exactly, Might this have been a store of some sort?"

Kirstie noticed he had slipped something slim into the keyhole of the lock, and was rotating and twisting the tool at different angles. With a purse of his lips and a final flicking movement, the padlock obediently snapped open.

Kirstie couldn't help herself showing her appreciation of David's hidden skill and applauded him with a little clap.

"Bravo— David. I always thought when they did that in

films; it was just a sleight of hand. Making it look easy by using a padlock that had previously been undone— or something."

David Chapman softly chuckled, "I am out of practice. That took far too long for my liking— Still I can't moan. After all,— at least it can now be opened..." He slipped the lock from the sturdy clasp and pulled the heavy door towards him.

They slipped inside a darkened room. He felt around on the wall to his right, the small effort rewarded as a number of fluorescent tubes flickered noisily to life.

Kirstie gasped at the sight of pure white Hazmat suits hanging in a long line. Suspended from a rail that disappeared behind a wall of concrete blocks at the rear of the room. The other side of the space was filled with numerous yellow fifty gallon drums painted with the word Disinfectant in stark white. The remaining space was filled with stacked steel cages, with small scuba air tanks stacked inside.

"Looks like they were ready for something bad to happen. I just remembered, this room was previously filled with steel-toe capped boots and camouflage outfits. Wonder where that overhead rail ends up behind that wall?" Queried David, already picking his way through various other boxes strewn across the floor.

Kirstie followed close behind, managing to avoid the random boxes David was kicking out of his way. He appeared to be totally unconcerned about whether their contents were possibly volatile or not. "Can you see anything?" she called, as David casually stepped out of sight behind the room divider.

"Only a door," he called back. Kirstie excitedly scrambled round the corner, eager to see what David had found. "Oh— It's just a door," she said in a disappointed voice.

David laughed, "I did say..." He reached forward and touched its surface, "Not just any old door, though. We were told that the fortress had multiple access points. This one appears to only open from the other side. I suspect it is probably going to be a couple of feet thick of solid steel."

Although Impressed with David's description of the door, Kirstie's ear had picked up on only one word. "Fortress?" she asked, stretching the syllables to make the word sound longer than it was.

"Yeah— fortress," David replied with a deadpan face. He slipped past her and headed back outdoors.

Disappointed that the subject had simply been dismissed, she followed behind him heading to the next nearby building.

✱✱✱

Pamela heard the squawk of the walkie-talkie clipped to her belt, quickly followed by the sound of Paul's voice moaning. "I am starving and thirsty. Can somebody put the kettle on?"

Another squawk and Kim's voice replied, "What did your last slave die of? Besides the hot water is in the large flasks outside the Multigym..."

234

The third voice of David chipped in beginning to giggle slightly. "I rather fancy a meat pastie, was there any in there— did anyone notice?"

Pamela couldn't help responding and found herself squeezing a transmit button as well. "Well I happen to know there are only seven bananas in there, so someone is going to be sorry."

George's deep baritone voice sharply interrupted any further banter. "Okay— this sounds like a good time to have a break. Everyone, please leave what you are doing wherever you are, and make your way back to the meeting point for a snack."

Nancy looked at Pamela and saw her smile. Pamela clapped her hand on Nancy's back, signalling for them to make a move, and after shutting the door of the building they were currently investigating. They both began walking back to meet the others, for a nice strong cup of tea.

✳✳✳

Sat in the shade under an enormous palm tree in the courtyard. The conversation was subdued as the gang wolfed down sandwiches and cold drinks out of cans. A peal of laughter from all filled the air, as Paul poured a plastic bottle of glacial water over George's head.

Further laughter rang out as George responded by poking out his tongue and pretending to lap at the water as it ran down his face. They discussed with each other what they had found, as far as the girls were concerned it was all pretty boring stuff.

Eventually, the mood turned to one of seriousness. George stood and raised his hand, and everyone waited for him to speak. "Okay, first question, did anyone find anything that looked like it had been inhabited?"

"Only the Barracks— But David and I could have told you that beforehand." Said Pamela, wiping away a bead of sweat from her forehead. "As we said before— the Fortress was where my sister had lived."

"Look— as Pamela and I seem to be the elephant in the room. I admit we were involved in working for her majesty's government for the best part of our life. As were Pamela's mother Angela, and her sister Helen and the nicest chap in the world Adam Bridges.

I am pretty sure I am still unable to speak about the fortress. But I suspect we will have to breach its ramparts to be able to find out more about what has happened to Helen and Adam."

David spoke with a firm voice, possessing the rare quality of clear delivery that demanded you listen. Totally surprising Kim, who had only ever known her dad as a mild-mannered man. His confident demeanour appeared totally out of character. Until she realised, she had just witnessed David as he really was. George shook his head, trying to clear his thoughts, "Amber kept that little gem to herself. I think there will be words sooner rather than later."

Paul broke the growing silence. "Now you have got us all back here outside this structure." He jerked his thumb towards the innocent looking building behind them. "What is your plan?"

"Okay, the only place we haven't explored yet as far as you have told me is the subterranean gym." He walked over to the pile of equipment and selected a couple of long nylon climbing ropes. "Paul, David follow me, and we can explore the building below ground."

"What about us?" Kim said indignantly, "Only big brave men for this job then?"

George recognised the look on her face; he was in trouble. "Sorry Kim, I know we invited all you girls as well. But this will be a bit too physical for you, we think."

"You think!" said Paul, "Keep me out of this Walsh. Women can make up their own minds. Just let them come into the gym to see how we are going to have to abseil to the lower section. Then ask them again..."

The three men tied their ropes to a set of bike parking frames, located just outside the gym, and began lowering themselves noisily to the section below.

Maria called out cheekily, "Does the grunting help you grip the ropes then?" Kim and Nancy began to snigger uncontrollably.

Ignoring the heckling from above, the men disappeared into a side annexe filled with weights and hi-tech exercise equipment.

"Right— follow me," said Pamela, a large grin spreading from ear to ear. She trotted at a fair pace, and the younger girls had a job to keep up as she sped round the perimeter to

237

end up standing at the rear of the building. Others arrived panting a few seconds behind her..

Pamela began feeling along the surface of the wall muttering, "I know it has been a while, but I am sure it was somewhere around here?" She kicked off the wheel locks of the nearest giant dumpster and heaved it away from its home beside the rear wall. "Bingo," She exclaimed loudly, standing back to admire her handiwork.

The girls looked first at the wall, then Pamela and finally back to the wall again. Pamela laughed at their expressions shouting a loud "What?"

"Our chance to show the guy's we girls can use our heads with results much better than muscle— watch." She chuckled and walked straight towards the wall.

Expecting Pamela to bounce painfully off the wall, the girls automatically leant forward ready to catch her as she fell. Their jaws dropped in synchronisation— as The floor dropped away and a number of steps appeared to disappear downward where a section of wall had now apparently evaporated.

Without breaking step Pamela vanished from sight.

With just a brief look at each other to reassure themselves that they had all witnessed the same thing. In a strict line they followed Pamela down the newly revealed stairs.

December 21st 2021

"Hey, you two we are supposed to be searching for clues, not playing with the toys..." George sighed impatiently.

Now completely exasperated as he thoughtfully watched the other two men race each other on the high-tech motorbike racing simulators.

Paul and David were sitting on the seats of two powerful bikes, attached to a complex series of pneumatic pistons.

The pair were purely focussed, while reacting instantly to shifting terrain on an illuminated screen in front of themselves.

The sensors and pistons on the simulator provided the feel and punishment of the imaginary landscape as if it were authentic.

George finally hit the large red emergency button at the corner of the simulator booth. The screen instantly went blank and all movement of the bikes froze.

The pair of riders looked around slightly dazed, not thoroughly comprehending what had just happened. At that moment they saw George— sitting across a wooden lectern with his legs hanging over the front, looking totally cheesed off in their direction.

"Sorry George," apologised David.

"Me too," confessed Paul "You've got to admit they are so cool though, it makes anything in an arcade feel like total rubbish."

The grin on his face was infectious, and George couldn't help but reluctantly agree.

"I must admit, when the British Government makes their mind up— it's always the best stuff money can buy," said David unintentionally inducing a sombre mood back to the room at the mention of the government. "I could murder a coffee, anyone else?" he asked Paul and George.

"Got a magic wand then David? The flasks are still topside..." observed Paul.

David smiled sneakily, "I might know where we could find some— I was here before— Remember. Helen revealed to me how to get into the instructor's canteen, when they left us alone and went up top for a smoke."

"Lead on Macduff, mine's a large cappuccino thanks," chuckled Paul. He followed closely behind David, and George brought up the rear, as they entered a corridor signposted 'showers.'

Half-way down the corridor, they stood beside an anonymous reinforced door. It's only difference from any other door was the electronic key code unit mounted to its right.

"Don't tell me you know the secret code David. I don't think I could remember random numbers after all these years — especially at your age..." George chuckled.

"Less of the 'old'— young man, I am still fitter than you will ever be," grinned David while entering a long numeric code into the keypad. His action was rewarded by a simple beep and a loud click as the door unlocked.

David pushed it open and a sensor aided light blazed out, followed by the clunking noise of multiple fluorescent lights bursting into life.

He strode across the windowless room, towards a large Italian made coffee machine. That would feature as the preferred tool for any self-respecting Barista.

Expertly he poured coffee beans into an open glass hopper on the top and activated the grinder. "You might as well sit down, this isn't a fast process if you do it properly."

Tall cushioned rotating stools, lined up along a long tall worktop. Paul and George lifted themselves up to sit comfortably while they waited.

"Spill, how did you remember that code then David, it looked pretty long. It must have been at least six or seven digits," George looked at David with new-found respect.

"Eight actually— 28111962." offered David.

"Umm, must be a number that means something to you spy types if you remembered it that easy," said Paul inhaling the fresh smell of steamed coffee.

"Last day of the Cuban crisis actually, more than enough incentive to remember something if you ask me." The three sat in a reflective mood before they were interrupted by David asking George a simple question. "What are your intentions towards my Daughter?"

Again grew an atmosphere of silence— interrupted only by George gulping deeply. All he could manage was a short "Erm."

"I didn't think you were the shy sort George; I'm still waiting by the way." David teased.

George tried vainly to escape, by partially repeating the original question, "Intentions?"

Paul silently sat enjoying the sight of his friend squirming on the spot.

George decided there was going to be no way out of this unless he confessed his inner feelings. "Well she is funny and makes great coffee."

David simply stared, while offering a cupped hand to signify he wanted more than that.

Paul laughed and placed his hand on George's shoulder, "And?" He teased, "What was it you were telling me the other night?"

George's eyes opened wide, he had always been a gentleman when in Kim's company. "What are you talking about?" He could feel his face beginning to burn in unwarranted embarrassment.

David's eyebrows demonstrated his concern and began to furrow into an upside down 'V.'

"You know, you were telling me how good-looking she was and couldn't understand why she wasn't already married. Then you told me, if I remember correctly, that if you ever managed to pluck up the courage. You just might ask her yourself..."

George felt he couldn't be any more embarrassed, and was about to tell Paul to shut up. When, he was interrupted by a curious voice from behind.

"What might you ask and to whom?" Asked Kim who seemed keenly interested. She stood in front of him awaiting an answer, while impatiently tapping her right toe against the tiled floor.

Pamela and the other girls walked into the room from behind a second door. "Thought I would find you here. Especially after I caught the whiff of brewing coffee." She asked, then noticed Kim staring intensely at George. "Err - did I miss something?"

David caught her eye and hissed, "Not yet, and you should have a grandstand view— if I know our daughter."

Pamela scrunched up her nose in confusion, just before Kim made her next move.

"Well, I'm still waiting for an answer George Walsh. I am not going anywhere so you might just as well spit it out." Kim said in a determined voice. She turned quickly towards her friends, making sure that George couldn't see the smirk appearing on her face.

Forcing a blank look to hide her amusement, Kim turned back towards George ready to continue teasing him. At first glance she thought he had disappeared, until she noticed he was now kneeling on one knee.

Everyone else but George took a sharp intake of breath.

Kim giggled in uncertainty, "What are you doing George?"

George looked upwards towards her blue eyes, "What I should have done before today Kim."

Paul's jaw dropped— He had only been teasing his best friend. He had been about to apologise to everyone for his wicked sense of humour when George's face had adopted a serious look.

George looked first at David and said simply, "Would you mind?"

David acknowledged him with a small nod of his head.

Turning back to look at Kim, he could see her visibly shaking in anticipation of what he was about to say. He smiled warmly and reached up to take her hand to reassure her. "Kim— I know we haven't known each other for very long. But for me it feels like a lifetime, and I can feel your presence in a room even if I cannot see you." He coughed as he felt the warm flush returning to his face.

Kim smiled in appreciation of his words.

Paul called out, "For god's sake George. Spit it out— my coffee's getting cold."

Everyone laughed as the tension in the air dropped a few degrees.

Five pairs of eyes returned to the couple in the centre of the room as George adjusted his leg, now twitching a little with the cramp.

Kim reached forward and placed her hands on either side of George's cheek and smiled. "Before you burst a blood vessel, the answer is yes…"

George continued holding her hands against his face as he stood up.

He looked visibly shocked and deliriously happy at the same time. "I'm sorry I hadn't meant to ask you so soon."

Kim looked at him in mock horror.

"No— I didn't mean it to sound like that. I sort of had a nudge in this direction. I confess I wanted it to be a little more romantic, if you know what I mean." George apologised.

George felt Paul push something into the palm of his hand. He looked at the item and smirked.

Kim was already in full flow with her family and friends when George nudged her with his elbow. "Hey Gorgeous lady, just one more thing."

Kim twisted sharply towards George and grinned expectantly. "What would that be then George?" She asked coyly.

"Never let it be said that George Walsh doesn't complete the task." He said solemnly and proceeded to slip onto her finger; a loose pull ring from a coke can that Paul had drunk earlier.

Paul stepped over to speak in a low whisper into his friend's ear. "Congratulations mate, just one thing. Those few words, might jump up and bite you in the bum."

George cocked his head waiting for an explanation to the curious statement.

"Well, put it this way. If Kim ever repeats the bit about you finishing a task in front of Miss Amber Prevett, I will be attending a funeral instead of a wedding."

George looked thoughtful for a number of seconds before replying. "Excuse me - did I say you were invited to our wedding?" he said seriously.

Paul looked shocked. "I'm sorry— I just assumed..." he stuttered slightly in uncertainty.

His best friend looked at him sternly before replying. "I don't believe it is customary to have to invite the best man and his guest to your wedding?"

Paul looked at his best mate, unsure how he should answer the strange question— then he twigged on to George's meaning.

"You swine— you had me going for a minute. I accept on one condition, can I bring a lovely lady with me?" Paul asked. He looked across to Maria whose ears had detected his comment in between everyone else's chatter.

She turned towards him and looked questionably at his face.

Paul smiled and mouthed one word — "You."

David brought the festivities to an end. "Sorry to be a pain, but as I recall we came here looking for clues and stuff.

To discover what has happened to my wife's sister and her husband." He swigged the last of the coffee from the bottom of his cup. "I suppose we had better examine this room thoroughly, before moving on?"

Five simple nods verified everyone else's agreement with David's suggestion.

With a buzz of excitement, they began exploring the nooks and crannies hoping to discover any elusive clues.

Soon after, Kim saw her mum and dad furtively whispering to each other while occasionally looking over in her direction. Every time they noticed her staring back, they abruptly turned away and resumed their animated conversation.

Kim wasn't certain whether she should just come straight out and ask them if she represented or had a problem— when they moved silently to her side.

David held up a solitary finger and said in a solemn voice, "We need to talk Kim, follow us into the toilets and don't say a word to anyone else— Even George."

Kim's eyes opened wide, slightly panicked inside wondering what the hell they had to say that no-one else should hear.

They shuffled into the limited room and stood adjacent to the sinks and mirrors opposite the door. Making sure they could become silent if anyone else innocently walked in.

Kim felt tears forming in the corner of one eye. One minute she was so thrilled after George' proposal, now she was nervously about to cry in anticipation of what they were about to say. She hated emotional roller-coasters.

David spoke first, "Kim we have been trying to tell you something since your eighteenth birthday. It wasn't that we were spies, as there was never going to be a need to reveal that." He could see that his daughter was under intense stress, and he felt awful with what they were about to admit.

Observing that her husband was unlikely to continue anytime soon, Pamela took the lead. She took both of Kim's hands wrapping them with her own. "Kim sweetheart, we never thought this obsession of yours looking for my sister would ever crop up. We have no idea how you came to be in possession of that personal material of theirs. To be honest, it makes everyone's life change…"

Kim waited impatiently for her mother to continue, her fingers tapped a beat relentlessly against the porcelain basin.

"Anyway," Pamela sighed. "You did manage to track down the Fortress with the help of your Ermm fiancé, and here we are today."

"Okay, what has that to do with what you want to tell me? You obviously already knew where they were living, so is that the big secret? Duh old news Mum..." Kim said, feeling frustrated that she had got worked up over this damp squib of news.

Pamela looked at David hoping for some support.

David obliged. "Well the long and short of it Kim— They are your real parents!"

Kim's jaw dropped, "You can't be serious" she stuttered. You are my mum and dad, not somebody else— please tell me what you have just said isn't true." She began to sob uncontrollably.

The toilet door burst open and George gallantly marched in, putting his arm protectively round Kim's shoulders trying to console her while staring accusingly at her parents. "What the hell is going on? Why is my fiancée so upset? Five minutes ago she seemed to be on cloud nine, until you two furtively dragged her in here for some reason or other."

David pushed out his chest aggressively, I may be thirty years your senior, but I am warning you now I am an eighth dan martial arts specialist. So don't try anything stupid. Even if you think you have a chance— think again."

Pamela nodded to George to confirm that David's threat was valid.

"George stood down and apologised. "I'm sorry— but I take Kim's welfare seriously," he held up his hand in restitution and uttered another sorry.

David simply nodded, "I should think so, I am glad you have met Kim, I know you are the right person for her. I am sorry as well, George." He held out a hand for a handshake.

George took David's hand and shook it hard. "Okay, is anyone going to tell me what has got Kim so upset, after all, I am about to become family." He smirked cheekily, while awaiting an answer.

"I am afraid we have just revealed the fact that we are her adopted parents while Helen and Adam are her real Mum and Dad." said David, bringing George up to speed.

"Kim", said Pamela sombrely, "I'm sorry but there was something else we needed to tell you as well. I also have to let you know that Mike is not your twin brother. I was coincidentally pregnant at the same time as Helen was and was working away when he was born.

By the time we got back home your Gran had managed to spirit you away from Spain and everyone thought I had twins. Your current birth certificate had been specially made by a government department, for a future life with us as a family..."

Kim seemed to have accepted the situation as it had now been revealed to her. But Kim being Kim still had questions to ask. "Can I point out the elephant in the room please? Why did Helen and Adam give me to you? Wasn't she a good parent or something?"

"Far from it," soothed Pamela. "Helen was a wonderful mother, and Adam, is one of the best dads around. But the job had caused an issue where your safety had reached an untenable situation."

"What do you mean exactly?" asked Kim pointedly, already forgetting the shock to her system only moments ago.

"Helen, Adam and your Nan, were working on a mission in deepest Bulgaria. They had managed to organise a meeting with a member of the local branch of mafia, who had deep contact within the Russian branch sometimes called Bratva.

Cutting the story close, they had to flee for their lives when it had all gone badly wrong. Long-term threats were fired in their direction, and it had them so worried, they decided to evacuate you permanently into our care."

"That means that Gran knew all the time that you were not my biological parents. I thought we were so close..." Said Kim, disappointed that things weren't always as they appeared.

"Your Gran loved you very much, and that was the main reason she had never made you aware of your hidden past. There was no-way she would expose your real background with the Mafia threats still valid." said Pamela making sure that Kim's childhood memories weren't deflated.

A terrible thought was beginning to form in Kim's mind as a realisation of something awful happening. "Nan was visiting Spain when she died, does that mean she was killed by the Mafia?" She said quietly.

Pamela and David remained mute for a moment, and the tension was released as David gave a simple nod before answering. "She was Kim, and that was the reason that Helen and Adam decided that the only sad thing they could now do, was to isolate themselves in the impregnable fortress.

They had intended to introduce themselves on your twenty-first birthday, but there was no-way that could happen after your Gran's murder."

"Oh my god, I had no idea..." Kim burst once more into tears.

George looked at her with a serious look on her face, "Oh my god as well Kim, if I had only known I was in danger of drowning at short notice, I may have had second thoughts..."

She looked at him with shock apparent on her face, in reaction to his strange and out of character comment. Then she noticed his shoulders moving up and down slightly with suppressed laughter.

"George Walsh you are simply— Wicked." She punched him on the arm— Hard.

Rubbing his sore arm, he grinned, "You are always so easy to wind up. See— Even you are smiling now. Things aren't always as bad as they seem." He concluded his piece of smug wisdom with a chuckle. "You know what— we have another problem to sort out now."

They looked at him with interest.

"I think we should draw lots on who will leave first, because I would lay on odds that if we all left at the same time we would become the subject of perverse gossip for years to come..."

✳✳✳

December 21st 2021

"David— Over here. I think I may have discovered something?" Paul yelled excitedly, standing next to a long wooden work surface.

David ambled over to his side and the others followed to promptly see what Paul had found.

Standing back slightly, Paul pointed to a large cork notice board on the wall. He lucidly tried explaining the content that looks like some sort of contest. "According to this, people can post on here. It looks like the challenge is to see if anyone has managed to generate an unbreakable code, according to the slip of paper pinned near to the edge." He gently unpinned the piece of paper for the others to examine.

Nancy examined the note and began scanning the contact on the notice board. "Pretty boring stuff for the likes of you and me I suppose. All I can observe is a blur of numbers, letters and shapes. There are so many entries, and what use would they be to us anyway?"

Kim smiled, "I think I can spot why Paul is so animated. Anyone else?" She stepped backward to make some room and managed to step on George's foot.

He had slipped behind her and was about to place his hands on her hips. George shifted and jerked his foot from beneath her heel as a spontaneous reaction. This unbalanced her footing and Kim twisted towards him, instantly falling into his arms.

Still supporting her against his chest, he examined her eyes while asking if she was okay. Feeling herself beginning to feel flushed again, she merely nodded her head and set her arms round his neck.

"Ahem— Get a room you two," teased Kirstie.

"Not while I am around, they won't— May I remind you that it is my baby girl you are talking about..." Said David, observing his wife chuckling at his paternal concern.

"C'mon, spit it out Kim, what have you and Paul spotted that us mere mortals are unable to see?" asked Maria, while edging closer to Paul and the notice board.

George saw the reason straight away. "I might have guessed you would spot that Kim." He reached forward and pulled at a piece of paper, pinned at the bottom right of the board. Glancing quickly at it to confirm his suspicions, he laid it on the work surface for the others to see.

"Jesus wept," gushed Maria in surprise Able to see what had obviously first caught Paul's eye, now she could see it close up and in isolation. "Signed by Helen Taylor and Karen Taylor. That is definitely an eye-opener, considering you didn't even know she existed."

"Yeah, no sign of Adam's name on there— unless it is concealed in the gibberish on the rest of the paper sheet?" George said, while thoughtfully handing it to Pamela to examine, "Any ideas?" He asked.

Her eyes flicked left and right looking for any obvious clue, but this was a coding competition set for any eager spies. "Sorry, not a sausage I'm afraid," Pamela said with an overtone of disappointment in her voice.

Nancy held up her hand in the air, as if vying for attention whilst at school. The others turned in her direction, waiting for her to speak her mind. She reached forward to the notice board and pulled away yet another competition entry.

"This one contains Adam Bridges name just plonked into one line. You can just about spot it amongst the other gibberish on the page…"

Kim looked at George, he looked like he was deep in thought. "Penny?" she offered.

It had been a couple of seconds before he acknowledged her presence. "Eh, sorry Kim did you mention something?"

"You looked as if you were somewhere else George. Are you concerned about something?" Kim examined his eyes, illogically hoping to read his mind for a reason.

George stacked his cards close to his chest, not sure whether this was the time to put forward his theories or not. He decided to hold back on revealing one idea for the moment, but did offer one opinion to the rest of the group. "I wonder if any of you have also thought about something I am a little confused about. In particular, the gap between the two worktops?"

Nancy wrinkled her nose, "I'm sorry George— I know I am just a mere female school teacher. You would think— not being rude, that I would probably be of above intelligence."

She smiled wryly, "I know you are a mystery author. But for god's sake, what is it with all of these guessing games?"

Paul coughed and gave a raucous laugh, "That's telling you George— Nancy does have a point..."

George was visibly shocked, nobody had ever mentioned that part of his character before. His bottom lip slightly protruded as he managed to mumble "I'm sorry, I never realised I was being so irritating, I thought I was just stimulating your minds."

Kim nudged his arm gently. "If it's any consolation George, I only find you mildly irritating." She made a noise in her throat that sounded suspiciously like a stifled laugh.

Pamela stood nearer to George as well and gripped him gently round one bicep. "Well I rather like my prospective son-in-law."

She purred, "I haven't noticed anything remarkable about a gap in the worktop, why don't you divulge to us with what you have surmised, George."

Not aware of Kim's jealous glance towards her mother, George preened himself in readiness, then he smiled and announced. "Why is there a gap in between two worktops when the only thing the gap leads to is a wall?" Feeling the stares and noting Kim mouthing, "Why?" He decided it would probably be prudent to continue.

"Well my thought process says to me— Why go to all the unnecessary work needed to separate a worktop, if there wasn't a practical reason?" He stepped closer to the wall and began wiping it across with a solitary finger. "I think I can feel a microscopic cut in the surface." He turned towards Pamela, "Why don't you have a go?" He invited her.

She placed her entire hand onto its surface and simply pushed. A whole section of wall dropped into a slot below floor level. With a short yelp of surprise, she fell forward into what appeared to be a concealed passageway behind the wall.

Before she could stand back up or anyone else could react, the wall rose back up sealing the temporary entrance.

David flew forward and began banging fruitlessly on the hidden portal to the corridor beyond. "Pam', Pamela— are you okay?" He yelled, panic-stricken whilst unable to contact his trapped wife.

Everyone nearly jumped out of their skin as Pamela's voice boomed through an overhead speaker set in the ceiling. A small video monitor fixed to a wall burst into life, displaying

Pamela's slightly dishevelled visage gazing towards them. "I'm fine, relatively speaking." She nodded, happy to be viewing her family from the other side of the wall. "The lights came on as soon as the door closed. This video phone was already showing you all staring at the wall..."

"Video phone?— You must be Inside the Fortress Pam'. It's probably there to act as a spyhole to the outside world," concluded David. "I've tried everything to re-open the door from our side. It must relock after one activation, to stop anyone else from following a person inside. There should at the least, be a way of opening the door from your side?"

They could see Pamela's head bobbing side to side, as she frantically searched for a trigger of some sort. "I can't detect anything, she said in a panicked voice. "Hang on, there is a button on the side of this metal strut..."

Her face disappeared from the monitor for a couple of seconds. When she returned to view, her face looked at them defeated. "The button opened a panel on the wall— it revealed a ten by ten grids of numbers, letters and symbols.

There is no way I am going to discover the code to open the door." She sniffed and turned away from the camera to conceal her tears of despair.

"Dad, what can we do?— we have to get mum out," sobbed Kim.

David thought quickly— "Pam'— don't panic, we will get you out of here. Have a mooch around if you want, I will assign a volunteer here in the canteen. Sorry it won't be me stopping, but I might be of more use searching for another way to enter the fortress."

He looked around, and the others silently nodded in agreement. "I'll stay back," said Maria. "I'm presumably the most unfit of us all, I suppose?"

Paul received the hint and winked at her. "In my eyes Maria, you are most likely the fittest here." Maria felt slightly disappointed when he hadn't additionally offered to stay behind and keep her company. "However, we aren't officially going out yet, so I suppose I will have to let that one slide."

She consoled herself with that regretful thought for a moment, as she placed another cup underneath the mouth of the coffee machine.

"Okay David, as you seem to be in a privileged position with regard to this place and the mysterious Fortress. What do you suggest we do next?" asked George, tapping his fingers in frustration on the work surface.

David was lost in thought for a few moments before he answered. "It's a while since I was last here, and we were always dissuaded from snooping around or mentioning the

Fortress. But if my memory is still ticking over correctly, I seem to remember every time we came across Helen or Adam, they seemed to appear round one side or the other of this building in particular."

George looked at David and nodded, "Okay, that would mean that the rear of the building would represent the obvious place to start looking."

Paul agreed, "Pamela escorted you girls down here from an entrance hidden at the rear. Do you suppose you could guide us all out that way?"

Nancy piped up, "Shouldn't present a problem I would have thought Paul. Kim was almost trampling Pam' out of the way in her haste to get down here with George. So if— we let her follow her nose back out there…" Nancy gave Kim a questioning glance.

"Yeah, sure— Not a problem shall we go now?" asked Kim, already sliding her bag back over her shoulders. "Come on then."

George held up his hand as a signal for them to wait. "Hold on a sec' can someone leave a walkie-talkie for Maria?" Paul nodded, "She can have mine as there are plenty of them between us. Maria took the handset from Paul as if it were a personal gift and held it close to her chest.

George indicated he was satisfied and clung to Kim by her elbow, leading her towards the exit and the rear of the building.

※※※

"I think you need to push the big red button Kim," said George— with his tongue planted firmly in his cheek.

Kim thought he was probably taking the Mickey, as the 'Big Red Button' was complimented by a large sign saying 'Push Red Button to Exit Building.' "Yeah— Yeah," she grinned and pushed the aforementioned Red Button and watched the door disappear once more. They clambered up the brief flight of stairs and found themselves standing by the large dumpsters, their profiles accentuated by the elongated shadows of an impending sunset.

Nancy looked at her watch, it was nearing five forty in the afternoon. "Thank goodness the sun is starting to drop. I hate the sun when we aren't able to lie down beside a pool, and hold a nice cold drink in my hands." Nancy stared at the bins, realising that they were emitting a horrible stench. "That's another reason I don't like the sun— god that stinks."

"I agree," said Paul, and was about to comment further when something attracted his attention. "Why would you need to bolt down a dumpster bin?" he asked himself, while walking to examine the tallest bin conspicuously standing away from the other bins.

George followed in his footsteps. "What's up Paul— what has caught your eye?"

Paul pointed to the bolts installed underneath the wheels, fixing them firmly in place. Together they examined the bin closely.

The bin had two lids, each supported normally by hydraulic stays. "George, would you mind giving me a boost? I want to see if what I suspect exists— is present on top of that bin."

259

George cupped his hands and lifted Paul up as soon as he put his foot in the human stirrup.

Paul found himself on top of the bin and knelt down to examine the top. "Just as I thought," he commended himself.

"Minor question George can you see the lid release catch down there. There is no way this size and height of the bin would allow someone to merely lift the lid up.

George mooched around for a short time and spotted a stainless steel grip. "Found one Paul— Tell me when you are on the opposite lid, and I will give it a good yank."

He heard Paul shout out okay, and pulled on the catch release as hard as he could.

The high-pitched hiss of the hydraulic lid struck his ears, and he leapt back in surprise as the front of the dumpster split and a section folded outwards. It was followed by a concealed step apparatus silently extending towards George.

The rest of the gang sprung to stand beside a slightly shocked George, waiting to witness what was going to happen next. "I must admit, I should have expected something like that— but it still caught me out, "George laughed nervously as he gathered his wits.

He began ascending the makeshift stairs until he stood next to Paul still standing at the top.

Paul indicated a large amount of scuffs across the surface of the lid he was standing on. "Looks like this was a veritable highway, by the amount of traffic it would have taken to wear the top away like that." He turned towards the nearby flat roof, now easily reached from his perch on the bin. They witnessed him leap onto the building and he disappeared from sight for those still at ground level.

One by one they made their way to the top of the bin and jumped the limited distance to rejoin Paul. Who by now was standing by a peculiar construction at the centre of the building. It looked suspiciously like a nuclear bunker with its aerodynamically shaped slopes and tremendously impenetrable walls.

An incongruous looking steel sheet of metal spread across three quarters of one side. On a stainless steel pole sat an almost familiar pad, immediately coming to mind when compared against the description, that Pamela had described previously.

David wiped his hand across his forehead, "I don't believe it— we are stuffed" He almost choked with dismay. "How the hell are we going through the door to get Pam' out now?"

✳✳✳

"They are on the roof Ma'am located next to the Fortress entrance, do you want us to intervene? As it looks like they are unable to bypass the secure lock, just the same as us I'm afraid— Over." The drone operator waited for the go-ahead from Major Nadine Spencer.

"Negative Delta-Oscar One. Sustain your position for just a bit longer. I have this gut feeling one member of this group is about to surprise the entire staff of the British military intelligence." Nadine advised.

She watched as the operator replaced the field of view with a telescopic lens focused solely on the roof rather than the whole estate.

"Okay Amber Prevett, I hope to god for the sake of the remaining staff in the Fortress. That your boys come out of this victorious, and everyone lives happily ever after. This must be getting pretty desperate in there by now…" Nadine Spencer said to no-one in particular, wringing her hands together in tension.

Her attention was again focussed on the unfolding drama happening only a few miles away from her present location.

She picked up the coffee cup from the dashboard holder and took a long draught. Glad that she had the foresight to make sure she would remain refreshed at her enforced vigil.

✳✳✳

"I can't stand this silence any longer, is anyone going to even attempt anything?" Kim appeared distraught and slightly panicked by the surrounding inactivity.

The three men raised their eyes towards her simultaneously. George spoke first, "Sorry Kim it looks pretty hopeless at the moment. We have no idea how to crack open this door, which as it happens hopelessness is probably the main justification for the industrial strength lock."

Paul shifted the subject slightly after reflecting on how Maria was coping on her own. "I hope you guys don't mind? I'm just going to give her downstairs a quick buzz on the walkie-talkie..." He pulled off the radio that was tightly clipped to his bandolier and squeezed the side-mounted transmit trigger.

"Hiya Maria— Is everything okay down there?— Over."

It had been a couple of seconds before he got a reply and wasn't sure if it was Maria talking. It appeared to be gobbledegook emitting from the small speaker.

Paul heard a couple of snorts and what sounded suspiciously like a burp before he heard Maria reply intelligibly. "Sorry Paul, I was kind of busy."

"Errm, busy doing what exactly?" He asked already with a reason in mind.

She began coughing a little and acknowledged him truthfully,

"Phew— the crumbs got stuck in my throat, I thought I was going to choke for a moment then. You made me jump with that walkie-talkie squealing in my ear, just as I had put the third chocolate and raspberry roll into my mouth."

Paul smirked, "You've found some goodies to eat then?"

"I was actually looking for a packet of crisps to be honest; I always get the munchies when I am bored." She explained."

Anyway, I started to mooch through the cupboards and found a massive box full of my favourite snack."

Paul could only just manage a simple, "Uh Uh" as a response.

She waffled for a couple more minutes before pausing and ultimately asking him a question. "I'm sorry Paul— but I tend to rabbit after being on my own for a bit. So how is it going up there?"

He had scarcely known her for a short time, but already felt that Maria was his sort of woman. She was determined and gawky, both at the same time sometimes.

He could feel himself falling in love with her already. "Regrettably, we haven't come across any snacks yet," he teased, while imagining her staring at the walkie-talkie as if she had just misheard.

Paul decided he had better adopt a little decorum and inject some seriousness into the conversation. "It's not going well this end I'm afraid to say. But we have come across another of those keypads that Pamela saw on her side of the wall. We are almost at the point of giving up, without a code—well, we are kind of stuffed..."

Maria sighed, if only she could help. A buzzing noise came from the speaker on the wall and then Pamela's voice boomed out. "Is there anyone still out there?"

Making her way quickly to the site of the hidden door, Maria called back once in front of the camera. "Hey Pam', are you okay? What's up?" More than a touch of concern in her voice. Remembering she had already been in conversation with Paul, she decided to quickly call him back. "Hang on Paul, Pam' has just shouted out. I'll let you know what she wants as soon as I find out."

A simple "Roger" was all she heard, as she waited for Pam' to reply.

"Maria, the corridors are long down here, but they all appear to terminate at more of these doors fitted with the super-locks. I finally got fed up with wandering about, and this particular notion entered my mind." Pamela sounded enthusiastic.

"Okay, I'll buy it— what thought came to mind then," Maria replied, eager to discover Pamela's idea.

"Well— it may be something or nothing, but do you remember those sheets of paper that needed decoding on the competition board. Could it be just possible Helen and

Adam had pinned those on there? On the off chance that if something went wrong here, I would come looking for them sometime in the future." Pamela stopped speaking for a moment.

Maria took the opportunity to reply, "I see where you are coming from. Do you think they contain door codes or something?"

"I do, but I have no idea why they would have found the need to go to the lengths of leaving door codes to be discovered by anyone. The Fortress was reportedly impregnable anyway..." Observed Pamela, her voice trailing off slowly.

Maria sounded optimistic. "That would be something we could maybe talk about later. So, do you really think those codes will be useful? If the answer is yes, I will rush them upstairs straight away."

"If they are still lying around, there is at least a chance," Pam' stopped mid-sentence. "But I have no idea how they are going to crack the code, though..."

Maria heard the catch in Pamela's voice made at the end of her reply. Making up her mind immediately to convey the codes to the gang up top. "If we don't try, we will never find out. I will come back as soon as I can Pam'."

With those concluding words, Maria snatched the code and walkie-talkie on the worktop. Disappearing from Pam's sight, already on her way up-top. Pamela prayed she was maybe embracing the solution in her hand, otherwise she would not be going anywhere soon.

✳✳✳

"Hey guys, Maria has just spoken to Pam', and she suggests we try to use the sheets of code to try to find a way in. Maria will only be a couple of minutes before she reckons she will reach us," Paul said excitedly.

They heard the clunk of Maria's heels on the metallic steps of the dumpster and her beaming smile greeted them all. Slightly out of breath, she waved the expected sheets of paper and delivered them with a grin to Paul.

Paul examined them carefully once more. Hoping something they had all missed previously— stood up and revealed its identity to everyone. No such luck.

Something was nagging at the back of George's mind, but he couldn't quite put his finger on it.

David Chapman spoke up with a serious look on his face. "I admit it's a few years ago now, but I recall one instructor directing us, look at an object and see what it really looks like." He waited for a reaction.

Nancy obliged with the first question, "That sounds downright weird. But on the face of it. I suppose you could say they are pieces of paper, with characters written on them."

"Good start," nodded David, "Anything else?"

"They have Kim's paternal parents name on them." Kirstie offered.

David bobbed his head, and his answer was slow and drawn out. "I don't think so Kirstie. Helen and Adam's name are only there to capture our attention. Not actually part of the code I am afraid." He looked around again, "Anything else?"

Kim put her finger on one sheet and flexed her finger up and down on its surface. "I'm probably not very adept at this, but there seems to be a hell of a gap between each line of text.

Probably half an inch I suppose. I know it's nothing to do with the code, but it sort of shouts out something to me."

George began slapping at his jacket pockets, mumbling, "I'm sure It's in here somewhere?"

The group stared at him— wondering if he had got a sand flea or something invading his person.

Suddenly remembering his jacket also had a couple of zipped pockets on the sleeves. He pulled on each zip and pushed his fingers inside searching for something. With a short shout of "Yes," he extracted something and clasped it tightly in one hand.

"Well?" Paul looked patiently at George, who was grinning like a maniac.

"I think I may have something that may assist us decode the message," said George, selecting a sheet of paper from Kim and spreading it flat on the surface of the roof. He extended his hand to allow the others to identify what had got him so excited.

"My plectrum!" Kim blurted out.

"Actually it's technically my plectrum darling; you abandoned it in the Library when you were going through paperwork back in May— Remember?. It's a good job I had the sense to pick it up, isn't it?" Said George placing the object on top of the paper.

Long shadows, from the almost out of sight sun impeded their view of George's activities. Recognising that they could not see what he was doing, he asked them to all take out the storm lamps he had provided to each of them.

The soft light given off the lamps mixed with the redness of the late sun giving an eerie effect to the proceedings. George began explaining his theory.

"First things first, I have only read about this method in an old wartime novel. So if it doesn't work, don't shoot the messenger.

The plectrum is used as a code cypher. By itself wouldn't be too bad, but I had already suspected there was going to be more than one method used. After all— you don't just leave the secret code for a fortress on a notice board— do you?" He secured their attention, all waiting for him to continue.

"I expect this is going to take some time, but one of these sheets of paper is the key to the other. My eyes aren't brilliant in this sort of light. Who here feels they have the best eyesight?" George asked, noting Kirstie had her hand up straight away. He waited for her explanation.

"I suppose it would be me; I am looking at numbers and stuff all day long working in a bank." Kirstie said. The others just nodded in agreement, although none of them were uneducated, they didn't have the day-to-day practical experience Kirstie had.

"Right what is the plan then George?" queried Kirstie waiting for instructions.

"I am going to have a stab in the dark here. The first one that has Kim's real name on it is probably a bit too obvious to be the one to embark on. I suggest we start with the one bearing Adam's name instead.

There are a number of ways that we can approach this with the plectrum, but the principle is the same throughout."

George turned to Kim, "I nearly forgot, can you get out the notebook and pen please. You are going to need to write out the numbers, letters and shapes that Kirstie calls out." He next looked at David, "We are going to need a starting point key as well though, any ideas?"

"I am inspired by your thought process so far George, maybe we should recommend you for a change of career?" Said David, quickly carrying on as he noted a deliberate blank look on George's face.

"It may be as unsophisticated as Adam"s name, For example, Kirstie if you put the top hole of the plectrum over the first character and read off what is shown in the bottom two holes please."

Looking slightly confused, Kirstie complied with his request. "A and Triangle," she said while Kim wrote down the sequence in the notebook.

David gave Kirstie the next step in the sequence. "Move across four for the letter D and again note the characters down."

Getting the gist of converting the letter into the positional number in the alphabet. Allowed Kirstie to forge ahead on her own, calling out characters until she reached the S of Adam's surname 'Bridges'.

Everyone looked at David for the subsequent step in the process. "Right this is where the puzzle part takes over. Pick up the other sheet and turn the plectrum around so that the two holes are at the top.

Start looking for A and Triangle fitting into those holes by running the plectrum along each line. When found, call out the unique character for Kim to write down." he advised.

"What if I can't find a match?" asked Kirstie, who was already sliding the plectrum smoothly across each line. David didn't answer, he merely lifted both hands, showing everyone he had his fingers crossed tightly.

Kirstie shouted out excitedly "Got a match, it's a square!" Kim rapidly copied the character down and called out the next pair to search for, then Kirstie began rapidly searching for the following sequence.

It occupied only a relatively short time to find all the other sets until with a sigh of frustration Kirstie announced she couldn't uncover the last one.

Kim thrust the notebook and pencil into George's hands and knelt down next to her friend. "I'm excellent at puzzle magazines; this doesn't look too different to some of those. Do you mind if I have a try?"

Kirstie put the plectrum into Kim's offered palm. "Fill your boots," she chuckled, totally relieved at the pressure being removed.

Everyone else began holding their breath as Kim also slid the piece of plastic fruitlessly backwards and forwards. "I wonder?" She said to herself and again began scanning the lines.

She screamed in excitement, "YES," and fist pumped the air.

"Write down a circle," she said triumphantly. George wrote down the final character, bursting to enquire how she unearthed it, when originally neither she nor Kirstie could.

Before he had a chance to ask, Kim explained. "I checked and checked and there was no way that the sequence I was looking for existed. I was beginning to suspect that Kirstie had decoded the other sheet incorrectly.

But I had a suspicion it had all been too easy so far, so I wondered if there was another source for the final code.

Then while staring at the current sheet— My eyes were suddenly riveted to the initial reason we spotted it in the first place. Therefore I used the initials H and K and bingo— I found a match."

George stood beside the keypad, notebook in hand. "Only one way to test challenging work," He said seriously and entered the first character on the page...

✳✳✳

December 21st 2021

George's hand was now shaking, as he prepared to enter the final eleventh character to hopefully open the door in front of them all. He glanced quickly round the group for moral support and could only discern blank stares as they impatiently waited for him to press the key. He stiffened his forefinger and stabbed downward to hit the appropriate key.

Only the sound of multiple sharp intakes of breath disturbed the nervous silence. While they nervously awaited for the door to unlock.

A small steel shutter slid to one side followed by the whirring noise of a servo-motor. A single camera extended from behind the recess and began to pan left and right.

Nancy queried no-one in particular, "Okay, what does that mean, is that a favourable sign or are we about to observe a reaction to an incorrect door code?"

David nodded. "Good question, but to be honest I have no idea what the protocol will be. When, for example, someone effectively knocks on the massive metal door and is expecting to be let in..."

A whispering hiss came from somewhere at the left-hand side of the entrance. Followed by the sound of receding piston driven bolts within the door frame. "Looks like the key worked after all," chuckled David happily, thankful it was a satisfactory conclusion. He hadn't possessed the heart to

273

reveal the fortresses defences were something NORAD would be proud of. If they had been invoked, it would have been unlikely they would still be alive, and celebrating the entrance being revealed.

With another sonorous hiss, the door began swinging open under the control of hidden powerful hydraulic rams. LED Lamps within instantaneously burst into life, revealing a steel-lined corridor with a concrete stairway leading downward.

George smacked David hard on his back, "David— Splendidly done, what a brilliant overall idea."

"No, it was thanks to you really George, retaining the presence of mind to pick up the plectrum off the floor," David replied.

"My plectrum actually," piped up Kim. David merely nodded in recognition of her misguided attempt at garnering praise. Simultaneously, George stepped towards her and put his arm round her waist.

※※※

Major Nadine Spencer was frustrated as hell. "Delta-Oscar One confirm the status of the team on top of the building. I am anxious I can't believe what I am witnessing, and need confirmation— Over."

The reply was instant from the operator of the overhead drone. "I have double-checked the situation and have now instigated Infrared as well as enhanced optical to make sure we do not overlook anything."

274

"I didn't ask how well you could observe anything. I distinctly requested a status report, please comply." Nadine's voice began to distinctly become angrier.

Suitably chastised the drone operator answered, "My apologies Ma'am. The impassable door seems to be open."

"I can witness that, but what the hell is the team doing?" Exasperated, Nadine could scarcely wait for an answer.

"If you require a straightforward answer Major, I will say absolutely nothing towards a rescue. I can see one male with his arm around a female. One more elderly male tapping his foot impatiently." He paused as he conducted a longer appraisal of the situation below. "Sorry about that, I couldn't identify what the second male was doing with one of the other red head females. He was— "

"I don't want to know. But would you agree there appears to be no sense of urgency to proceed into the Fortress?" Nadine tapped her pen impatiently against the steering wheel.

"I would tend to agree Ma'am." the operator stated with conviction.

I suppose we had better nudge them then— oh, I forgot we hadn't spoken in the past." She chuckled lightly, I think we had better introduce ourselves Delta-Oscar One, let's arrange a chat..."

❋❋❋

"C'mon you lot, we are supposed to be rescuing Pam and her family— Remember?" David implored.

"Hang on a sec,'" Paul interrupted. "Did you hear that?"

They looked at him dumbfounded and chorused together "Hear what?"

"That buzzing noise— somewhere above us," he held a cupped hand to one ear, "It's getting louder…"

"George Walsh— attention— George Walsh," a curt woman's voice boomed out. From what appeared to be a flying tube with stubby wings and an unfeasibly large propeller mounted at the rear of the craft. It was circling in a tight circle mere tens of metres overhead.

George and the others froze in response to the unexpected interruption. He recognised the device as a military drone from documentaries on television.

Remembering their main purpose was observation rather than assassination, he warily raised his arm while waving his hand to indicate he had heard the broadcast.

There had been a pause of several seconds before the female voice began speaking again. "Much appreciated for your acknowledgement Mr Walsh. My name is Major Nadine Spencer, and yes we have already met recently at the car hire centre. Pleasantries over I would like to get down to the business in hand. Taking into account your recent activities, combined with the presence of David and Pamela Chapman.

I will work on the premise that you are aware you are currently about to enter an extremely restricted area."

She paused until George realised that she was waiting for him to acknowledge he understood. He brandished his arm again, waiting to see if that was the reason she had paused.

"Thank you— Under normal circumstances you would expect to see a division of trained tactical operatives in a helicopter hanging over your position. However, time is of the essence, and being in foreign climes it is extremely difficult to arrange military assets at short notice. I am currently talking to my opposite number in the Spanish Military, so additional assistance may remain a little time away before they reach your position.

In the meantime, can I urge you to proceed with caution? We have been unable to establish any form of contact with the occupants within. We have no idea why the Fortress went into lockdown. Good luck and Godspeed." Nadine Spencer signed off with a little emotional cough in her voice as she uttered the final sentence.

The drone headed directly upwards to continue prowling overhead and out of sight.

"Well there's a turn up for the books, Major now eh?" said David.

George sharply turned towards him. "You know Nadine Spencer?"

David looked mildly astonished at George's reaction. "George, more to the point how do you know her? Ms Spencer is strictly an enigma within the intelligence community. I'm not being facetious, but unless she expressed a particular interest in you, you wouldn't even know she existed…"

"Must have been my good looks," George muttered, receiving a sharp elbow in his ribs from Kim for his throwaway comment. He looked around at friends and hoped they would all be okay. Knowing it would be pointless asking Kim to stay behind, he restrained his tongue from making the effort.

Paul piped up sounding suspiciously like a drill sergeant, "I suppose we had better get started then, I'm glad to see everyone still has their backpacks in their possession. We may still need their content. I will lead, and George can bring up the rear. Everyone else arrange yourselves into a single file and move forward."

Maria smiled, "If I had known beforehand he was so bossy, I might have had second thoughts." She flashed Paul an enhanced false grin, and stepped behind him. He reached backwards and clutched her hand, squeezing it affectionately.

The line carefully began negotiating the stairwell. Lighting appeared to perceive their presence and clicked on as they approached. Darkness prevailed behind them as each light extinguished after the last person had passed underneath its luminance.

✳✳✳

The warble of the Satphone ringing commanded her attention. Distracting her from her vigil, following the remotely transmitted video from the orbiting drone. Nadine saw a withheld number. "If that is someone telling me I have experienced an accident, they are likely to receive one themselves." She chuckled softly as she pressed the answer key.

"Major Nadine Spencer, how can I help?" Nadine asked curtly.

"Ahh Major Spencer, this is Colonel Garcia of Grupos de Operaciones Especiales. Sorry about the mouthful, we are also known as GOE and are the special operations forces of the Spanish Army. However, enough of the introductions it's time to get straight down to business. I have rung to update you as we currently have a team heading your way by helicopter.

They are acutely aware of the particular conditions surrounding your facility. It goes without saying we hope you have not got anybody else entering the ah, Fortress?"

Major Spencer bit the inside of her lip, "Ermm about that last comment of yours, it has just become a little more complicated..."

✳✳✳

"What— is that smell?" Kim moaned, looking suspiciously at George.

Paul laughed, Well it's not me. I made sure I stayed clear of those ripe bananas. But, I did see Maria stuffing them down her throat."

"I will have you know Paul Carter, I really like a banana or two whenever I get a chance." Maria said indignantly, about to remonstrate further when she realised she was having her leg mercilessly pulled by Paul. "Smug git," was the only response she could think of, as she was currently feeling a little distracted and embarrassed.

"Nice little story guys, but that smell is really beginning to bother me— oh my god, it's not what I imagine it is— is it Dad?" Kim looked at her father imploringly waiting for him to validate or deny her suspicions.

David carried on walking, snuffing the air like a gun dog. "I don't think its human remains if that's what is worrying you Kim. He breathed in again deeply, "Smells like sewage to me?"

Nancy and Kirstie declined to comment, and silence again prevailed as they followed the long downward sloping corridor. Five minutes later, they were still descending the metal-clad corridor. The stench was getting stronger and more overpowering.

"Might be a reasonable idea to pull out those builders' full-face masks I bought this morning." Said George, already rummaging through his backpack. "They are in fact class P3, which means they filter out harmful vapours. The sole thing I am concerned about is gases, but I'm not certain how they will cope with those..."

"It's going to mess up my hair isn't it?" Maria moaned while struggling to stretch the elasticated strap of the mask over her head.

Paul stood behind her to assist by tightening the straps when in position. "By the level of the stench already reached, I think you won't be worrying about your hair. The sole thing you will experience is feeling grateful for the mask instead."

Upon reaching an abrupt change of direction to the right, they could conclusively identify the source of the mysterious odour.

They stopped abruptly, only just managing to accommodate two people across the width of the corridor. As a result the girls were shuffled to the front, so they could observe the scene ahead without obstruction.

David took charge, "Okay, that looks suspiciously like straight forward sewage. If you look to the right side of the corridor, there appears to be a panel split. The contents of a sewage pipe are emptying into the corridor as you can see."

He coughed loudly inside the mask. "It looks like the floor grill which would normally drain rain water away from an open door above has become err clogged. That overhead aeration duct never stood a chance, it must be overwhelmed trying to extract the air as fresh sewage keeps pouring in."

George took a roll of all-purpose webbing tape from out of his back and began creating a temporary seal across the leak in the wall. Affixing multiple layers atop each other until the fluid stopped. "Well that was a simple fix, what next?"

David trailed a foot over the drainage grill, allowing the remaining fluids to drain away. "I suspect the Fortress went into an automatic shutdown when the gas was detected out here. The artificial intelligence that regulates the security must have decided the facility was under attack and..."

Paul held up his hand, "Yeah we get the picture, but I don't see any of those keypad thingies. Therefore, how do we get the AI to open the door again?"

David delivered a sombre look, his expression half hidden by the lower half of his face mask. "We have to get rid of the source of the gas." He stated positively:

Maria looked confused, "Well, how will we do tha'..." She stopped half-way through the sentence, after suddenly comprehending what David was about to suggest.

"Don't worry about that, I suggest all you ladies head back up to the rooftop, While us men clear up here. We will obviously be up and down the corridor ourselves, so we will keep you informed what is going on."

The girls simply turned around and headed upwards as suggested.

✳✳✳

"Sorry to disturb you Major, but radar has just detected an incoming helicopter towards our monitored building. They have contacted us to say they will presently take over the situation and will report back when they have successfully concluded.

Do you want us to clear the area for the Spanish Special Forces or do you prefer me to just change altitude to clear the airspace while they land?" Asked the ever-present drone operator, keeping an eye on the proceedings below.

Nadine bit her tongue as she could feel her temper rising. "No way are we leaving the area for a bunch of testosterone fuelled egotists? Change the altitude as you suggested for the time being. Anything new happening down there yet?"

"No Ma'am. Hang on a sec; the three females have just exited the stairway. They all appear to be wearing gas masks?" Replied the operator, noting that there seemed to be a male just exiting the stairwell also.

He continued with a running commentary. "One of the men has just emerged as well and appears to be carrying a heavy bag. The females are moving well away from his path, as he has just thrown something liquefied over the side of the building. He appears to be making his way back into the Fortress now."

"What the hell is going on?" wondered Nadine as the Drone Operator reported yet another man had just thrown something over the side as well.

✳✳✳

George was about to wipe some sweat from his eyes, and at the last moment thought twice about it. "That was close," he muttered grimly to himself. "Only a couple more bagfuls David reckons, and hopefully the AI will release the doors once the gases dissipate through the air vent."

Kim took a step closer to him and stopped short before he could put his arms around her for a cuddle. "Be quick then George, the sooner you can finish the more reasonable chance you will have of getting a shower. To be honest you stink, and I want to give you a cuddle." She fluttered her eyelashes coquettishly and giggled.

George was just about to smack her backside for her cheek, when David appeared at the top of the stairs.

"Why is it, every time I turn up where you two are, you are just about to manhandle my daughter?" David said with an anxious look on his face which quickly morphed into a smile, glad to see his daughter so happy after her breakup with Andy King. He felt there must have been more to that particular situation than Kim had let on. David Chapman was confident it would all come out at some point when she was ready and willing.

"Is that a helicopter I can hear?" Nancy asked.

"Probably that Drone thing is still buzzing around overhead," suggested Kirstie.

"Nope, definitely a helicopter, it's getting louder— it's coming from somewhere over there. Stated Nancy peering into the darkness, anticipating some movement against the stars. Night-time was completely in place, and the rooftop was lit with the bone white glow of the moon.

A voice they all recognised boomed out from somewhere above. "Is that you Mr Walsh? Your masks make it difficult to identify anyone conclusively."

Major Spencer waited for George to confirm his identity in the same manner as before. Paul appeared, struggling with a particularly heavy load, flinging its contents over the side. "That's the lot— Did I just overhear that military woman speaking through the drone again?"

As if she had heard him speak, Nadine Spencer recognised his presence by calling out to him from her virtual position overhead. "Aha, Mr Carter— Good. That means the gang are all here." She gave an obvious false laugh. "As I am sure you will soon be very aware, we have an inbound helicopter approaching your position. They are representing the Spanish Special Forces. As we have no jurisdiction for a military presence, they will be taking charge of effecting an extraction from within the Fortress. Could I ask you to not impede them from their mission please."

They found it difficult to comprehend the end of her transmission. As the Spanish helicopter was now directly overhead, the rotor wash underneath made it difficult to stand, let alone hear.

George manoeuvred Kim away from large aluminium cases being lowered by steel cables onto the rooftop. Paul did the same for Maria and the others quickly followed suit, avoiding the descending boxes of equipment.

Suddenly a multitude of cables fell downward, their tips barely striking the rooftop. The sight of seven strapping men dressed in black rappelling downward towards them, infused them with apprehension.

The soldiers quickly disappeared down into the stairway and the helicopter moved away to acquire a suitable landing site in the adjacent grounds.

Kim moved closer to her father and clung to his hand. "They will get Mum out Dad," she said reassuringly. He squeezed her hand back lightly. "I know Kim— I know they will sweet-heart."

A salty tear formed in the corner of his eye, establishing a visible path through the accumulated sweat on his face, as it slid down behind his mask.

Two soldiers wearing what looked like oxygen masks, appeared from the doorway, and ran straight towards the boxes of equipment located at one side of the roof. They cracked open a box and began placing items round them as

if searching for something. Two other soldiers arrived and hauled what looked like a couple of heavy cylinders and a long pipe about six-feet long. The first pair presently appeared to have pinpointed what they were looking for, and followed the second soldiers back underground.

Nancy carefully stepped closer to the rooftop edge. "I can see car lights approaching. It's going to get quite crowded on this rooftop soon."

Kim and George looked out into the darkness and could also see the headlights moving up and down. Validating someone was heading towards them at speed, over the rough terrain around the estate. "Bet that is Nadine, you can tell it's a woman driver by the way she doesn't bother avoiding the craters even though they must be shredding the tyres to pieces."

Kim disregarded his comment, displaying no reaction at all, as she was now becoming familiar with his particular sense of humour. Vaguely disappointed that his teasing had no effect, he sought a different tack instead to garner her attention.

"Wonder how Roger is getting on with your brother?" He asked innocently, while pleased as punch when he saw her snap her head in his direction. "Why would you ask that, you've just reminded me how much I am missing the little blighter?

She was immediately distracted by the sight and smell of acrid smoke billowing out of the stairwell opening.

"Looks like they are employing a thermic lance to cut through the door. That's what the big pipe and gas bottles were for. I believe they represent the cutting tool of choice for safe crackers..." David informed everyone, assuming they

286

would be interested in what was likely to be happening underground.

A significant booming noise followed by the wailing of sirens piqued everyone's interest, and they all automatically stepped closer to the entrance. A voice from behind, made them jump with fright. "Can I ask you to step away from there? In fact, it's not a request it is a direct order." They twisted around to face Major Nadine Spencer, still dressed in a smart pair of slacks and a cool blouse.

Realising the group was staring at her attire, Nadine rapidly explained, "Sorry to disappoint you all, but I haven't been back to change at the hotel. I have been keeping an eye on you 'lot' all day long…"

She sighed profoundly and resumed the conversation in a less harsh voice. "You may be interested to know, as I reached the compound I received a positive update from a

Colonel in the Spanish Special Forces. He has advised that his team has managed to breach the final door below.

The Colonel appeared to be a little embarrassed, when he admitted the door had opened under its own power at the same time they were trying to cut it open. It seems that whatever you had been undertaking previously had worked.

The Fortress AI had been convinced it was now non-toxic, and decided that the door was safe to open again."

They overheard voices coming from the stairwell. Instead of the expected soldiers, men and women dressed casually emerged instead.

"Looks like the inmates have been released," joked Paul as a continuous line of weary looking people was forming on the rooftop.

287

Ignoring the out of context attempt at humour, David looked concerned. "No sign of your Mum yet Kim," he said, disappointed that no-one had managed to release Pamela from the corridors below yet.

Kim entertained a burning question for David. "I know you are concerned about Mum Dad, so am I. But I have to ask the obvious question— Are any of these men and women, Helen or Adam?"

"No Kim, I'm afraid not. It's strange they are not here, and there doesn't seem to be any more people coming out." David said, noting that the Spanish soldiers had just made their way out as well.

George had overheard Kim's question, so he turned to converse with one of the military men standing nearby drinking from a can of cold cola.

"Have you seen a man and a woman who stayed behind, there may have been another woman with them too?" He asked politely, not really expecting a favourable answer.

The man shrugged his shoulders, "I am not positive who you actually mean señor, but a man and woman who seemed to be in charge told us they would be staying behind to check everybody had got out. They had fancy CCTV screens on one wall, with movable cameras everywhere as far as I could make out.

We were only tasked with getting access so that everyone trapped could leave. No jurisdiction to force anyone to leave, though…" He shrugged his shoulders for a second time and turned to converse with a colleague.

Making his way back over to David and Kim, he related a conversation that he had only just had with a member of the military.

David smiled and appeared to visibly relax with the good news. "Well, that sounds like Helen, last man out and all that. I hope she and Adam manage to identify Pamela wandering around like a lost soul in those corridors.— She'll be okay though, she had the same training as me, and it wasn't for wimps I'll tell you."

Kim made a noise in her nose, almost unable to hold back her suppressed laughter. David looked at her with an incredulous expression on his face. "Excuse me!" He said firmly, "And what was that laughter all about, young lady?"

"Come on Dad, what with the window peeping and stuff, I am finding it hard to take you seriously as a spy," Kim chuckled.

Pretending to be hurt, David pushed out a sulky bottom lip. Just as quickly a beaming smile appeared on his face as he spotted three people emerging from the Fortress.

He began rushing across to urgently greet them and thrust his arms around Pamela's waist, while simultaneously placing a kiss onto her smiling lips. Hugging his wife tightly, he turned to the couple who had accompanied her out and mouthed a silent 'thank you.'

Kim rushed to their side, clearly crying with happiness at the sight of her mother safe. It only took a few moments to realise that a nearby man and woman were watching her closely. She instantly knew who they were, and started crying once more.

The man stepped forward and put his hand onto her shoulder, "Hi Karen, sorry it's Kim now isn't it," he smiled waiting for her to acknowledge his existence. Kim managed a shy smile. Encouraged, he introduced the beautiful woman at his side, who was intensely staring at Kim. "This is my wife Helen, say hello to your other Mum..."

Kim flashed a look at Pam' and David as if to ask their permission to acknowledge her biological parents. Pamela simply nodded and smiled to give her the go-ahead with their blessing.

Shaking inside she turned to face Helen and looked into her eyes. "Hi Mum," was all she could manage, her throat felt dry, and she felt it was slightly difficult to breathe.

Helen held Kim's hand lightly, lifting it to her lips for a simple soft kiss. "No need to say anything at all my dear, I think we are both feeling rather emotional at the moment. Let's get back to your hotel or wherever you are staying. I have had enough of this place to last a lifetime..."

#24 Wednesday Seven AM

Kim could not stop grinning.

What a day they had yesterday, she discovered her biological parents represent the couple she had spent so much energy and time trying to discover their whereabouts. What's more— there was the rescue itself, topped by George proposing to her as well.

She sighed with satisfaction, as her mood quickly changed to one of excitement. Kim vaguely remembered that Helen and Adam had stayed overnight as well.

They spent a short time talking, before deciding everyone was far too tired to remain lucid. They scarcely possessed the energy to bother with an evening meal. Sooner or later they were forging their way to their rooms, after promising they would all meet up the following morning.

Major Nadine Spencer cried off meeting first thing, as she received urgent business at the Fortress to conclude before she was going to be freed from work.

She swiftly pulled on a pair of shorts and a vest, after sorting through for suitable underwear to go underneath. Kim applied a little lipstick and mascara and flung open the door, stepping into the corridor outside.

"Hey Kim, are you just going down to breakfast?" Nancy called out, only just vacating her room and wrenching the door to pull to and latch behind her.

Before Kim could reply, the loud click of another door being unlocked broke her concentration, to be followed by a monosyllabic cry of greeting from Kirstie as well.

"Hi," she shouted out towards Nancy and Kim from further down the corridor, "Are you two just going down to breakfast? I am starving and could eat two cooked breakfasts at the same time." She offered, while breaking into a trot to reach them both before they disappeared into the stairwell, mere yards away. "Morning", announced Kirstie, "Did you both sleep alright? I've been sitting on the balcony for the last couple of hours drinking coffee, and on the phone catching up with Dave back home."

In unison, they began descending three flights of concrete stairs down to ground level. "Everything okay back home then?" Nancy asked. "Umm," uttered Kirstie, usually quite verbose. Assuming she accommodated other things on her mind, Nancy promptly overlooked the way Kirstie had untypically answered.

As they walked into the well lit restaurant, Evandro was standing in his customary place by the door, waiting to escort them to their regular table. Perfectly located by the sliding door leading out onto the expansive patio outside. It would be a straightforward matter for the door to be closed if inclement weather was expected, otherwise the fresh air on a good day boosted the poorest appetite.

After greeting the girls like lifelong friends, Evandro smiled oddly, and entrusted them to wander up to the main buffet to collect items for their first course.

"Wonder where everyone else is." asked Kim, looking round the restaurant for familiar faces.

"Well— If they had already come down, I would have thought they would only just be in one of two places. Sitting here— or already filling their plates to the brim at the buffet," observed Nancy. Evandro stepped silently behind her and placed a steaming cafetière on the table to her right, immediately melting away to serve another adjacent table.

All three turned towards the entrance to watch for the rest of the group to arrive. From behind their backs, a loud "Ahem" startled them and made them jump. They twisted sharply round to see George grinning at them inanely.

"Got you," he laughed raucously. As he shook with laughter, other giggling faces appeared in the open patio doorway. It was so infectious Nancy and the other two couldn't help but begin to laugh along too.

They all sat at the table and waited for Evandro to bring more coffee and tea before collecting some food.

"What are we going to do today then?" Paul queried, "Whatever it will be, I suspect it's going to have to be something amazingly wild to be able to top yesterday's adventure."

"Helen and Adam said they were going to be down for breakfast soon," mentioned Pamela.

"Well, I'm sure Pam and Kim will require an enormous catch up. I reckon that should be on the cards to start with," offered George.

Kim looked at her mum questionably, "I think that sounds great, shall we ask Adam and Helen when they come down." Pamela inclined her head in agreement. David chipped in quickly to say that Adam had already implored him if he possessed any pictures of Kim growing up— stored somewhere online. "He will regret asking that, there are thousands," he chuckled.

Paul, having turned away, had been chatting to Maria, utterly oblivious to what had just been discussed. "I fancy a day out at the water park," he offered. The group instantly became silent. "What— what did I say? He said worryingly. Nancy bent over and muttered something into his ear. He appeared incredulous that he had missed so much, "Really?" Was all he could manage before adopting a goofy grin and apologising for his stupid and untimely suggestion.

Evandro dropped off a couple more cafetières, and a large bright blue teapot. He looked up, someone had caught his attention.

"Morning everyone," called out Helen as Adam and herself strolled into the restaurant. They had spotted everyone sitting at the enormous round table and were currently making a bee-line directly towards them.

George rose from his chair and shook Adam's hand in greeting, David looked slightly miffed and asked, "Hey George, you never shake my hand every time we meet?"

"The amount of time we see each other daily, If I did— our hands would have fused together by now!" George chuckled. David saw the funny side, and tongue in cheek blew out an exaggerated "Humph" and simply smiled in response.

Adam offered a suggestion, "We could meet at our local casino, they have a private area on the balcony overlooking the gaming room below. It's normally used as a VIP meet and greet area, so it has an adjoining high-class kitchen and restaurant if anyone should feel peckish.

"Not being funny," said Paul, but we don't all earn a fortune like some people..."

Adam shrugged, "Not a problem, the owner is a big buddy of mine. He said he thought we had all emigrated, when we hadn't bought any staff or new clients into his establishment for two weeks." He curled two fore fingers closed and open when mentioning 'new clients'. "Anyway, it's all buckshee. All food, drink and a hundred Euro each for use in the casino if you get bored."

"Blimey, you must bring in a lot of business for that kind of generosity?" Paul sounded thankful. "We do, believe me, we do..." Adam answered, leaving only their imagination to fill in the reasons.

Nancy interrupted the conversation by announcing she was starving and was going to finally head to the buffet for some food.

"Me too, I'm going to grab a couple of croissants and some fruit as a take-away," announced Kirstie. "I have a little errand I want to complete before we head out this afternoon. What time are we expected to arrive at the casino Helen?"

"Around three if that's okay with everyone else?" Helen suggested, answered with a positive nod from everyone still sitting.

Nancy flounced away, while everyone else still resisted getting food themselves. Feeding only on conversation and laughter instead.

✳✳✳

George pulled in behind David's large people carrier, parking in the refreshing shade of the casino's underground car park was really appreciated by all passengers. The humid

296

heat in the streets overhead was overpowering, as new records for the time of year were being created every day.

Kim wiped a bead of sweat rolling off her forehead, as it was threatening to fall into her eyes. "Right, we are all here apart from Kirstie. Did anyone see where she went?"

"Well not local— if the out-of-town taxi she climbed into was any sort of clue. It was one of those yellow and brown ones, like we saw everywhere in the main city of Alicante." Nancy replied, swinging her handbag over her shoulder.

Kim pursed her lips; it wasn't like Kirstie to act like this. They were routinely all joined at the hip, with no secrets between them. She hoped her friend was okay.

"Right how do we get in there?" George inquired Adam.

"See that guy in the suit with his muscles almost tearing the jacket, well he is the lift attendant. So make your way over there in a single line, so he can observe all of us at the same time." Adam directed them towards the lift with his forefinger extended.

"Bit O T T isn't it?" Maria said, not thoroughly grasping the security implications of a private entrance into restricted areas within the betting establishment.

"They are one of only a few groups of employees allowed to use firearms in Spain apart from the police and army." Adam advised as they could all see the shoulder strap holster just under the guys' open suit jacket.

Helen smiled at the man, "Good morning Manuel, lovely day today outside."

The lift guard known as Manuel destroyed the stony visage. As his face cracked a grin and sighed. "Morning Mrs Bridges, as I have assured you maybe a thousand times, I haven't observed the sun for five years. I arrive in the dark and go home in the dark. Even the kids have begun referring to me as Dracula..." He chuckled, as he thought to himself *"Maybe I should dress up when I head for home? Count Drac' walking through the door would cause chaos."*

Manuel waited for the last guest to enter the spacious lift before closing the doors.

When the doors finally peeled apart, they were escorted out into a room practically devoid of people. On their left were a walk-up bar, one member of staff behind the counter and two at the ready on the nearest side.

To their right a circle of plush chairs had been arranged round a low thick wood table. What appeared to represent a single-polished slice, hewn from an enormous redwood tree. Another set of tables and chairs lined a low glass barrier, allowing an unrestricted view of the action in the casino below.

A smartly dressed Spaniard with a hundred watt smile, walked towards them— Arms outstretched wide in hospitality. "Adam, Helen— I am overjoyed to appreciate you and your family could make it."

298

Adam ignored the assertion that they were all family when that was patently inaccurate and casino owner Philippe Trascor discerned it. Philippe was the consummate professional when it came to greeting guests and was eminently successful at convincing the party everyone was welcome.

A group of friends were directed to the impressive table and the awaiting waiters swooped in and offered free drinks and snacks. A woman dressed elegantly in a long sparkling blue dress, silently appeared and stood nearby.

Phillipe introduced her as Sondra, who specialises in what would normally be known as street magic. Sondra greeted everyone in what sounded suspiciously like a Liverpudlian accent. She walked over to Paul, "Hello chuck, what's this behind your ear?" Appearing to struggle, she incredibly seemed to extract a mobile phone. Sondra announced slightly sarcastically, "Might be easier to turn the ring volume up next time love..." She was rewarded by a peal of laughter, and proceeded to mystify them with her next trick.

✳✳✳

Sondra was presently sitting amongst family and friends, a drink in her hand, laughing gaily in conversation.

Kim was standing with Nancy and Maria looking over the glass fence to watch and listen to sounds of people winning and losing on the slot machines. It was too early in the day for the main tables to open. But, the machines were active— eating and spewing euros, from the moment the hotels finished breakfast.

Kim looked concerned. "Wherever has Kirstie got to, I am getting damn worried now." Maria looked sympathetically at her friend who was looking more than a little tearful. "I'm convinced she is fine," she cooed.

The sound of the lift door opening with a muted ping distracted them. Out walked Kirstie, followed by two male strangers.

Kim peered a little closer at Kirstie's accompanying men. "Mum, it's Mike and Kirstie's brother Dave," she squealed, waving towards her mother whilst already heading rapidly towards the newly arrived guests.

Arriving at her destination, she was temporarily hesitant who to hug first. And after only a second's hesitation, plumped for Kirstie rather than her own brother Mike. Which was just as well, because Mike was almost pinned against the wall as Pamela flung her arms around him whilst still in motion.

"How come those two are over here Kirstie?" Kim was still surprised and excited to witness the lad's arrival.

"I was on the phone to Dave briefing him about all the fun we have been having, and he mentioned he wished he was here as well. As a result I asked him why not, it meant we could all spend Christmas together." Kim looked at Mike questionably, and Kirstie admitted with a goofy grin that he was an afterthought.

"That's a point Mike Chapman, what have you done with my best friend Roger? I thought you promised you would safeguard him with your life?" Kim sounded annoyed.

Mike tried defending himself, "I'm not quite sure that I considered any reckless decision to offer my life for him, but he is in safe hands."

Kim looked at him uncertain of what he could imply.

Mike explained, "Kirstie had telephoned me to ask whether I would want to join Dave to fly out for your wedding. I had initially explained a big fat no. It just so happened purely coincidentally that I saw Betty Warburton in the corner shop. I was merely getting his highness some cats milk chocolate."

He grinned as he could see Kim's temper beginning to melt away. "In any event, I was disclosing to her about my wasted opportunity to watch someone else suffer my sister." Mike paused and gulped, realising he may have taken the conversation a step too far. He quickly recovered. "I mean, to see how happy you would be. At any rate, Betty had perked up by saying she loved cats and would love the opportunity to feed and fuss Roger until we got back in the new year. Needless to say, I quickly got another key cut, and phoned Kirstie straight back with the good news."

Kim wasn't sure what to say, but she had to admit the extra guests would be welcome. As she suspected that any church would be rather empty with only the group there. She brightened up, "Come on it is good to see you both, come and help yourselves to some food from that table over there. It is replenished with fresh snacks every thirty minutes and the samosas are simply divine," she gushed.

Others had noticed all the commotion and had gathered around the additional visitors to ask questions about home and things in general.

"What's new?" asked Maria not really expecting a lot to have happened, the short time they had been out of the country.

Dave took the helm, "Not a lot happened that you wouldn't have until now seen in the newspapers." He took a step backward and announced dramatically "But!"

They looked at him with bated breath, urging him to reveal whatever he was teasing them with. "Well to begin with, Miles Quinn has been arrested and charged with attempted manslaughter." Dave looked at Maria in particular. "The authorities added a myriad of driving offences as well. They apprehended him after an appeal in the local newspaper brought forward multiple dash cam videos of his attempted attack on Maria."

Maria grinned at the news of the evil Miles Quinn, ultimately getting his comeuppance.

Mike held up his hand and uttered the catchphrase of a famed Irish comedian from the nineteen seventies. "Hang on— There's more..." He had tried imitating an Irish accent, but it sounded suspiciously like Pakistani.

"There was additionally another arrest made, this one might interest you Kim. If I remember correctly, the local news item on the telly went something like this..." Dave coughed and put on his best exaggerated 'BBC voice'. "Police made an arrest today after an anonymous tip had been received, regarding a serial con man attempting to cheat potential females out of property and money. By worming his way into their lives, moving into their home from a rented property, and getting married. He would after a short time file for divorce, demanding half of the property value as a settlement." Once again Dave cleared his throat and winked at Kim. "Here's the best bit— Andy King was adamant that he was innocent but incontrovertible evidence was made available. From what the police were dubbing the anonymous whistleblower, had also provided high definition video and audio to seal the case tight."

"I have no idea who that anonymous person could conceivably be..." Laughed a instantly familiar voice. Major

Nadine Spencer had snuck in quietly from another entrance, courtesy of Philippe Trascor.

"Sorry for arriving unannounced to your family gathering Kim, but I genuinely would like to convey my most heartfelt thanks. Especially to everyone involved in reopening the Fortress." Nadine laid a hand on Kim's elbow and directed her away from everyone else— so she could talk privately on her own.

"I have to admit I nearly burst out laughing, when you poured that hot soup into Andy King's lap at the Indian restaurant. I confess I was trying to get closer to you to try to find out whether you already had contact or something from your real parents. We consider security very seriously at the Fortress and frown on unknown entities having contact with anyone residing there.

I suspected that if you had told anyone it would most likely have been your fiancé. From the first time I introduced myself to him, I sensed he was a Bad'un. Rather than losing my cover I worked under the pretence that I was additionally in the 'con profession' to gain his confidence. After your fated appearance, I dropped all contact with the rat, and decided to send the police a couple of files I currently had in my possession."

Kim just remained stock still, staring at the woman standing in front of her. "Is that why you kept appearing like a bad penny everywhere I went?"

Nadine smiled, "That's absolutely correct Kim. Seems like that fellow of yours used the info I fed to his agent to good use."

Kim looked a little confused, "Agent— do you mean his ex-fiance Amber Prevett? Why would you have presented information to her?"

"Captain Amber Prevett, was one of the best we had. Very little ever slipped past her, and she could sniff almost anything out from the most meagre of information." informed Nadine.

Kim wasn't sure what to think, as her fiancé had she deduced been colluding with the enemy. She mentally struck her hand— Hard. They worked together, it wasn't as if they were still an item for goodness' sake. "Thanks Nadine, for all of your help seen and unseen. I hope we remain friends and encounter each other sometime in the future?"

Nadine nodded in assent and said under her breath, "We will Kim Chapman, we will do both of those— Mark my words…"

"Mum— Can I ask you a question?" Kim examined her mother's eyes for a response.

Pamela elevated her eyebrows before hesitantly replying. "Kim, I am confident you are old enough to know the bird's and bee's stuff by now surely?"

Kim nearly choked in surprise at Pam's response, "Mom! What the hell are you thinking? These are modern times, and we discovered all that stuff at school from teachers." She paused, tongue firmly nestled in her cheek. "Not like when you were at school— behind the bike shed…"

Pamela was speechless for a couple of seconds, steadfastly refusing to resume the conversation upon the current lines. "What was your question then Kim?"

"I know this is most likely a cliché, but did you already know you wanted to marry dad before he proposed?" Kim said purposefully.

Pamela grinned, "To be honest, Kim— no, I didn't. I had been only thinking five minutes before he dropped onto one knee, what the hell am I doing with such a scruffy sod?"

"Mum…" was all Kim managed to utter.

306

"Weeeell," Pamela produced the word out longer for effect. "He was always unkempt until we got wed, then he miraculously changed. I suppose— it might have been me always pestering him to get tidy, or maybe it must have been divine intervention..." She smiled in reflection of days gone by.

"So I suppose that means I am going to be lucky in love then, I haven't seen one thing that George makes me cringe about," said Kim earnestly but with a touch of naivety.

Pamela decided it was better not to try to convince Kim that all men were the same and left it at that instead.

A knock at the door made them both jump slightly. Kim called out "If you are female come in, but if you are not— naff off it's bad luck to see the bride on her wedding day!" She muttered softly underneath her breath, "Even if I don't have a wedding dress..."

After they heard another knock, the door swung slowly open, revealing the rugged face of Adam smiling nervously. "Sorry to barge in when you have, erm— just advised me not to. I am bearing gifts if that helps?" He pushed the door open a little wider to reveal he had contained in his arms a bulky parcel covered in tissue paper.

Kim felt a flutter in her heart as she asked, "Is that what I conceive it is?" She stuttered slightly, stepping forward to greet her Paternal father.

"It might be," Adam teased with a twinkle in his eye. "And what would your imagination assure you I am holding?"

307

"Well to be truthful my imagination would love to see a beautiful white wedding dress. But it's Christmas Day, and even with your powers of persuasion. I can't see any shops opening up specially for you today." Observed Kim while partially holding her breath.

Pamela looked at her daughter's face, looking like a small child being given a gift by father Christmas, both wondrous and inquisitive, sharing the same expression.

Adam placed the package onto the bed, "Okay, have a look for yourself and see if you are right or wrong." He stood back to allow Kim complete access to the parcel.

Kim looked once at Adam and proceeded to gently lift the delicate tissue away from the object beneath.

She gathered a breath of surprise as she surveyed the content presently lying on the bed. Ever practical Kim couldn't help herself blurt out, "Oh my god, What size is it?" She held it up to try to visualise wearing it.

Pamela poked the elephant in the room by stating, "What a beautiful wedding dress. It looks practically pristine?"

"Not exactly new, but it has never been worn." Adam apologised with a smile.

Pamela and her daughter waited patiently for an explanation for the dresses appearance.

Adams' eyes shifted and seemed to look through Kim and Pam, focusing on something behind them. They glanced around to identify what he was gazing at, and were rewarded by a blank wall.

"Sorry," Adam apologised,"I just recollected something." He smiled and asked absently, "Where was I?"

Kim reminded him.

"Thanks Kim," he continued his response after gathering a deep breath. "The dress is rather special. It belonged to Helen. It was given to her by a Russian oligarch, who was atypically grateful. At short notice, she had managed to arrange for the man's wife to leave the USSR. The man had somehow managed to upset an influential man in the Polit Bureau and was desperate to escort his wife to safety…"

"Helen was in Russia?" Asked Kim, slightly surprised, "I thought we were at war with Russia at one time?"

Pamela and Adam began to chuckle as Kim looked slightly offended at their response to what she thought was a valid question.

"Sorry Kim, we weren't laughing at you, it was your description of the situation we were distracted by. The war wasn't about war and bombs and killing at that time, it was more about what they believed someone could present to them. Your mum is a very compassionate woman and wouldn't see anyone die as the result of a needless punishment. She accomplished what she could— and it resulted in a life being saved." Adam sighed profoundly and looked sorrowful.

"Okay, he gave her the dress, but why didn't she use it?" Kim asked respectfully.

Adam swallowed deeply, "The man's name was Vasily, and she was exploiting him as a 'go between' to allow her to access certain restricted buildings. Regrettably, the debt of the insult had been allocated to a government assassin, and Vasily had received his punishment after all. Helen was distraught afterwards and was unable to use the dress. This was because the occasion prompted her sadness rather than happiness.

Kim looked at the dress again and beamed. "This is absolutely fantastic, George will undergo a massive shock…"

Adam coughed, "There is something else as well, Kim— Vasily had also made sure that the bridesmaids we kitted out as well. There are a massive number of unique styles and sizes in an air-conditioned room downstairs. You can go with your friends if you want and fill your boots, "He chuckled. "Don't forget the wedding has been arranged for 18:30 sharp, and then it's straight to the reception in the main canteen."

Kim squealed with delight. "Okay, do you mind if I could enjoy some privacy now? I am itching to try this dress on,"

With a meaningful stare, Kim pointed at him; Adam took a hint and left the mother and daughter alone.

Kim pulled the dress on and it was an instant fit— no seamstress was going to be required today. Pamela took note and advised Kim that she hoped the rest of the day was going to go along identical lines.

"C'mon mum, let's gather the rest of the girls and find out where this room is," Kim enthused and began to drag her mother out of the room urgently. "Do you by any chance know where it is?" Pamela inclined her head and laughed contentedly to herself seeing her daughter getting ready for a wedding of her own...

✳✳✳

David, Mike and Dave stood on one side of the chapel representing the bride, George and Paul sat down the other. They fidgeted with cufflinks and ties, nervously waiting for the ceremony to begin. The lack of people sitting at the side of the aisles felt somewhat disappointing to George. He had been going over it in his imagination for the last few minutes.

Although he had felt remorseful, he hadn't really squandered a lot of time this past year contemplating marriage with anyone. There were rare times, though, when the subject had fleetingly crossed his mind. He had imagined that he would be getting betrothed with more people than were going to be here today.

He shuddered inside, how could he have forgotten? This was nothing like the disaster with Amber a few years ago — at that time, the aisles were full to capacity with friends and family. He knew they shouldn't have got engaged in the first place, but she had this way of convincing him that black could be white. That they really should be married, and everything would be rosy for the rest of eternity.

He had already made his mark as an author and was determined to work even harder to release a virtual stream of his creations. They had begun to argue regularly. The straw that finally 'broke the camel's back', was when she had demanded he gave up his mates. Forcefully trying to convince him, he would be unable to allocate any time for them. Especially when she would be introducing him to her circle of friends instead. They argued continuously on this point, and she was adamant it was the way forward for his career, not by writing more thrillers.

When it came to the wedding vows he had to walk away, apologising that it would not represent a sensible move for either of them.

George felt an elbow jab sharply into his ribs.

His best friend chuckled. "Just checking that you are fully aware mate— Although I have to admit once again you have fallen on your feet, with a beautiful girl heading to the altar. I wish I had your luck." Paul inspected nervously around in case Maria was lurking nearby and overheard his comment.

George realised the reason for Paul glancing round the large chapel within the grounds of Finca Nunca Aquí. "She never gave me any bother when I used to visit her in the hospital..." He teased whilst raising an eyebrow.

Paul tried to deflect George's correct assumption that he was thinking about Maria. "I was thinking about Amber actually," He suddenly realised he may have mentioned the inappropriate thing, as George looked at him like thunder.

Paul raised his hands in a posture of supplication, "Sorry George..." He managed to stutter, maintaining a wary eye on George's next move. It certainly wasn't unheard of— to witness a fight at a wedding. But they were customarily drunkards at the reception after the ceremony proper. George's face began to relax, and the muscles in his tightened shoulders decompressed.

George bestowed Paul a lopsided smile, "Yeah, I was thinking about Amber as well to be honest," he admitted and flailed an arm over his most reliable friend's shoulder. Paul mirrored George to repair and secure their already watertight friendship.

They perceived the sound of more than one pair of high heels clip-clopping down the aisle, and naturally turned to identify who it was. Pam and Helen were walking arm in arm talking animatedly to each other. They stopped opposite

George as they were about to be seated and waved coyly whilst conveying him a beaming smile.

"*Ahh, two mothers-in-law...*" Paul was about to taunt George again but luckily thought about it twice before uttering those exact words. "They look nice," was all he could manage instead. George surmised that if both had only just arrived, they had finished helping Kim get ready and his prospective bride was about to arrive.

As if on cue, they heard the strains of 'Here comes the Bride' from the overhead tannoy system. Unable to help themselves, everyone already sitting turned in their seats to observe the bride walk down the aisle. George and Paul stood and walked to the centre of the aisle to wait for Kim. George faced forward as Paul twisted around to sneak a look.

Paul hissed in George's ear, "There is no-one there, and I don't want to unsettle you any more. But, have you noticed there is a distinct lack of clergy to conduct the ceremony as well?"

George looked across towards Pamela and Helen to see if they looked concerned— In fact their demeanour was quite the opposite. They looked as if they were completely waiting for something else. Looking towards the doorway, with smiles on their perfectly made up faces.

The music suddenly stopped, and in the midst of the ensuing silence they heard the rattle of a door handle. Fully expecting to hear the organ music begin to play once more.

George and Paul were surprised to detect the sound of many varied voices, of people about to enter the church.

The door swung inwards and an orderly crowd began to swarm inside. Some sat on the left and others on the right.

Paul looked confused, "Do you know any of this lot?" He asked George, watching as a stream of smartly dressed people were still noisily entering the room. George could only manage to shake his head, words currently failing him.

Helen rose from her seat and stepped up onto the upper level and walked over to the lectern at the side. Reaching underneath, they heard as she switched on an amplifier to allow her to utilise the microphone on the stand.

In time honoured fashion she tapped the microphone and uttered the obligatory "One two – One two." She held up a hand for silence before she made her announcement. "Ladies, Gentlemen and errm Roy."

Roy held up his hand to acknowledge his presence and to let everyone admire his new sparkly dress.

Helen smiled in return and continued her address, "I would like you all to accept my thanks for attending this wedding at such short notice. Of course you probably hadn't managed to get far enough away to escape my clutches yet." Everyone laughed at their leader; she was loved by all of the employees at the Fortress.

"At any rate, if you would all enjoy the day as you support the bride and groom in their hour of greatest need," More laughter ensued.

George could only stare at Helen in awe, "*What a powerful woman,*" he thought. "I can see where Kim gets her attitude from..." he murmured out loud.

Paul poked George, "Well I think you are going to get your chance to inform the missus real soon. Someone has left the door open, and I can see somebody in white walking across the courtyard."

The music again burst into life, as Helen sat down beside her sister. They could completely see a gathering of females outside, with one lone man manoeuvring beside the woman in white.

The procession moved forward entering the church through the wide-open door.

Heading the group was Kim and David, followed by a trio of young women dressed in matching peach outfits.

Maria was closest and was acting as head bridesmaid, proudly clutching the long veil behind Kim.

Nancy and Kirstie followed a step or two behind clutching peach-coloured bouquets created from an incredible mix of peonies, garden roses, ranunculus, and dahlias.

As the procession drifted closer, George looked at Kim and smiled proudly. David released his arm from Kim's clutch and proudly directed her elbow towards the 'groom in waiting.'

Bending over towards his bride, George whispered gently into her ear. "I am almost speechless, you look irresistible and I love you, Kim— whatever your surname is..."

Kim looked innocently at George, "I suppose you think you are funny - Just you wait."

George smiled with a twinkle in his eye "I'm already looking forward to it."

"I am still standing here you two, and can gather every word you mention," Paul said in mock horror, his playfulness given away by the wide smirk on his visage.

"Seriously, though," he confided in a conspiratorial tone. Still no sign of the clergy - looks like you may have to book a plane to Vegas after all..." He overheard someone moving behind him. "Sorry I'm delayed, I had a job to find an Elvis outfit at short notice."

The bride, groom and best man spun around in unison, to be greeted by Adams' grinning face. "Only joking," he mimed.

Dressed in an extremely elegant light blue suit, complete with a pale shirt and dark blue tie. Adam looked less like a member of the clergy than was possible.

He looked at Kim. "I hope you don't mind me conducting the service myself, after all your other dad got to

317

convey you down the aisle." David lifted a hand in acknowledgement.

Adam continued, "Anyway, this is all above board, as I have the authority to perform weddings and other duties needed in an enclosed society such as the Fortress. Though it may seem strange, spies get married you know!" His latest comment invoked a peal of laughter from the congregation.

He waited for the last 'titters' to die away before continuing. He looked round the church and pronounced, "Well looks like everyone needed today is present, so I suppose we had better begin…"

✳✳✳

#26   Friday Ten AM

After he had woken, Paul had received an early morning phone call. He was informed that Maria, himself and the rest of the wedding guests had been invited to spend Boxing Day at Adam and Helen's home. Provisions had been made for the rooms they would all be using, to be hastily prepared by independent specialists for an overnight stay.

No sooner had they finished their breakfast at the hotel, a luxurious coach had pulled up outside the building. Conveniently arranged to transport them all to Finca Nunca Aquí as soon as everyone was aboard.

Each person had packed a suitcase handed to them by the driver of the coach, given with compliments from their hosts of the day. They subsequently forged their way outside the front door to allow the driver to load multiple cases into the storage compartment below his awaiting vehicle.

After the party last night, the after effects of too much alcohol and bodily exertion during the entertainment, had drained almost everyone. Manifested, as they now sat in quiet contemplation of what the day was about to deliver. Transport pulled up outside the main complex in front of a number of boxier buildings. The journey had ended with a

319

hiss of hydraulics as the doors opened allowing them to disembark the vehicle.

Adam and Helen had been waiting patiently in a stone seating area for their arrival and stood to graciously greet their guests.

"Good morning everyone, I trust you experienced a pleasant journey?" Announced Adam, noting there appeared to represent a few hungover expressions amongst the select gathering. A few mumbles and nods of solemn heads responded.

He continued his greeting regardless. "As you are aware, we have allocated each of your separate living quarters to use as you see fit. The staff that formerly occupied the premises have decided that weeks of incarceration have provided the impetus to visit their families as an escape from this place. To be honest, nobody would condemn them if they had second thoughts about returning."

Helen began offering everyone a simple key fob, explaining they were pre-programmed RFID Tags that controlled the door locks and other features within the compound. The first time you entered a guest area, the RFID tag present was recognised as the primary key for that room. Any other RFID tag presented afterwards would be unable to unlock the guest room ensuring security for the occupants at all times.

Presently everyone was comfortably settled into the guest rooms, within the outer buildings of the complex. After thirty minutes or so, Adam and Helen had graciously invited their guests to forge their way to a substantial nondescript building. Paul remembered it was one they had previously been unable to access. To a large extent because they had not discovered a solitary door on any of the four featureless walls.

As the group approached, they could see the building had miraculously transformed beyond recognition. The construct was facing inward across the courtyard outside the main Fortress complex.

A number of openings have appeared on every side, with sun canopies over most. A considerable section of the courtyard had disappeared and been replaced by an enormous swimming pool, complete with water-slides and surrounding sunbeds.

Pamela and David's faces sported reasonable impressions of a Cheshire cat; their grins being so expansive — almost threatening to split their face.

George submitted a slightly sarcastic comment, "Something you've only just seen delighted you eh?" He raised his eyebrows in mock surprise.

David was all but drooling with anticipated pleasure, "They've reopened the Galaxy," He exclaimed as if it were the meaning of life.

The only reply he provoked was a sea of blank faces.

David appeared to visually calm down, explaining his unknown reason for the outburst. "It's the entertainment complex for the whole complex. It was recommended by some psychiatrist or something who said -'A happy Spy is a competent Spy." He shrugged nonchalantly, "Nope I don't appreciate why he said that, but who cares. The Galaxy is the absolute answer to boredom..." Comment finished, he picked up pace heading towards his Nirvana.

The rest of the gang followed him through one of the nondescript openings at the front of the building. Once inside they could only stand and look around at the garish decoration and signage. David disappeared through a door with a picture of a car emblazoned on its surface. Meanwhile, the rest of the group scattered round the enormous hallway, eager to explore the delights within.

"Hey Maria— look at this," called out Paul excitedly, waving to her in a come hither movement.

She shuffled over to Paul and looked up at the well lit sign overhead. One word flashed on and off repeatedly, 'Cinema.'

They walked closer to the entrance and could see an unmanned foyer inside. "Wonder what's on." Observed Paul, looking around for a notice board or something with a schedule.

Initially, Paul found nothing until Maria called him over to the other side of the foyer desk. They found a narrow bank of touch-sensitive LED screens, each displaying an independent film to watch. A second line of monitors presented a selection of hot and cold food and drinks. The ominous thing they both noted at the same time was that no prices were displayed.

Maria smiled, "It appears everything is free," she stated while already flicking her finger over the screen choosing popcorn and drinks.

"Hang on," said Paul "We haven't even selected a film to watch right now..." He began browsing the screens displaying the films available to view.

"This can't be valid. These films aren't anticipated for release until just before the Easter holiday, and that is three months away— Look," said Paul disbelievingly.

Maria squealed in excitement, "Oh-My-God, it's the sequel to my all-time favourite Romcom. Can we watch that pleeease."

Unable to resist the look of pleading on his friend's face. Paul quickly grabbed some treats for himself, and began trailing her towards the indicated number of the screen that would be playing the film for them. They entered a V-shaped sloping room, where a screen occupied the broadest part of the V allowing an unrestricted view from anywhere in the theatre.

The rest of the room was obviously empty, so they selected two loungers in the centre. Paul wriggled slightly to get comfortable and laid down his arm over Maria's shoulder.

Soft music began playing, as if the room had sensed there was now someone in occupation. The lights began lowering in brightness and Maria snuggled closer to Paul.

He looked at her and smiled, "I hope this film doesn't cause me to go to sleep," he admitted with a sleepy and relaxed look upon his face.

"It won't happen, I have an unusually sharp elbow," she chuckled and plunged her hand deep into the giant tub of popcorn wedged between her knees.

✳✳✳

The boys had found a compound with numerous vehicles corralled round the rear of the building. It contained a number of one man hovercraft, sand buggies and Segway's. A smattering of petrol-powered tricycles and go-karts completed the external line-up. A large tarmacked racing track was revealed, which they had recently commandeered with the go-karts racing around at full speed.

Meanwhile, the girls had found the stables within, had now been re-occupied with Helen's horses— reinstated from the safety of their temporary homes.

Helen had offered to take them out for a trek round the boundary of the grounds to look at an oasis like valley hidden from sight.

In the centre of the depression was a lake with a boathouse, and a small jetty extended from within. They made their way along a beaten path through a small wood, to arrive beside the wooden building in a short time.

"Has anyone been feeling peckish yet?" asked Helen, dismounting and leading her horse to the cool water of the lake.

Nancy and Kirstie looked at each other and together exclaimed loudly a resounding "Please!" Pamela steered her horse over to the water, dismounting to stand by her sister and nodding a simple yes. "Thank you for this Helen; you didn't have to go to all this trouble..."

Helen looked into her sisters eyes and stated, "I did Pam - for more than one reason." She dropped the horses reign to the floor and turned to stare across the lake at nothing in particular. Helen allowed a moment before continuing her explanation to Pamela. "I had spent too much time locked up inside with people - you only think you recognize them, until their true self exposes itself with pressure of the unforeseen incarceration."

She pointed towards the boathouse to indicate they were all headed inside. "I wanted to be surrounded by family and friends enjoying themselves, rather than hearing complaints and tales of woe from people convinced they were never going to escape."

Helen pushed open the unlocked door to enter the farmhouse kitchen, complete with a central aisle and wood-burning stove.

Simultaneously, the two girls searched through the double-height fridge for something cool to drink. Pam' touched her sister's elbow and said lightly,"You said there were two things?"

Helen bobbed her head and offered her a squat bottle of San Miguel, after knocking the cap off on a tool affixed to the worktop. "I appreciate you will think me stupid, when you have already given Kar - I mean Kim, everything she desired or needed up to now. But I nevertheless have this maternal urge inside that says I want to support our daughter as well."

Pam smiled at the use of '*Our Daughter*, and nodded that she appreciated her sister's feelings. "Anyway, what was this mention of food?"

"Conceivably I suspect I am going to require everyone's help on this one," she turned and walked back outside and the others followed.

A rickety looking wooden garage had been installed onto the left-hand side of the boathouse. She lifted the substantial latch and hauled the door open.

Inside lay sails, fishing rods and other water-based paraphernalia. Helen pulled on a tarpaulin to expose a substantial stainless barbecue and some enormous propane gas bottles. "If you could all give me a hand to wheel and roll this little lot outside. You will discover an intimate gravelled area with some brick grills and a pizza oven. If you could position them somewhere near - that would be great."

Collectively they organised the cooking equipment and loaded the grills and oven with charcoal. Helen led the girls back inside to confront an enormous American fridge-freezer with a door to a larder at its side.

While they prepared salad and bread rolls Helen contacted the guys by walkie-talkie, and asked if they could make their way to the mini-oasis.

Watching the credits rolling down the screen, Maria turned towards Paul and noticed a tear in the corner of his eye. She motioned for him to turn towards her and grasped his chin with her left hand as she wiped away the tear with her right forefinger. "There - You big softy you, " she cooed, still holding his chin she leaned forward and kissed him fully on his surprised lips.

Maria leant back to try and gauge Paul's reaction. Instantly a massive grin split his face, "Wow, that was worth waiting for Maria. I'm not being greedy but is there any more available where that one came from?" Without waiting for a reply he placed a hand behind her neck, and pulled her slowly towards his lips to give her a chance to pull away if she wanted to. He needn't have worried, as she hungrily settled on his lips for a longer, more passionate kiss.

They spent some time consuming each other before Maria pulled away, gasping for breath. Paul looked into her eyes, "Not being ungrateful, but what brought that on?"

"I want to spend more time with you Paul, I just wanted to make sure we were fully compatible before I asked if I could become your permanent girlfriend. I don't want what we have together to just be a holiday romance."

Paul just grinned, "As long as you promise to drop the bossiness a level or two..." He almost regretted the comment, as she swung an open hand his way to give him a playful slap – Almost, but not for a single second were there any real regrets.

✳✳✳

"Yeah, I've managed to find Paul and Maria, they were a bit emotional after watching a chick-flick or something. We will be there in ten minutes or so - Save me some burgers, love you Mrs Walsh, over." George clipped his radio back onto his belt and turned to see where Dave and Mike had got to. He had asked them specifically to start packing up whatever they were currently doing, as the girls were preparing a barbecue. He told them he thought they could come back later that day to continue the game they were currently playing.

He tapped his foot for a few more beats before trudging off to find their whereabouts. George heard yells for help coming from a different area to where he had last seen them.

George pushed open the heavy swing doors leading directly into a large L-shaped hall, which at first glance appeared to be gym related. "Hello, is there someone there?" Moaned a pitiful voice from around the corner of the L. Another voice equally pathetic "Please can someone help?"

Both slightly worried and intrigued, he trotted around the corner to be confronted by an unusual sight.

Two men, dressed in yellow and black bee suits, were stuck halfway up a wall with their arms frantically flailing to try and get down. Dave managed to twist his head around, surprised to spot George standing hand on hip chuckling for all he was worth. "Can you please help George?" He asked conversationally as if they were just there for a chat.

George couldn't hold his giggling any longer and began to roar at the sight he beheld in front of him. "It's not that funny..." said Mike belligerently.

Paul and Maria joined George at his side, they had wondered what the laughter had been about and were eager to see what was so funny. Unfailing, the sight forced them to curl up laughing as well.

Maria laughed so much at the sight, exaggerated as Dave had now slipped around ninety degrees to his left into a superman position. She eventually had to excuse herself, hoping to get rid of the developing uncomfortable feeling inside.

Eventually, she returned to be met with the sight of Paul and George standing on a cushioned floor. Each separately tugging on one of Mike's legs, to try and tear him off the wall coated with industrial strength Velcro..

With an ear-splitting crack followed by a shrill tearing noise, Mike and his two rescuers fell to the padded floor in a heap of laughter and moans.

Kim's brother stood up first and stared malevolently towards his rescuers, "Did you have to pull in two different directions?" he accused, "I feel like a damn ballet dancer now," he rubbed at an inferred soreness. Paul shrugged, "Well you are down now aren't you, and there are barbecue goodies waiting for all. Paul smiled— already beginning to grasp Dave's wrist. While George manoeuvred to his right, to attach a hand firmly onto an ankle.

Dave squealed like a baby pig, "Don't hurt— don't hurt m..." With a final squeal and tearing noise, three fell in a heap again.

Mike stood nearby Dave, as his newest friend got to his feet. Mike turned to the others to explain how they had ended up in the weird predicament in the first place. "We had just come from the games room next door on our way to meet you in the foyer, when we noticed these bee suits hanging on the wall over there." He pointed vaguely toward a sturdy looking coat stand. "Anyway, we worked out that the velcro on the suit and the wall would allow us to stick like flypaper." He looked vaguely at his costume. and wondered whether bees normally fell to the same fate.

Dave spoke up, "What my friend has failed to tell you, is after we had donned the suits, we had without thinking both ran at the wide ramp and flung ourselves into the air." He paused thoughtfully, "Neither of us had given a consideration, of how we were going to get back down before we jumped — Oh well at least we know the velcro suits worked." He sighed deeply.

George clapped Dave on the back and gave a final chuckle. "No real harm done, apart from upsetting my appetite. Let's get this show on the road, boys and err girl."

With those final words, they made their way to jump gingerly into his awaiting four-wheel drive, standing outside in the warm baking sun.

✳✳✳

Ten minutes later, they were standing beside the coolness of the lake, choosing hot meaty food to place onto slabs of warmed bread. The girls circulated handing out long glasses of San Miguel beer and chilled fruit juice as they devoured the surrounding food. George stepped to stand beside his wife, sliding an arm around her slim waist and squeezing gently. "Well Kim, I know it's been a whirlwind romance. Wed after just two days of me proposing, and I don't even know what you like for breakfast at a weekend yet." He saw her smile, "Well I have to say, I am more than happy to have chosen you as my wife. I'm not so sure my mother would say the same though, she was always a fussy bugger." George noticed a strange look appearing on Kim's face.

"Mother? You never told me about your family, have you, George? Every time I tried to broach the subject you tried to give the impression that you were a result of immaculate conception or something. You simply changed the subject to something else of interest. In fact, it was so smooth, I had never realised that we had changed the conversation until now.

332

George looked like a naughty child caught with his hand in the biscuit tin. "Ah, sorry about that," He said morosely, while taking a large bite out of his burger. Uncommitted to an answer while trying to dismiss the subject, and ignore her pointed accusation.

Kim wasn't going to let this drop, "George," she prompted, "Are you going to tell me about your family or not?" She raised an eyebrow to emphasise her inquiry.

George sighed, "Okay, just a potted history at the moment then, I will regale you with all the details when we are back in blighty" He informed her, and took a long swig of the cold beer. They moved to stand under the shade of a tree, before he continued.

"Okay, first, by spooky coincidence I am adopted. My real mother was a full time crack-head, and I was parted from her company by social services after a chance call found me with massive sores as she hadn't bothered to change me for several days. Apparently she hadn't put up much of a fight to keep me, which was more than lucky as she died a couple of months later with a massive heroin overdose." He took another swig and Kim nodded her head, urging him to continue.

"I had been adopted by a couple who could not, for biological reasons, have children. My father was and still is a military planner," Kim looked at him to clarify what a military planner was? "I am not sure what the job entails, but we travelled all over the world with him attending high level meetings— So, I suppose it must be something important…"

Kim looked thoughtful, "So that would make you a 'military brat? I think that's what they are called isn't it?" George nodded, "Yeah, and if you asked my mother she would have told you that I was the biggest brat going."

"It sounds like your mother didn't think much of you?" Kim said, feeling concerned for George, and it showed in her voice.

"Oh, don't get me wrong, my mother thought the sun shone from my proverbial. She was being honest, if I told the truth, I was out of control, with no friends I could speak to half the time, apart from Paul. Made me a pretty lonely and frustrated little sod every time dad was on manoeuvres, and we left home for months at a time." George slapped and scratched at a mosquito bite he had just received on his arm.

"Okay, you seem to be indicating that your adoptive mum was actually a nice person? Tell me more about her please George.

George built a short précis in mind to describe his mum. "Her name is Trudi, and she was born with the surname of Kennedy. Oh, umpteen years ago— I'm sorry I can't remember how old she is. Her father was a mega-rich industrialist who hailed from the centre of the industrial revolution in darkest Dudley in the Midlands. She had met dad at a university dance, and to cut that bit of the story short— they had hit it off and got married in just a few months."

"Sounds a bit like us?" Suggested Kim.

"Sort of, except they spent the next few months desperately trying for a baby." Said George. He was amused watching Kim beginning to go red with embarrassment, while addressing the subject of 'making babies'.

They finally had the courage to visit a private clinic, who promptly pronounced she had a gynaecological defect, which meant zero chance of conceiving. They began the long process of applying for adoption— and here I am." George concluded his tale for now, and looked across to the rest of the gang laughing at Dave trying to juggle a number of apples and failing dismally.

He smiled and grabbed Kim's hand, pronouncing he could juggle and was going to show them all how it was done.

She followed her husband towards their laughing friends. "*I must be the happiest woman on earth today?*" She thought to herself, with a skip of happiness in her step.

"Does anyone else want a hot drink at all?" Shouted Paul, trying to be heard over the cacophony of animated feminine voices.

A flurry of hands raised vertically into the air, their owners still talking nineteen to a dozen. "Okay, I'll try being a bit more specific. Can I have a show of hands for coffee first please?" He called out, desperately trying to count hands as they began lazily sinking downward.

"Six," said George standing to the side of Paul, "I can tell you the rest are going to be tea except for Kim, who regardless of the weather will be drinking hot chocolate."

"Are you psychic or something?" Asked Paul, slightly sceptical of George's suggestion.

"Nope, but I can tell that you haven't been on hot drink duty over the last couple of days have you?" George replied in a slightly sarcastic tone of voice.

Paul flashed him an inane grin, "Nope, but you are the one who is going to require the practice. When you are waiting on hand and foot for your wife and her coffee mornings with other mums."

George only just about grasped the concluding word that inferred babies and shivered unconsciously at the thought. "Are you trying to frighten me off Paul? I'm nervous in my unfamiliar role as a husband— as it is…"

His most trustworthy friend chuckled. "Merely checking that you are fully aware mate— Although I have to admit once again you have fallen on your feet, with a beautiful girl heading back home with you. I wish I could enjoy your luck." Paul surveyed nervously around in case Maria was lurking nearby and overheard his comment.

George rapidly realised the reason for Paul glancing round the vast hall, set within the vast passenger terminal of the Spanish airport. He wondered where Kim had got to as well, she had not left his side since their wedding day a week ago. She had told him she needed to talk to Helen in private and had wandered elsewhere to rejoin the other group to try to find her.

They wandered up to the café counter and placed their order with the adolescent girl at the till. "Do you require food as well?" She queried Paul in a listless Spanish voice, chewing heavily on some sort of gum.

George smiled, choosing to ignore her depressing attitude. "Not at the moment thanks— conceivably later if the planes aren't on time," he replied, picking up some napkins and spoons from the desktop dispenser.

"That'll be thirty-eight Euros and sixty-eight cents please." The girl informed Paul straight-faced, while picking at some gum sticking to her teeth.

Paul sucked in a generous breath while trying to utter one coherent word, "What?" He said totally exasperated with the unforeseen cost.

The girl was clearly used to irate customers moaning about the inordinate prices charged and began to chant an obviously rehearsed answer. "Would you prefer me to break it down? It was twenty-four euros for coffee and five…"

Paul moodily flung two twenty euro notes onto the counter. "Forget it, all the times I have flown, this is the biggest rip-off yet." He snatched the given change as George began loading up two large trays with hot drinks.

They began wandering back towards the source of laughter indicating the location of their group. George almost laughed out loud with his amusing thoughts, "*I hope Kim gets back soon. Paul will go ape if he thinks he has wasted money on her precious Hot chocolate at those extortionate prices…*"

✳✳✳

Kim had noticed Helen had disappeared five minutes ago without saying a word. She had supposed that her Paternal mother had wandered elsewhere to find the ladies

338

toilet. So, she hung about to the side of her friends to patiently wait for her.

Her face broke into an undisguised grin of pleasure as she spotted Helen and another woman walking in her direction. The other woman possessed ebony hair and looked kind of familiar. It wasn't until they both got a bit more adjacent, could she identify the woman as being Nadine Spencer.

Nadine held out her hand to Kim in greeting, "Hi Kim, you look a little lost?"

Kim shook the offered hand and apologised, "I'm sorry Nadine, I think your hair colour fazed me." She paused in realisation. "Oh my god, you are supposed to be in disguise— aren't you?"

Major Spencer laughed out loud, "Supposed?" Helen was in a fit of giggles at the inadvertent comment.

Kim began to blush, "I'm sorry Nadine..."

The Major presented a hand towards Kim and said forcibly, "No more sorry please Kim, it's beginning to sound like an echo." Kim set her chin in a slight sulk after the admonishment. But after a few moments she realised the Major was tormenting her.

"I hope you don't mind; I had borrowed your mum for a while as we possessed significant things to discuss." Nadine explained looking at Helen openly. "I am not completely overjoyed with the outcome, but she has indicated she would like to return to the United Kingdom for a while.

Helen has suggested it might be beneficial for a field agent to escort you both through your initial training with Her Majesty's Secret Service. Before you ask, Adam will be staying here. Someone has to hold the fort; the pun intended." She chuckled softly, waiting for Helen to speak.

"Believe it, or not Kim, I have had a flat in the town centre you visit almost every day. In fact, I have this wicked Indian restaurant about a hundred yards away, You might recollect it?" Asked Helen conversationally.

"If you are going to say Asian Ari's I will scream with happiness," Kim threatened.

"In which case I had better acquire you a muzzle, before I reveal the restaurant's name is indeed— Asian Ari's." She chuckled as she saw how excited Kim had become and was about to squeal. She set a solitary finger to her lips to prompt Kim to let her know where she was.

Kim responded by leaping forward and clasping her paternal mother in a bear hug with happiness. Nadine attempted assisting Helen by starting to peel Kim's arms from round her. The operation quickly backfired after fashion, and as soon as Kim's arms were taken away from Helen, she twisted around to start hugging Nadine instead.

"Whoa young lady, enough with the visible demonstration of happiness or I will fracture your arm if you don't desist immediately." Nadine advised Kim with a snake-like expression on her face.

Kim took the hint and stepped back clear of Nadine's intended threat.

Nadine reacted by bursting into raucous laughter. "Your face, you looked as if you were going to end up wetting yourself," she guffawed uncontrollably. "Rule one of becoming a successful spy, do not make the opposition laugh…"

Kim wasn't sure what to think or say, but she did see the funny side. She noticed Nadine's normally immaculate make up had taken a turn for the worse, with Mascara running down her face courtesy of a myriad of laughter tears.

They jumped in unison as an unexpected masculine voice asked a straightforward question. "Is this a private 'laugh in', or can anyone join?"

Kim spun round as she instantly recognised the owner's vocal cords. "George— Where did you come from?"

"Well to be honest, there was no urgent reason to approach stealthily. I thought you were all having a fit or something the way you were moving hither and thither. I'm not sure, but I think an ambulance has just pulled up and the driver is carrying what looks suspiciously like a pack of straitjackets…" George smirked and stepped sideways preventing a playful punch from his wife.

An announcement overhead ended their reverie, "Could all passengers for flight 4326 TIU airlines, please make their way to departure lounge 5A…"

Nadine looked disappointed. She leant forwards and presented each of them a kiss on the cheek, followed by a lingering hug., "Take care all of you, and have a safe flight home." She looked at Kim and George in particular, "Especially you two— you have only just embarked on a life together, and long may it continue."

Kim thought she saw a tear forming in Nadine's eye, but refused to mention it. Just politely nodding in agreement instead.

The three members of the family turned away to head towards the rest of the group, currently employed gathering their hand luggage together.

Waving towards Nadine, they began wandering towards the indicated departure lounge, ending their adventure in sunny Spain.

Kim squeezed George's hand tightly as they walked down the final corridor to their destination. George surprised her by pulling his hand away, rubbing it softly as if it had been injured.

Totally panicked all Kim could think to say was, "What's the matter George, have I hurt you?"

He looked at her with a candid face, "No - but that hand is going to need all the pampering it can get. After all, there is a massive load of typing I will need to do to complete this novel."

Kim quickly realised that George was back to jerking her leg yet again. "Yeah, but once that has been finished the sole use you will have for it— is flicking your fingers through my hair." She said jokingly, while unconciously pushing a bang of her own hair back into place.

George smirked, "Err about that, had I already mentioned that Amber has texted me to say she has acquired some more material to be investigated?"

Kim could solely think of one thing to carry out at present, and that was to wrap her arms round him and invite him closer for a lingering passionate kiss...

✳✳✳

ABOUT THE AUTHOR

Marilyn L Palmer — Born 1953 in Bedfont, Middlesex in England. The youngest of 6. Marilyn was a shy and sensitive child. Preferring to help her hard working mother to undertake the daily housework, rather than spending her childhood outdoors. Married with two boys and three grandchildren, it wasn't until approaching retirement, that she considered working with the one constant love in her life — Books.

As with any other Author climbing the ladder of recognition, Marilyn encourages her current audience to tell other potential readers about her work. Contrary to belief, there is a substantial amount of work self-publishing your own manuscripts. Mention the words proof reading and formatting to any author, will normally induce a pale looking individual typically moments after their utterance.

If you enjoyed Hidden Past, please post your comments on the respective Amazon page you purchased this book from. Every comment boosts the success of the Author.

Thanks Everyone — stay safe.
Marilyn. Xxx

Printed in Great Britain
by Amazon